KNOCK
ON
WOOD

PRAISE FOR THE BARKERY & BISCUITS MYSTERIES:

Bite the Biscuit:

"Kicking off a cozy new series, prolific Johnston blends mystery and romantic intrigue."

—*Kirkus Reviews*

PRAISE FOR THE SUPERSTITION MYSTERIES:

Lost Under a Ladder:

"Doggone cute."

—*Library Journal*

"A town built around superstitions, a heroine looking for answers, and a murder. It's your lucky day! Cross your fingers and tuck yourself into a cozy chair, you're going to love this new series."
—Sparkle Abbey, bestselling author of the Pampered Pet Mysteries

"Cross your fingers, grab a rabbit's foot, and take a walk down Fate Street with a charming new sleuth."
    —Connie Archer, bestselling author of the Soup Lovers Mystery series

"Rory Chasen comes to the town of Destiny with her dog, Pluckie, and gets her first taste of superstition—even though she's a non-believer. She finds mystery and romance in this delightful tale by Linda O. Johnston. Thoroughly enjoyable!"
        —Joyce Lavene, bestselling author of the Sweet Pepper Fire Brigade Mysteries

"A town called Destiny, superstitious residents, a broken mirror, and a lucky dog—the perfect setting for a mystery. Linda O. Johnston has created a fresh and clever world that you'll want to visit again and again."
    —Krista Davis, *New York Times* bestselling author of the Paws and Claws Mystery series

A SUPERSTITION MYSTERY

KNOCK
ON
WOOD

LINDA O. JOHNSTON

MIDNIGHT INK
WOODBURY, MINNESOTA

FIRST EDITION
First Printing, 2015

Book format by Teresa Pojar
Cover design by Kevin R. Brown
Cover illustration by Mary Ann Lasher Dodge
Editing by Patti Frazee

Midnight Ink, an imprint of Llewellyn Worldwide Ltd.

Library of Congress Cataloging-in-Publication Data

Johnston, Linda O.
  Knock on wood / Linda O. Johnston.—First edition.
     pages ; cm.—(A superstition mystery ; #2)
  ISBN 978-0-7387-4552-7
  I. Title.
  PS3610.O387K66 2015
  813'.6—dc23
                          2015014197

Midnight Ink
Llewellyn Worldwide Ltd.
2143 Wooddale Drive
Woodbury, MN 55125-2989
www.midnightinkbooks.com

Printed in the United States of America

As always, to my husband Fred. I had the best luck ever in finding and marrying you!

And again, this is dedicated to my readers. You can be sure my fingers remain crossed that you each have fun reading *Knock on Wood*, and that every one of you also enjoys continuous and wonderful luck.

ACKNOWLEDGMENTS

Once again, I thank my wonderful agent Paige Wheeler as well as my delightful editor Terri Bischoff. I also thank my publicist Beth Hanson and all the other fantastic Midnight Ink folks—as well as the other Midnight Ink authors who are all so wonderful and supportive.

Thanks also to those who read and critiqued and helped me polish the *Knock on Wood* manuscript. I always appreciate your input!

ONE

My customers, a young married couple, were having a hard time deciding which collar and leash to buy for their gorgeous, friendly Labrador retriever, who sat at their feet.

It was one of those times when I, Rory Chasen, manager of the Lucky Dog Boutique, would have considered handing these nice but very indecisive folks over to one of my two able and extremely patient assistants.

But this was also one of the days when those assistants had both been around at the same time and had ducked out of the store for their customary half hour to share coffees and conversation. That left just me there, along with my very sweet and very lucky little black and white spaniel-terrier mix, Pluckie. She was a lot more patient today than I was, too, and had been trading nose sniffs with the Lab.

"Any of the colors would look great on Lady," the woman said. She was perhaps mid-twenties, dressed in a Destiny T-shirt over jeans. The man with her wore the same thing, but his shirt was green and hers was white.

She had draped three leashes over her hand, one black, another white, and the third blue. All were decorated with designs representing superstitions. Of course. After all, this was Destiny, California, the world headquarters of all things superstitious. That was undoubtedly what had brought the young couple and their dog here.

"I'd go with the blue," said a voice from behind me. A familiar voice—but one I'd not anticipated hearing for another day.

I pivoted. "Gemma. What are you—"

She ignored me and approached the customers. "I'm a librarian," she said. "I did a lot of research on superstitions before I came here to Destiny, and I learned that blue is one of the luckiest colors there is. And the fact that the leash has a waterfall of rainbows depicted on it? You and your dog will have all the good luck in the world!"

"We'll take it, then." The woman's grin was huge as she put down the other two leashes, then picked up the blue collar with rainbows that matched the blue leash; she held both the leash and collar out to me.

Gemma winked at me and stood there, arms crossed, as she watched me lead the customers to the counter where I could ring them up on the electronic cash register.

My bff, Gemma Grayfield, is a very pretty lady, with short brunette hair, dark eyes with endless lashes, and a real fashion sense, even when she's dressed casually in a work shirt and jeans as she was now.

In a way, we're opposites—in appearance, at least. My hair is longish and blond, with highlights and bangs. I want to look nice since I have to appear professional to customers. Today, I wore jeans, too, and my pink Lucky Dog Boutique T-shirt with my lucky black dog hematite amulet that I nearly always wore on top of it.

Another group of customers walked in as that couple left. Darn. I wanted to talk to Gemma. Despite her smile, I could see something less than happy percolating behind her expression. Maybe I could just take her aside—but that wasn't going to happen. Not yet, anyway. Two male senior citizens approached the counter and began asking me questions about ingredients in some of the dog foods we carried.

I sent Gemma an apologetic look as I talked to the men. As I spoke with them more customers walked in. Normally, I'd be delighted. I was doing all I could to increase the Lucky Dog's sales; they'd been relatively healthy even before I started managing the shop over a month ago. Even so ...

The Lucky Dog was a small shop, as were most in Destiny. Like the others, its basic theme focused on superstitions—in this case, those related to pets, especially dogs. I had helped to reorganize how stock was displayed and was quite proud of it. I was also working on other merchandise for the store to carry.

Toys? Oh, yes, we sold ones that could be enjoyed by pets and people alike. Some of them were stuffed animals, like black cats and black and white dogs, and horseshoe shapes. Then there were the collars and leashes, some decorated in rhinestones and some stamped with superstitious themes, like rainbows or four-leaf clovers.

The foods all had lucky-sounding names like, well, Lucky Cat Food. We also had pet clothing and bedding decorated with superstition themes. Plus, we had a glass counter filled with amulets that could be attached to collars—or human necklaces—that had smiling animal faces and more.

The walls, too, had superstition-related decorations in some locations, including a wallpapered area designed with cute puppy and kitten faces.

Gemma was seeing it all for the first time, but I got the impression she wasn't taking it all in—at least not yet.

These men seemed to want to hear not only about the food but also about everything else we sold here. Plus, a line was forming behind them with other customers holding products they apparently wanted to buy.

At this rate I'd never get an opportunity to break away and greet Gemma properly, let alone ask any questions about why she was here early.

But this was my job now. My calling, of sorts. I'd promised the store's owner, Martha Jallopia—a very nice but ailing lady who lived upstairs—that I'd be here at least for a while.

That was after I'd helped to clear her of the murder of a neighbor, but that's another story.

"Yes," I said to the shorter of the two men before me. "I believe that all the dog food we sell here is excellent quality. But if your pet has allergies or anything else, you should read the contents on the label."

If I'd been impatient before, now it was all I could do to continue smiling and acting like a consummately patient store manager. I saw, from the corner of my eye, that Gemma had started walking along the aisles, examining the products. And she didn't own a pet. I loved her anyway, although I'd suggested adoptions often when I'd lived near her in L.A. There, I'd been an assistant manager at one of the best MegaPets stores in the area.

I finally rang up a five-pound bag of dog kibble for these two men, and the next customers stepped up to the counter, their arms filled with cat toys and food. I smiled at them—and then my smile turned broader when I saw my assistants, Jeri Mardeer and Millie Weedin, walk through the front door. I caught Jeri's eye first and motioned for her to join me as Millie approached another group of customers over by the glass counter that contained charms and amulets representing pet superstitions.

"Hi, Jeri," I said. The lovely young dark-complected woman, who wore a long, white Heads-Up Penny Gift Shop T-shirt over slacks, immediately stepped in and began ringing up the customers' purchases. Of course she'd know what to do and why, maybe as much as I did. She also worked part-time at her own family's Destiny store— yes, the Heads-Up Penny.

I went in search of Gemma then. She was behind one of our tall displays that held an assortment of pet toys; she was looking at a wand for cats from which a fake rabbit's foot on a string dangled. "Oh, hi, Rory." She sounded somewhat surprised to see me.

"Hi yourself. Come with me while I can get away for a few minutes." I gestured for her to follow me to the back of the store, where I quickly led her through the flowing mesh drape adorned with shapes of dog bones into our stockroom in the rear. I finally had the opportunity to hug her in greeting. "It's so good to see you," I said.

"Likewise." She hugged me back, her closeness emphasizing that she was shorter and slimmer than me.

When we both stepped back, I motioned for her to sit down on one of the chairs at the card table. "Okay," I said, taking the other seat. "As glad as I am that you're here, I want to know why you came a day early, and why you didn't even text me to let me know you were arriving today."

A look of sorrow and something I couldn't quite interpret washed over her pretty face. I wanted to stand and hug her again since I sensed she needed emotional support for some reason I couldn't fathom ... yet. Instead, I merely waited.

"I had to get away sooner, Rory." She stared at the table like it was a library book that had captured her attention. But then she looked up, straight into my face with her cinnamon brown eyes, and said, "I just broke up with Frank and I needed to get away. Fast. And don't ask me why. Not yet. I'll explain, but not right now."

The tears that shimmered in her eyes punctuated her words, and I didn't even consider pushing her. Not now.

There'd be time for that later.

———

Things had finally quieted down at the store, but I still couldn't spend a lot of time with Gemma. First, we had to get her checked in at the Rainbow Bed and Breakfast, which was where I had been staying since I'd come to Destiny.

But as much as I liked the place, I no longer felt it was my destiny to remain there. I was considering renting an apartment. Or maybe, if I found the right situation, even buying a house.

For now, my room was too small to invite Gemma to stay with me. I'd reserved a separate room there for her, starting tomorrow. I felt reasonably sure that the owner, Serina Frye, would be able to accommodate Gemma for tonight too.

I hoped so. I didn't really have time to find her someplace else. I was presenting "Black Dogs and Black Cats," one of my programs on superstitions involving animals, at the Break-a-Leg Theater tonight.

Gemma walked out the main door of the Lucky Dog in front of me. She'd told me she had parked her car in a lot a block away, and I figured it was better to leave it there for now, till we knew for sure she'd be staying at the B&B that night.

I had Pluckie beside me on a leash, one we sold at the store that had representations of four-leaf clovers on it. My dog hopped right onto the sidewalk and began sniffing the air. I wondered what scents she picked up from the crowd and figured she was most likely zeroing in on the smells of other dogs. A lot of tourists brought their pets to Destiny for good luck.

As always, Destiny Boulevard was jam-packed with tourists walking slowly along its length, most careful to avoid the myriad cracks in the sidewalk that I felt certain had been designed there so one of the most well-known superstitions had to be dealt with right up front by all visitors: "Step on a crack, you'll break your mother's back." Not too many visitors here had dogs with them today.

"How far away is the B&B?" Gemma asked. As if by osmosis, she'd picked up the need to stay away from sidewalk cracks. Or maybe it was because of all the research on superstitions she had done to help me before I came here … when I'd needed closure after my fiancé Warren had died after walking under a ladder.

I gestured toward our right, beyond the nearest visible intersection. "A couple of blocks up that way. Nearly everything in Destiny is within walking distance of everything else."

"Including that shop." She pointed to the building next to the Lucky Dog Boutique. Like my pet store, the Broken Mirror Bookstore was in an ornate, attractive structure that had been built back in the California Gold Rush era.

I nodded.

"It's the one—" she began, and I quickly interrupted.

Keeping my voice low so only she could hear it, I said, "Yes, that's the store where all the ... er, problems occurred. Superstition-related ... well, it's been made very clear in Destiny that to talk about what happened is extremely bad luck, and so we don't."

I still wasn't sure whether I believed in the reality of superstitions leading to good or bad luck, but I did agree that, for Destiny to remain the wonderful tourist attraction it was, discussing the superstition-related deaths of the two men who'd owned that shop was a good thing to avoid. And so I did, even with Gemma.

We managed to reach the B&B in a little over ten minutes despite the crowd, Pluckie's usual dog sniffs and squats, and, yes, finding one of the heads-up pennies—locals often seeded the sidewalks to make tourists know they were lucky being here—as well as Gemma walking slowly to take in all the stores in this area.

As I expected, my librarian friend sucked in her breath in delight as we entered the lobby. The Rainbow B&B was also an ornate, three-story building. To get inside, we had to walk under a horse-shoe mounted over the door. In the lobby, near the registration desk, was a pot of gold—or at least something that resembled gold. In a way, this place was a depiction of the rumored founding of Destiny by a couple of forty-niners during California Gold Rush Days who'd followed a rainbow to its end ... and actually found gold.

Our hostess, Serina Frye, stood behind the desk. She was chatting earnestly with a tall, slender man in a plaid shirt and dark slacks. As always—well, nearly—she was wearing a dress that would have looked appropriate in Gold Rush days, and her hair was in an upswept do on top of her head.

She noticed me right away. "Hi, Rory." She gestured for me to come closer and I stooped to pick up Pluckie. "I'd like you to meet our newest guest. He arrived yesterday. He works for the publisher of *The Destiny of Superstitions* and was its editor."

"Really?" Gemma responded even before I could. She hurried toward the man, who had turned to face us. He had a thick head of light hair and even thicker eyebrows that almost met over his prominent nose. He didn't necessarily look like a scholar or editor but his solid build suggested an interest in athletics.

"Hi." He held his hand out to Gemma. "I'm Stuart Chanick."

"I'm Gemma Grayfield," she responded. "And I'm a librarian and bibliophile and a real admirer of editors."

She was laying it on rather thick, I thought. Surely she couldn't be attracted to this man that fast. But maybe, since she was now unfettered by a relationship with Frank, she had decided to test the waters of possible dating.

Or perhaps she actually was impressed that this man had had something to do with the late Kenneth Tarzal's book that had helped to increase Destiny's popularity as a tourist destination.

As the two of them started chatting, I used the opportunity to approach Serina. I was still holding my dog. "Is that your friend who's supposed to arrive tomorrow?" she asked. I'd already mentioned to her that Gemma was a librarian.

"Yes," I said. "She decided to come a day early. I hope—"

"That I just happen to have a room available?" Serina's grin seemed rather sly, so I waited for the answer. She didn't disappoint me. "In fact, I do—but it'll cost you."

"Cost me what?" I asked suspiciously.

"I've got a couple of other guests who got here unexpectedly, both with dogs, and I hadn't made reservations for them for your talk tonight."

Happily, my discussions of pet-related superstitions had been growing in popularity. In fact, the first time I gave it, the crowd overflowed the backroom of the Lucky Dog, so I had to move the discussion to the theater, with the approval of the local mayor and others in charge. And already, the growing crowd sometimes meant a lack of seats.

But I always had some reserved in case I needed them for customers who had made especially generous purchases at the Lucky Dog.

"I'll find room for them," I said, "if you find room for Gemma."

"Done."

Pluckie and I hung around only a little longer. I spoke briefly with Gemma and her new friend Stuart. "I've got to head back to the shop now to pick up my notes and paraphernalia for my talk," I said. "I hope to see you later at the theater."

"Can you join me for a quick dinner first?" Gemma asked. She looked first at me, then glanced at Stuart as if she was inviting him too.

"Unfotunately, no," I said.

"But I'd be glad to," Stuart said.

"That's great." The beaten, worried expression on Gemma's face had been replaced by her usual devil-may-care, librarians-know-all look, and I was glad.

I just hoped she wasn't setting herself up to double her hurt. But, of course, I didn't know what had caused her breakup with Frank in the first place.

I'd make sure we had time to talk about it while she was in Destiny.

I said my farewells and Pluckie and I headed back onto the relatively empty sidewalks of Fate Street, home of the B&B, till we reached busy Destiny Boulevard again.

We crossed the major street at the intersection, again passing by the Broken Mirror Bookstore. I was aware that family members of both deceased owners were on a protracted stay in town deciding how best to handle the store's ... well, fate. I wondered how new arrival Stuart Chanick would fit into the equation.

That wasn't really my concern. I saw a couple of customers exit the Lucky Dog with bags in their hands and I smiled. More sales. And even more to come. The days after my talks always seemed to be particularly busy at the store.

Once the customers had gotten onto the sidewalk, I approached the front door, careful to avoid cracks on that sidewalk and giving Pluckie one more chance on this outing to relieve herself.

Then we went inside. And I stopped. And stared at the person near the display of superstition dog toys who was staring right at me.

I felt my breathing stop, my mind race for what I should do next.

He made it simple for me. He approached Pluckie and me, his expression grave and pleading.

"Hi, Rory," he said. "Please, I need to know where Gemma is."

Of course I couldn't tell him. Not without thinking, and holding a conversation first.

The man coming toward me was Frank Shorester, Gemma's newly ex-boyfriend.

TWO

FRANK LOOKED LIKE THE epitome of a male librarian. I'd met him before in L.A. and had thought him cute with his dark, curly hair pushed forward over a receding hairline, a short, somewhat squat body, and glasses. He worked at the same library branch as Gemma, in Westwood.

They had been dating for about a year, and it didn't appear to become more serious. Not like it had been between Warren and me ... before I'd lost him. In some ways, Frank seemed more of a convenient date to Gemma than a potential long-time lover or husband.

Yet she'd left L.A. after breaking up with him, or so she'd said.

And here he was, following her.

That seemed somewhat ominous to me, but it might just mean the guy was a lot more committed to the relationship than my friend was. I'd have to find out.

But not now.

"No, sorry," I said after he asked me for maybe the tenth time if I knew where Gemma was. I'd put my hands behind my back to cross my fingers—a good thing to do when lying, if you happened to be superstitious. It helped the fates forgive you.

I hadn't yet fully decided whether I was superstitious, but enough things had happened that made me lean toward believing. Somewhat, at least. In any event, my agnosticism hadn't removed my tendency these days to follow what rules I knew, just in case.

By then, I stood behind the sales counter, Pluckie lying on the floor beside me. Frank faced me over the glass case. The store was crowded, and though Jeri had left, Millie was still there helping customers. If I hadn't been tied up in this difficult conversation, I'd have joined her briefly, although it was almost time for me to leave.

"Look," I said to Frank. "I'm not sure what's going on, but I have to keep on the move right now. I've got plans for this evening." He could think I was going on a date or whatever he wanted. I wasn't about to tell him about my program on animal superstitions in case he decided to come.

Since Gemma would be there, that would be a bad idea in many ways.

"But—" His eyes locked on mine, then dipped to look at the floor. He looked so sad that I almost felt sorry for him. No matter what was going on between them, though, Gemma was my friend and he wasn't. I'd be supportive of her—as she had been in helping me move on after Warren's death.

It was thanks to her, in fact, that I'd come to Destiny to seek closure by learning all I could about the validity of superstitions.

"Sorry," I said. "If I happen to see Gemma, I'll let her know you were here."

Would I ever.

Would she be surprised? Whether she expected Frank to show up here or not, she might want to avoid him. That meant it would be a good idea for her to know if he was staying here and, if so, where.

I hoped it wasn't the Rainbow B&B.

"I assume she's got your phone number in case she wants to call you," I said. A geeky-looking guy like him surely had a smartphone.

He nodded without meeting my eyes. "But she's not answering when I call her."

"If I happen to hear from her, should I tell her you're on your way back to L.A.?"

He shook his head slowly. "I think she's here, or coming here, at least. I've booked a room for tonight and maybe longer, at that place down the street, the Black Cat Inn."

I already knew where most businesses in small Destiny were located, and the inn wasn't far from here. Plus, I'd eaten at its restaurant a few times.

"Okay," I said. "So maybe I'll see you around." With a wave, I picked up Pluckie's leash and headed first toward Millie. She smiled at her customers and took a step in my direction. "I'm going upstairs to see Martha," I told her quietly. "I need to make sure she's got someone helping her to the theater tonight. If she feels like it I'll want her to say hi and talk about the Lucky Dog."

I gestured around. This shop was the reason I gave the presentations, to help increase its business while teaching people superstitions about animals.

Martha, who'd owned this shop for quite a while, was a great addition to the talks when she was able to attend, say hi, and add to what I said. But she was aging, and with her health issues, she was too frail to get there on her own.

"That would be me," Millie said. "I'll bring Martha to the theater."

"Great!" I said. I appreciated Millie, and I believed she appreciated me. When I'd been ambivalent about staying to help Martha, her encouragement, although annoying at first, had been one of many reasons my decision had been positive. "See you later, then."

"Sure." She looked over my shoulder, then whispered, "Who's that guy? He's giving me the creeps."

"He's a former friend of a friend." I hesitated. "If he doesn't take the hint and leave now, I'll call Chief Halbertson."

My insides warmed at the idea. I didn't really need an excuse to call Justin Halbertson, head of the Destiny Police Department. He'd made that clear for a while.

I'd probably see him tonight at the theater, too. And siccing the local police chief on Frank, even if he had followed Gemma here, seemed premature to me.

Although if it turned out he was stalking her or otherwise doing anything besides giving himself one final try to win her back, I'd pull out all the stops I could to protect her.

"It's okay." Millie nodded toward my left side. "He's on his way out the door."

I watched as he did, indeed, exit. "Great," I said. "I'll go up to check on Martha and confirm to her that you're on for the night. Then I've got to leave too."

———

Not long after that, Pluckie and I were at the theater.

It was a charming place like many other structures in this town, with its golden Art Deco façade that had rounded arches outside and what appeared to be a newly restored auditorium inside. I used my phone to call a staff member to let me in since the building wasn't officially open yet for the night's festivities.

Pluckie and I had gone slightly out of our way before heading here. I stopped at the 7-Eleven store for a take-out sandwich for me, and I'd brought treats from my pet boutique for my pup. The 7-Eleven was the only convenience store in downtown Destiny, but with a potentially lucky name like that it fit right in.

I was getting tired of mostly eating prepared foods, or jockeying for position in the Rainbow B&B's kitchen with its owner and other guests if I wanted to cook—another reason to consider getting a place of my own.

Now, I put some signs I'd made on a few front-row seats I was saving for Serina's guests as I'd promised. Then Pluckie and I walked toward the stage of the auditorium with the employee who'd let me in, a young guy named Phil who was still in high school. I'd seen him before during the other times I'd given presentations here. It was probably a good thing he was so young. I needed help with some technical matters so I could show slides on a screen on the stage, and he knew just how to set it up.

Pluckie settled down immediately at my feet as I fiddled around for a few minutes, making sure I had everything organized just right. There was no platform on the stage as there had been the first couple of times I had come here to the Destiny Welcome programs. Tourists and everyone else were encouraged to attend the first Welcome given after their arrival, since it was good luck.

It had turned out not to be such good luck for Kenneth Tarzal, who had been the primary presenter at the Welcomes at the time. He was the guy who'd written the premier book *The Destiny of Superstitions*, and the first time I'd come here someone had left a container of milk at the edge of the platform so, when he strode down its steps, he knocked it over, spilling milk, falling, and causing himself bad luck.

He had been murdered shortly thereafter.

But I didn't want to think about Tarzal now, even though it was hard not to in this location. Instead, I went over my notes about the superstitions I'd researched and would be talking about tonight—most involved dogs and cats. In my earlier talks I used most of the same superstitions but always added others.

I didn't pay a lot of attention to the time, nor to the songs that played in background, including "Knock On Wood" and "Superstition," but I soon heard voices. I sat on a chair at stage right, and a couple of men approached me from stage left. One was Mayor Bevin Dermot, who always resembled a leprechaun to me, and probably everyone else, thanks to his plumpness and the way he wore suits, often with green jackets, and he even had a leprechaun pin attached to the lapel. His hair, including his beard, was silver and short.

I didn't know the other one.

"Hi, Rory," Bevin said in so hearty a tone that I expected something awful to happen next. "I want to introduce you to someone."

Presumably the guy with him, who didn't seem particularly evil or otherwise unpleasant. He was younger than Bevin, maybe around my age, mid-thirties, and had thinning blondish hair. He wore a suit too. His nose was prominent, and his toothy smile even more so.

"Sure." I smiled back at the other man. I felt a little underdressed beside them in my Lucky Dog T-shirt and jeans, but it was the appropriate outfit for me to give my talk on pet superstitions so I didn't worry about it.

"This is Public Affairs Director Lou Landorf. Lou's in charge of Destiny's public relations and has been on a goodwill tour across the U.S. on behalf of our tourism for the past couple of months. He probably left around the time you arrived, Rory. But he's back now."

"And I hope the contacts I've made will bring a whole flood of new tourists here to Destiny." Lou knelt down and knocked on the floor, which was clearly well cared-for wood. That stirred Pluckie, who sat up and went over to sniff his hand. "This must be the lucky dog I've heard so much about." He stroked Pluckie's head. Then, when he rose, he held out his hand for me to shake.

"I see you're a great resident of Destiny, Lou," I said. "I'm Rory Chasen, and I'm running the Lucky Dog Boutique for Martha Jallopia right now." And maybe for a long time to come, since, at least at the moment, that appeared to be my own destiny.

"I know, Rory," he said. "Bevin's been keeping me informed about everything that's gone on in town since I left." His smile disappeared into an expression much more grave. "Of course it's bad luck to talk about some of it, so I won't. But I've also heard about how your great little dog here helped to save Martha's life. Sounds like it's a really lucky thing that you're staying here to help her."

"I hope so." I wasn't about to get into a discussion about luck or anything else relating to superstitions with this man, or anyone else, right now. Fortunately, he and the mayor left the stage. I heard voices and looked down toward the seating area. People were starting to arrive.

Most were strangers, as they should be. Tourists, I figured. But among them was Martha, brought in her wheelchair by Millie to sit at the front, as we'd discussed. Gemma walked in, too, with that guy Stuart.

I'd also talked to Gemma briefly on the phone before, told her about Frank. She'd gone quiet, then said, "He wanted a lot more from the relationship than I did, so I had to break it off. And he—well, this isn't the time to talk about it." She'd paused, then continued, "I shouldn't be surprised that he followed me, but I'm definitely not happy about it. I've made myself a vow to look around and see what other, smarter, nicer men are out there. Frank won't like it."

I was sure he wouldn't. I was also still curious about Gemma's attitude, but that had filled up all the time we'd had to talk then. More to come, I hoped.

I had placed an ad in the *Destiny Star*, the small local newspaper, for my first program and had distributed flyers. I hadn't had to since then. Word of mouth, plus a mention with other events on the town of Destiny's website, had been all the publicity I'd needed.

Now, a lot of people were pouring into the theater. Among them I saw three I recognized after meeting them recently: the heirs to the Broken Mirror Bookstore. One was Kenneth Tarzal's sister, and the other two were his also-deceased business partner Preston Kunningham's mom and stepfather. Preston had died as an apparent result of superstition, but we didn't dare talk about that.

The couple of times I'd spoken with those relations, I had the impression that one thing the two factions had in common was mourning their losses, but they were not coming together on a solution for how best to keep the store in operation, at least not yet.

But surely they would succeed. It was one of the most successful businesses in Destiny, thanks to the popularity of Tarzal's book on superstitions. It wouldn't make sense for them to shut it down, or even to try running it themselves unless they had retail experience, although perhaps they could each sell their interests to someone else—preferably the same person or company—so whatever disagreements there might be now would disappear.

I wondered, then, about why Tarzal's editor Stuart Chanick had come to town. Had Tarzal's sister invited him? Preston's family? Both?

Or neither. Maybe he was here to see what was going on, and to find out if anything was necessary for the publisher to do to maintain the book's success.

Unless … well, maybe that publisher, or Stuart himself, had aspirations of buying the store.

I had to stop this speculation. The plush red seats of the theater were filling. It still seemed strange to me, after being in the audience a few times for Welcomes, to be up here with everyone waiting for me to say something.

If I'd been a shy and retiring person, I'd have felt very uncomfortable.

Even having gotten a business degree in school, being an assistant manager at a very successful chain pet store, and now managing a store myself, didn't exactly prepare me for this.

Determination did, I supposed. I'd gotten plenty of kudos for the other presentations I'd made, and the Lucky Dog Boutique had seen its sales skyrocket. That was exactly what I'd hoped.

When I saw Serina's guests, who carried a rainbow sign to identify themselves, come through the door, I waved them toward the seats I'd saved. Then, microphone in hand, I prepared myself to begin talking.

That's when I saw who I'd been hoping to see come through the door: Police Chief Justin Halbertson. I felt myself grin broadly, not even letting it fall a little when I saw who accompanied him: Detective Alice Numa, who'd been the one to interrogate me and Martha and others at the time of Tarzal's death. She wasn't exactly my favorite resident of Destiny.

I couldn't say the same about Justin. In fact, I wondered if he would soon become my very favorite person around here.

I'd decided to keep an open mind about it, at least.

I pushed the button on the microphone and began to talk. "Hi, everyone."

The hum of voices immediately grew lighter.

"Welcome to Destiny," I continued, "and to the Break-a-Leg Theater. Although I'm going to talk to you about superstitions relating to animals, especially dogs, do all of you know why this is called the 'Break a Leg'?" In case they didn't, I explained how superstitious actors tended to be. "If you wish someone who's going on stage good luck, then they're sure they'll experience bad luck. Therefore, if you tell them to break a leg, they feel a lot more comfortable that good experiences await them."

I got some applause, including from Justin, who grinned at me. I grinned right back for an instant, and then I began my talk.

THREE

THIS WAS MY FIFTH presentation of "Black Dogs and Black Cats." As I took a deep breath, I looked down from the stage at the audience after scanning the auditorium's tall ceiling, ornate chandeliers, and plain walls that spoke of the renovation I'd assumed had occurred once upon a time. So did the great condition of the rows of seats that were now nearly all occupied.

Then, after Phil halted the background music on my signal, I really got into my program.

I started out as I had before, describing how seeing a strange black dog is good luck, and running into a black and white dog is also particularly good luck when you're heading to a business meeting.

I mentioned how my lucky little black and white dog Pluckie, who stood up and wagged her tail on hearing her name, had in fact brought good luck to Martha Jallopia by finding her when she was ill and unable to attend a meeting—which I didn't describe. The rest of the world didn't need to hear that her now-deceased neighbors had wanted to buy her property. It might be bad luck to hear about it.

I used a slide show presentation program on a computer owned by the theater and set up by Phil to display photos of Pluckie on the screen at the back of the stage. As I spoke, Martha stood from her wheelchair and waved to the audience. She chose not to say anything that night, although she occasionally did speak at my talks.

I then did more standard stuff like mentioning how black cats crossing one's path are supposed to be bad luck in the U.S., but they're good luck in other countries, again illustrating it with pictures—including a representation of a black cat crossing someone's path on a local city street as they reached an intersection, with a car barreling toward them.

I didn't discuss Destiny's black cats tonight, yet there appeared to be a lot, or a few very active ones. I'd seen them often, sometimes in potentially dangerous situations, and since I was an inveterate animal lover I had begun to worry about them. I was assured by locals, though, that they were fine, that they were being observed and cared for, although those assuring me seemed uncomfortable talking much about it.

Besides, they told me, cats had nine lives.

And although black cats might cause people bad luck by crossing their paths, their presence in Destiny was essential.

So I wouldn't bore those townsfolk and others who'd come here to listen to me before, I next started on the theme of today's talk: dog and cat superstitions relating to weather.

"I recently moved here from Los Angeles," I said. "We tend to have fairly moderate weather, hot in summer, coolish and sometimes rainy in winter. I've asked around and done a little research, and I understand it's the same here in Destiny, which isn't too surprising considering how close it is to L.A., despite being a ways northwest. Other than drought, we may not be as concerned about bad weather conditions as people in other parts of the country, so the behavior of our dogs and cats that are omens of the weather to come may not be as significant—but it's still interesting. And fun."

I began to describe some of what I'd learned, including a few of the harbingers of changes in weather, such as dogs scratching or acting sleepy, or cats scratching a table leg. If a cat sits with its back or tail toward a fireplace, bad weather is on the way. And if a cat licks its tail or cleans behind its ears, the weather's about to turn rainy.

Plus, if a cat sneezes, the rain'll come soon. Although watch that cat. If it sneezes three times, that can mean either good luck—or that the people around it will get colds, which is definitely bad luck.

Once again, I punctuated what I said with pictures I'd mostly found on the Internet on free-use websites, although I'd staged a few myself with the assistance of Millie and Jeri at the shop.

There weren't a lot more superstitions that I'd found, but I embellished these and provided some made-up for-instances, then basked in the laughter and applause of those who were listening.

My programs weren't meant to last the whole night, and after my other talks here at the theater Mayor Bevin had come up on stage, welcomed the crowd, and thrown in some superstitions of his own, often those involving his Irish heritage.

This time, Public Affairs Director Lou Landorf joined the mayor, and they appeared to try to out-superstition each other. The audience seemed to eat it all up, which was fine with me.

When they were done, I added my farewell, including a reminder. "I hope you enjoyed my presentation and that you keep your eyes open for lucky, or unlucky, dogs and cats. And if you have pets of your own, or your friends and family do, please be sure to stop in at the Lucky Dog Boutique to buy them presents to help ensure that the luck they share with you is all good."

I grinned at the applause, letting my gaze roam around the audience, mostly looking for Justin. I saw him nodding and smiling as he clapped.

But then my gaze stopped on someone behind him: Frank Shorester, still seated and looking around.

Had Gemma noticed him? Had he noticed her? I didn't see her now in the crowd. People had begun leaving the auditorium. I scanned up and down the aisles. Even though I saw Martha in her wheelchair at the front, Millie at her side, I still missed seeing Gemma. Just as well, although my inability to place her didn't mean she was already gone … or that Frank also wouldn't see her.

I made sure that the young theater employee, Phil, picked up the computer I'd used for my presentation after I removed my memory stick. Then, hefting Pluckie up and stuffing her under my arm, I hurried off the stage, down the steps, and through the door that would take me to the theater lobby.

It was so crowded there that I had a suspicion everyone who'd seen my talk was gathering to discuss it. Or discuss other things connected with Destiny and superstitions.

Anything but leave the theater.

Even so, I saw Justin near the exit door. My gaze was drawn to him as if he had called and I'd heard him despite the combo of people and noise. Was there some kind of superstition about that, where people who were attracted to one another somehow felt each other even in the middle of a mob? I'd have to check that out. I realized that in some ways I was being presumptuous about Justin's feelings for me … although he'd certainly been giving that impression.

And me? Maybe I felt some attraction and was willing to admit it to myself. But ... And that was it. I still had a lot of buts.

Still holding Pluckie so she wouldn't get stepped on, I started making my way toward Justin, then heard Gemma's voice off to my right. I turned and saw that she was near a wall, in the middle of a group that included Mayor Bevin, P.A. Director Lou, editor Stuart, and the heirs to the Broken Mirror Bookstore.

As much as I'd have liked to join Justin, I realized that I needed to talk to Gemma and at least warn her about Frank being here.

Plus, okay, I admit it. I was curious about what the town administrators were saying to the people affiliated with the bookstore that was next door to my shop.

It took me a minute, and I had to be careful not to squeeze Pluckie too tightly or suffocate her, but I was soon beside Gemma.

"Hi, Rory," she said. "Your talk was delightful!"

"Thanks." I placed Pluckie gently on the floor. As I rose again, I tried to tell Gemma with my expression that I needed to talk to her.

But she looked back toward the mayor and the public affairs guy. "We were just talking about how important all the superstition-related stores around here are to keeping Destiny the wonderful destination that it is," Gemma said.

"Absolutely." Director Lou knocked on the wall, which was paneled in varnished wood. He beamed at Gemma as if she had just made the most important pronouncement possible for promoting Destiny's future. Interesting. Was he flirting with her—after knocking on wood?

"That's certainly true of the Broken Mirror Bookstore," Stuart said. "My employer, *The Destiny of Superstitions'* publisher, sent me here to find out how things are going in preserving the store and making sure it has a future."

"We do need to talk about that," said Nancy Tarzal, sister to Kenneth Tarzal who'd authored the all-important book. She was almost as tall as her brother had been, and her slim, reedy form was enhanced by a shapeless black dress that reached just to the bottom of her knees. Her stiletto shoes added to her height enough that I suspected she wore them on purpose to emphasize not only how tall she was but also how important she considered herself to be.

"We absolutely do," seconded Edie Kunningham Brownling, mother of Preston Kunningham, and her husband Brandon Brownling nodded his agreement enthusiastically. They were both silver-haired senior citizens, a whole lot shorter and rounder than their co-owner of the store, and both were dressed in button-down shirts with the tails out over their jeans. Apparently looking dressed up wasn't important to them, and so far I'd no idea what was. But I hoped it included the survival of the Broken Mirror.

And the loss of their son apparently because a superstition came true? I couldn't, wouldn't, talk to them about it. That was not only forbidden in Destiny but was also, arguably, bad luck. They were clearly grieving, though, even as they appeared to be trying to figure out how to handle things around here.

"Gemma, since you're a librarian," Stuart said, "I'd love to have you join us for a meeting tomorrow to discuss where the bookstore is heading. I suspect you'll be able to contribute some interesting insight into the importance of *The Destiny of Superstitions* having a primary location from which it's known to be available, not just from book distributors." The smile he leveled on her suggested they'd been talking a lot together and getting to know each other a bit more since I'd left them at the B&B. Interesting. Were they forming some kind of alliance—some kind of relationship?

I knew Gemma was interested in meeting more men now, but this seemed too much, too fast. Maybe I didn't know her as well as I thought I did.

Lou, who'd also been flirting with Gemma, seemed to notice it too. He edged closer to her. "I agree. And maybe with your knowledge you could hang around here for a while, help the new owners learn more about books, including their bestseller."

Did Gemma actually have men fighting over her affections already? She was certainly a pretty lady and, from my perspective, very intelligent and very nice too.

And if—

Uh-oh. What I'd anticipated was about to come to pass.

Frank Shorester had found Gemma and was moving his way through the now-dwindling crowd toward us.

Surely, with all these people around he wouldn't create a scene.

But if he tried to assert his possessiveness over Gemma around these two other men who apparently liked her, too, what was about to happen?

I decided it was time for me to edge my way toward Justin, who was still near the door. So was Detective Alice Numa.

"Hi," I said softly, looking at Justin.

He was a tall man, muscular enough that it showed despite his usual informal uniform of blue button-down shirt over black trousers. And handsome? Yes. He had angular features and, at this hour, a five o'clock shadow that emphasized those features. His hair was dark and his eyes a penetrating blue. Like many people in Destiny, he, too, wore an amulet—his was a small bronze acorn.

"I'm really glad you could make it and that you heard my talk tonight," I told him. "But right now I'm a little concerned about the people I was just speaking with and the guy who's about to join them."

Justin shook his head slowly as he smiled at me. "You do seem to have a predilection for getting into difficult situations. We need to figure out if there's some kind of superstition involved with a person who seems to invite trouble just by being around." He glanced at Alice. "You can leave if you'd like, or join me in seeing whether there's a fracas in the making here."

"I'm in," she said. She was a bit older than I, her skin a deep tan shade, her personality apparently dedicated to the seriousness of her cop job. She glanced at me with the humorless grin I'd gotten to know. "Let's go."

FOUR

To my surprise, when we reached the potentially contentious group all was calm.

Apparently that was because Director Lou had issued an invitation. "We're having a post-presentation party. A great one." He turned to the wall beside him and once again knocked on wood. "We're all heading to the Clinking Glass Saloon for a little nightcap. Care to join us?"

I glanced toward Gemma. Sure enough, Frank was beside her.

"Maybe it's not—" I began, catching her eye.

"It's a wonderful idea," she said firmly. She looked up toward Frank. "There's still a lot I don't know about Destiny, and having drinks with people with insight might help to remedy that—for me, and for my good friend Frank who's also come to check the place out."

His face seemed to whiten as he merely nodded at the implied invitation—possibly because he'd been described as a good friend and nothing closer.

"Okay." I turned to look at Justin. "I hope you'll join us too."

"Sure." He caught my eyes with his. Oh, yeah. Having a drink or two with him, even with the others around, was bound to be fun.

"I hope I'm also invited." I pivoted toward the sound of the familiar voice to my right. Carolyn Innes, owner of the Buttons of Fortune shop and my closest new female friend in Destiny, stood there. I'd glimpsed her in the audience before when she'd said hi to Martha, then sat down with a few other shop owners, but I hadn't seen her when my talk was over.

"Absolutely," I said, without bothering to check with the others around us, who included the mayor and Stuart Chanick. "I hope at least some of you will join Pluckie and me on the outside patio."

Nearly everyone in this impromptu party agreed except for Frank. If he chose to go inside while this group remained with me, maybe that would be for the best.

I saw Millie wheeling Martha toward the exit door and told them about the upcoming festivity. "I'd be glad to take you there, Martha," Millie said. "But I won't be able to stay."

I'd learned before that although Millie looked like a teenager, she was a little older—emphasis on a little. She was twenty, so she still was too young to frequent bars. Her pretty face was youthful, her dark brown hair was in a soft, straight style, and I could have hugged her for wearing a red Lucky Dog T-shirt here.

"No, thanks," Martha said. "I'm a little tired and just want to go home." She seemed in some ways the opposite of Millie, with silver hair and lines crinkling her aging face. But she'd been the first person I'd met in Destiny, and I remained impressed with her keep-on-going attitude despite her health issues. "I'll take a rain check if you ever do it again after one of your talks, Rory."

"Absolutely," I said. I watched as Millie wheeled her out the door, then joined some of my fellow partiers as they, too, left the theater.

Although the Clinking Glass was several blocks down Destiny Boulevard, nothing was terribly far away in this compact city's downtown. The group seemed eager to get to our destination, so we quickly passed Millie and Martha. Luckily, we could see under the glow emanating from the modern streetlights designed to resemble lanterns from the Gold Rush Era so that most of us could avoid sidewalk cracks.

As usual, those sidewalks were filled with tourists, but we still managed to reach the Clinking Glass fairly quickly. The tavern was crowded but most people congregated in the dark bar area inside. The outdoor patio was relatively empty and that's where I headed with Pluckie. Everyone else joined us, even Frank. As I'd noticed when here before, the patio was a lot quieter than the rest of the place, too, which could encourage conversations.

I chose a seat near the railing at the patio's edge. The tables were small and round and made of wood. I imagined that Lou would be glad. It hadn't escaped my notice that our public affairs director loved to knock on wood for any reason at all.

He took a seat at a table next to mine. Stuart and Bevin joined him, and, somewhat to my surprise, so did Gemma.

Not that I was lonesome. Justin, who'd joined Pluckie and me for the walk here, sat down at our table too. So did Carolyn.

Detective Alice Numa had gone the other direction after we'd gotten the invitation to party from Mayor Bevin before leaving the Break-a-Leg Theater. I assumed that, since all in this group was now under control, she didn't feel she needed to hang out with us. I wouldn't mind getting to know her better, I supposed, but I hadn't liked her attitude before when she'd been interrogating everyone. Remaining distant acquaintances, too, was fine with me.

I knew there was a difficult case that she was mostly in charge of. She was investigating the death a few weeks ago of a tourist after an apparent fall from a trailway up in the nearby mountains where town visitors often ventured. It was likely to be deemed an accident from what I'd heard, although the friends who had accompanied Sherman Ambridge to Destiny understandably remained shaken and upset and apparently said they didn't know what had happened either. They hadn't been with him at the time.

The guy had been a frequent tourist here and apparently loved superstitions. He and his friends had even been considering opening a store here.

Locals were demanding a resolution—including an official explanation. Had it been simple bad luck? If so, why? Or could he have been pushed—and by whom?

Having a visitor die here with no definitive reason was likely to negatively affect Destiny's tourism. In fact, it might have already. Some motels and inns had reported cancellations of reservations. Death of a tourist? No explanation?

No way.

Sure, there was that other situation relating to Tarzal's murder. No one could talk about that without incurring bad luck. But that involved locals, not tourists, and it hadn't seemed to affect the number of visitors here.

The tourist's death remained discussable, and apparently a lot of people wanted it finally resolved. The whole Destiny Police Department was under pressure to find answers. And most especially the head detective on the case, Alice.

Maybe she was heading back to the station to work on it—but that was just speculation. It was late. Maybe she just didn't want to party.

The rest of us did, though, or so I believed.

Because there were only four chairs at each table, I wasn't surprised when Frank, after staring glumly at the table where Gemma now sat, took a seat near me.

At the table at the far side of Gemma's sat the three heirs to the Broken Mirror Bookstore. I was a little surprised that they sat together since the two factions seemed at odds over what to do with the store. But having them share space while drinking might indicate a willingness to find some way to compromise. I hoped. I didn't just want the Broken Mirror to survive because it was the Lucky Dog's next door neighbor. I had also grown fond of Destiny and thought it important to have a venue here that focused on selling those special books of Tarzal's about superstitions—and Destiny's role in teaching people about them.

Before ordering, those at my table discussed what we wanted. Both men selected drinks with hard liquor. Justin was off duty now and chose a scotch and soda, which seemed to be one of his favorite drinks. He'd ordered it before when I'd been with him. And I suspected that Frank wouldn't mind it at all if he got drunk on his Bacardi neat.

Carolyn and I wanted wine. We chose a cabernet of interesting vintage from the menu and decided to split a carafe.

"We'll need to be careful how we pass it to one another, though," Carolyn said.

A server approached us. It appeared to be the same guy who'd waited on me here before, thin, in a white button-down shirt and a short white apron over his trousers. He took our orders, then left.

When he was gone, Carolyn started divulging wine-related superstitions. "We've both got to pass the carafe back and forth with our right hands," she said. "That's good luck to each of us."

"Just don't spill it," Justin said. "That's bad luck."

"Not always," Carolyn contradicted. "If you spill it while toasting, it's good luck. And the Greeks apparently think spilling it at any time is good." She turned her gaze from Justin to me. "One thing, though. If I want to get you drunk on just one glass of wine I'll need to shave a few slivers off your fingernails to drop in your glass."

I grinned, holding out my hand so everyone could look at my neatly shaped and polished but short fingernails. "Good luck getting anything off," I said.

We all laughed. Or at least three of us did. Frank managed a weak smile, at least.

"Maybe I should try getting some slivers from Pluckie," Carolyn said, looking down toward the patio surface.

At her name, my little dog woke and sat up alertly, looking at me as if waiting for a command—or, more likely, a treat.

"Good girl," I said, patting her head. I'd ordered a bowl of water for her from our server, and he soon brought it, even before the drinks for the rest of us. I also had some treats along but didn't intend to give them to Pluckie immediately.

When our drinks were finally served, those at my table clinked glasses, even Frank. I'd only taken a couple of sips when Gemma rose and came over to clink glasses too. How appropriate, I thought, for all of us, considering the name of this bar.

But Gemma had joined us with an additional motive. "Can I talk to you for a second, Rory?"

I rose and excused myself, handing Pluckie's leash over to Justin and bending to give my dog a treat so I could escape for what I was sure would exceed a second—or even sixty of them.

"What's up?" I asked Gemma.

She grinned. "Stuart has been checking out the Destiny Library and is going to give me a tour tomorrow. Lou also intends to be there. He knows the librarian in charge and wants to introduce me. Would you like to come too?"

"I'd love to if I can," I said. "What time?"

"Lou said around 11:00 a.m. Is that okay with you?"

I pondered for a moment. Only Jeri would be at the shop assisting me tomorrow, and she'd be there in the morning before heading to her family's gift shop to work. But I trusted her to do fine on her own.

"Sure," I said.

"Good. We can talk about it more tonight at the B&B, but I wanted to have a sense for who'd be there." We were both still holding our wine glasses, which we clinked again, and I took a sip of the deliciously tart red cabernet as I resumed my seat.

Justin's look asked me what the discussion had been about, but it wasn't appropriate to explain in front of Frank. That was okay. I knew Justin would walk Gemma and me back to the B&B tonight, while Frank's accommodations at the Black Cat Inn would take him in a different direction when we reached Fate Street.

For now, I just smiled at Justin, trying to convey silent assurance that we'd talk later.

His return smile was darned sexy.

Maybe it was a good thing that Gemma would be with me on that walk and staying at the same facility.

Or maybe it wasn't such a good thing, I thought, as Justin returned Pluckie's leash to me, still watching my face—and prolonging his touch to my hand before he let go.

FIVE

THE DESTINY LIBRARY WAS gorgeous inside and out, I thought the next day as I entered it for the first time. I'd passed it before while visiting the Destiny civic center without going in, but now I could examine it from many angles.

It was behind the police station, on Golden Road. Its architecture, unsurprisingly, matched the rest of the town—California Gold Rush eclectic. It was built of stone, four stories high, with curves and vaulted windows and a look that shouted of its wonderful history.

Maybe. It was so well preserved inside, without looking remodeled like the theater did, that I wondered whether it had been built more recently than most of the local structures but styled to match them.

No matter. I was a pet store professional, not a librarian, but found the place amazing. Judging by Gemma's awed stare as she pivoted to look around, she did too.

The front door opened into a large, high-ceilinged room with filled bookshelves lining all the walls. Even if I was wrong and the place had been founded around the same time as the rest of the town, it didn't have old-fashioned card catalogs but rows of tables with computers on them that undoubtedly displayed files of what books the library carried.

Gemma had arrived about the same time I did. She hadn't eaten at the B&B but had been taken out to breakfast by Lou and Stuart. I was curious about how that had gone since they both seemed interested in her. I'd have to ask her later, and how they fit in with her campaign to meet new men. I'd also press her to tell me the final straw in her breakup with Frank, which she had hinted about.

Gemma wore a tailored silvery gray dress today that made her look like a librarian—not a big surprise since she was one, and she'd known she was about to visit a venue that could feel like home. And me? As nearly always these days, I wore jeans with a Lucky Dog T-shirt over them, green today.

I'd left Pluckie at the store in Jeri's capable care. I didn't know if dogs were welcome at the library and wanted to be sure I could hang around to join whatever discussion was apparently about to be held here.

It was early enough in the morning that there weren't a lot of patrons present, although a couple of librarians—a young woman and an older man—sat behind the checkout desk staring at their computer screens.

Were there any superstitions involving libraries? I didn't know, but I'd have bet the people who worked here did. Maybe Gemma did too. In any event, there were several table displays of books about superstitions, including *The Destiny of Superstitions*.

Gemma had stopped near the door, and I approached her. I didn't see either of her breakfast companions.

"Oh, Rory." The smile that lit up her soft brown eyes was huge. "Guess what. They had something to discuss with me. Lou seemed to think they needed another librarian here."

"You?"

She nodded.

I looked around, feeling excitement rise inside me. "Would you really consider working here, in Destiny?" I'd been making friends in town, but how great it would be if my closest pal was around too. We could get together often. We could talk about everything, just like we used to—even superstitions.

I'd learned quite a bit about superstitions and why people did and didn't believe in them, but my opinion about their validity seemed to vary with whatever happened to be going on around me. Mostly. But I still sought answers. Gemma could be a great help in seeking them with me.

And the fact that she seemed, out of the blue, to have morphed from a sweet and quiet librarian to a man-hunting vamp? I was sure I needed to know more about her breakup with Frank to understand that.

"I don't know how long I might stay here," she said, "but the idea's intriguing." She glanced toward the door. "Here they come. Look, Rory, I'd have jumped at the opportunity in a second yesterday, when I essentially ran away from Frank after he started acting so horribly. And, yes, I owe you a better explanation." She must have read the inquisitiveness in my expression. "But since he caught up with me here," she continued, "and isn't acting like as much of a jerk as I was afraid he was ... well, I may just prefer going home. Oh, and visiting you here often." She must have also read the disappointment on my face. We knew each other so well—usually.

"Hi, Gemma. You ready for your tour and more?" That was Lou Landorf. He wore a blue plaid jacket over his dark trousers, and a contrasting striped necktie. He didn't look any more formal than the mayor, who wasn't with him, but neither did he appear to be attempting to look like a leprechaun. He approached Gemma with his hands out and grasped both of hers in a gesture that seemed more intimate than a simple handshake, while giving her the toothy grin I'd seen previously.

Gemma just smiled back, then looked toward me. I was standing right beside her, and Lou hadn't even glanced my way before.

"Oh, hello, Rory," he said. His grin was less pronounced as he aimed it at me, but he at least made an attempt to look friendly.

"Hi, Lou," I said enthusiastically, more to see his reaction than anything else.

All he did was turn, as if he was aware that, coming up behind him toward where we stood near the catalog computers, were Stuart Chanick and all three bookstore heirs. We exchanged greetings, and I continued to act friendly despite being torn with curiosity. Where was the head librarian? One of those who sat behind the desk? Surely that would be the person to offer Gemma a job here.

"Let's go into another room," Lou finally said. "After Stuart and I had breakfast with you, we all began talking." He nodded toward the bookstore heirs. "And now there's even more to talk about. I called ahead and reserved a room for us."

With a slight salute toward the male librarian who was now watching us, Lou led us past the row of computers and through an arched doorway at the far side of the long room. The room he took us into was small but also had bookshelves lining the walls. I observed that they were California history books with library call numbers primarily in the 979s. Besides the books on superstitions, I assumed these would be the next most popular ones the library carried. They were mostly about Gold Rush days.

A rectangular table filled the center of the room, and Lou directed us all to sit around it. I took a seat beside Gemma, still wondering why, if she was to be offered a librarian's position, these people were the ones meeting with her. Maybe that meeting would come later.

"Now, then," Lou said as he joined us at the table. "I think you've already met Nancy Tarzal and the Brownlings, haven't you?"

Gemma nodded.

All three seemed fairly dressed up, even the Brownlings, who'd given me the impression when I'd met them yesterday that chic clothing wasn't important to them. Today, Edie wore slacks and a black T-shirt, with a colorful scarf draped around her neck, and her husband Brandon wore a loose red vest over his blue shirt. Nancy again wore her stiletto shoes, but today her dress was white and hugged what curves her tall and slender body had.

"Stuart, you sit there." Lou gestured toward a seat next to him. Stuart, dressed in a white shirt and nice navy slacks, complied.

"Now," Lou said, "I'm hoping we're all going to have a very productive meeting." He lifted his right hand with its fingers crossed. "And that everyone agrees on what I'm about to suggest." This time, he knocked on the surface of the wooden table in front of him.

Judging by attire and the way all the others deferred to the public affairs director to run things, I knew this was a business meeting of some kind. But what kind?

Most likely it was the discussion they wanted to hold that Stuart had mentioned yesterday, about where the bookstore would be going and potentially how to get there.

Should I have brought Pluckie after all? My black and white dog might be what Gemma needed here for good luck.

She and I waited, as Lou looked first at the Brownlings, then at Nancy, and finally at Stuart. Then he said, "The five of us have met about this before: What is going to happen to the Broken Mirror Bookstore now that its original owners aren't with us? And I once again offer my condolences."

"As do the rest of us," I inserted, looking at Gemma, then Stuart, who both nodded.

All three of those who had recently lost family members looked around and thanked us. I could imagine how they must feel, since I had lost my Warren. But none of us could talk to them more specifically about their losses and their pain.

Lou took control again. "I believe that the agenda of all of you, including Stuart, is not only to keep the store going but also to make sure that books on superstitions, especially Kenneth Tarzal's, continue to be sold here in Destiny and elsewhere too. Did you know that the bookstore does a very good online business as well?" He glanced toward me, then Gemma. His eyes remained on her as he continued. "And it's really important that the right person runs it."

This was the discussion I'd anticipated and more. I suddenly had a very good idea of where it might be heading. But was Gemma the right person to ask?

Hell, yes. My good friend knew books, backward and forward, inside and out. She was also learning about superstitions.

But did she know the retail business?

She, too, had apparently figured out what was coming. But why hadn't Lou mentioned the possibility before? Why was he blindsiding her?

"You all know, don't you, that I'm a librarian?" Gemma asked. "I thought that was what I was meeting about here—a possible job at the Destiny Library."

"We want you to manage the bookstore, Gemma," Edie said earnestly. "Lou called us this morning after his breakfast with you—although we'd discussed the possibility yesterday. He told us how well your breakfast meeting went. We know your background doesn't necessarily include selling books for money, but as a librarian you must have 'sold' books to your patrons for what they were looking to learn, right?"

"Well, yes, but—"

"Maybe this isn't such a good idea after all," Nancy said. "We should think about this a little more. Maybe we could find someone to buy out our interests. Or even if we had to shut the store down—"

"No one is going to shut down the Broken Mirror Bookstore," roared Lou, standing up quickly. "None of you, or you'll all be sorry. Destiny will sue you, or we'll figure out something worse, like bad luck forever." He glared at the three heirs. "Now, we talked about this even before the potentially perfect manager happened to come to town. Stuart is an editor now but he used to be a bookstore manager in New York, and he can hang around initially to help. And with Gemma, it's even better than we'd hoped. Rory, who runs the Lucky Dog Boutique, is her friend, right?" For the first time, he did more than acknowledge that I happened to be present.

I nodded. "Yes, I could help. But it has to be Gemma's decision. Assuming that I understand what's going on here."

"Look, we miss our son," Brandon said. "But we're trying to be realistic here. We want to hire a book expert to manage the Broken Mirror." He looked at Gemma. "And we think we've met the right manager."

"I agree." Stuart's eyes met Gemma's, and I saw the mutual attraction there that, perhaps more than anything else, might convince Gemma to stay—especially with this man hanging around at first to help.

But was it a good idea?

"If she accepts the position, she'd be working there to help all three of you," I said, butting in before Gemma could say anything and acting somewhat as her agent. "I gather that the relationship among you isn't very cordial. I wouldn't want my friend to step into a situation where not only did she have to learn a partially new profession but, to do so, she had to walk on thin ice to please her new bosses—and maybe even act as their mediator. If she's officially offered this position and accepts, there has to be a promise of professionalism among you, at least in your dealings with her."

Gemma looked at me, her mouth pursed as she nodded. "What she said," she told the group.

"I'll tell you what," Stuart said. "While I'm around helping out, all meetings will need to include me. If things get dicey I'll help to find a solution—which may include allowing Gemma to bow out gracefully if things get difficult for her."

"We recognize this is sudden," Lou said, "but we only met Gemma yesterday and got this idea then. We also had to consider it further and run it by all of you." He paused, then spoke again. "You're willing to offer her the job under those conditions, right?" He demanded this of apparently everyone in the room, since he looked from one to the other, even at me. He was seated again, but his expression was grim—even as he once again crossed his fingers.

Under other circumstances, that might have looked ludicrous, and I might have laughed.

But this was Destiny. And Gemma's destiny, at least for the near future, might depend on superstitions, as mine did.

At least the aura of bad luck hadn't seemed to affect the bookstore itself, nor its new owners, but just those who attempted to talk about the fate of the prior owners. And certainly those prior owners themselves. But at least that shouldn't be Gemma's worry.

"Let's have a meeting at the store this afternoon," she said. "The three of you plus Stuart. Lou, I appreciate your efforts to convince me for the good of Destiny, and at this moment I'm thinking favorably about the opportunity—even though it's far from the position of librarian that I came here today about, assuming it was going to be offered to me. But if all goes well this afternoon, then I'll probably accept."

Lou stood and clapped so loudly despite his still-crossed fingers that I saw the male librarian's head come through the door. "Hear, hear," he said. "Thank you, Gemma. And thank you all. And, of course, my fingers will remain crossed until I hear that all has been worked out and Gemma will be running the store. Which she will. She has to." He crossed his fingers on his left hand, even as he knocked on the wooden table with his right.

SIX

We started to leave the library a little later, and I think I felt as bemused as Gemma must have. As we walked toward the bookstore, my phone rang. I checked the caller ID. It was Justin.

I'd been able to get a few moments alone with him after the presentation as I'd anticipated, and he had walked Gemma and me to the B&B last night. My good night kiss with Justin had been brief but warm, and suggestive enough to ensure that I would remember it.

Now, standing on the library's top step as the others filed past, I smiled at the thought as I pushed the button on the phone to answer. "Hi," I said. "I'm in your neighborhood now, at the library. We're about to pass the police station on our way back to the stores."

"Stores? Plural?"

"Long story," I said, "but yes. In fact, we're going to the Broken Mirror first."

"Sounds like a story I'd like to hear. Things are under control at the moment. How about if I walk with you?"

Of course I agreed. In fact, I knew I'd appreciate his take on the atmosphere among the people I was with. Were the bookstore heirs actually happy about the situation, or were they holding their tempers inside, along with their grief, as they were being ordered by the city employee, Lou, to compromise or face the potential wrath of the Destiny government?

And the wrath of those running a town based on superstitions could be pretty scary.

In fact, it might have been Mayor Bevin's edict that no one could talk about what had happened to the original owners of the Broken Mirror Bookstore that had rained bad luck down on those who disobeyed. Or maybe it had been whatever superstitions had been in effect that had caused the death of Preston Kunningham when the murder of his partner Tarzal was about to be resolved. Or a combination.

Afterward, there still had been all kinds of speculation in media outside Destiny—followed by stories of odd things that went wrong because of the resulting bad luck. True or not? I didn't know. But what I did know was that discussion and speculation in Destiny itself were quashed by that fortunately minor fire in the offices of the *Destiny Star* after their first and only inquiries and attempts at interviews. They of course ran no articles about what had happened.

A black cat had appeared, which was the norm around Destiny. Even the cops kept things quiet.

As a result, only a few of us knew what had actually happened and who did what—and we weren't going to talk about it.

Now, I lagged a little behind, watching Gemma chat with Stuart on one side and Nancy on the other. The two Brownlings walked in front of them. Lou had stayed in the library.

As I passed the police station, I saw Justin hurry down the steps of the attractive old marble building. I waited for him.

"Hi," he said, joining us. As usual while he was on duty, his uniform consisted of a blue button-down shirt and dark trousers. I'd not seen him wear anything that identified him as the highest-ranking police officer in the city. I supposed he didn't need to. When something needing his official attention happened, there were always other cops around heeding his orders.

"Hi," I returned, increasing my pace so we could catch up with the others. Justin matched my gait as I told him what was going on.

"Out of the blue they decided not to hire a stranger, Gemma, as a librarian." Justin's deep voice rang with amazement. "That would have been odd enough, but to have her manage a bookstore when that's not what she usually does?"

I glanced toward him, knowing that my expression displayed my own disbelief and wryness. "That's the story," I said. "And why they did it? I suppose the idea of someone who knows books is of greatest importance. Someone who has no ties to either of the factions who now own the store may also be important. And most important of all, something I think is even weirder than my being hired by Martha because she likes the luckiness of my dog?"

"What?" Justin prodded.

"I think it's because two guys tied to this venture are attracted to my good friend Gemma."

"I'd imagine that guy's one of them." Justin gestured his long arm toward where Gemma now walked only with Stuart, since Nancy had moved forward to be with the Brownlings. Both Gemma and Stuart were looking into each other's faces a lot and laughing.

"You've got that right," I said. "Did you meet him? He's an editor, the representative of the publishing company that published Tarzal's superstition book."

"So he's got good reason to want the store to survive and do well," Justin said. "And who's the other one? The boyfriend who followed Gemma here?"

"No, not hardly, although it's interesting that my relatively quiet friend has so many guys suddenly panting after her. I haven't had much of a chance to tease Gemma about that—and ask her secret—but I will."

I'd also ask what she was up to. I still felt sure she was being flirtatious because she felt insecure after the breakup of her latest sort-of relationship, even though she'd initiated it. But would she want a long-term relationship with either of those other guys? That was up to her, but I'd be interested to see which one she chose, if either.

At the moment, my bet would be on Stuart.

We were now passing the Break-a-Leg Theater along Destiny Boulevard and approaching my friend Carolyn's shop, Buttons of Fortune. Justin glanced down at me with a smile that didn't look amused. In fact, if I read it correctly, it was an expression holding a touch of regret. Had I made him feel bad by suggesting I might want to know how to attract a whole raft of men right now?

Of course I'd been teasing him. Or attempting to, in a snarky way. Gemma's current goals weren't mine, whatever they might be. For a long time after losing Warren I'd had no interest in attracting other men at all.

But at the moment, my snarkiness notwithstanding, I was willing to see whether Justin's and my initial attraction to one another grew into something more interesting, assuming I could move forward

49

after Warren. Which, even just by staying in Destiny, I now felt might be possible.

"Sounds good," he finally said. "Don't know whether Gemma's secret would work for men, too, but I'd appreciate it if you'd pass along to me whatever she tells you."

My lips puckered into something that probably resembled a grimace as much as a smile. "Touché. Anyway, the other man besides Stuart who seems eager to get to know Gemma better is none other than Destiny's goodwill ambassador and p.a. director—"

"Lou Landorf," Justin finished as I waved through the store window toward Carolyn, who was waiting on some customers. "Interesting. He's dated a few locals during the time I've been here—" Which was about two years, when Justin had been recruited from a nearby town to take over the Destiny police department. Or so he'd told me before. "But he seems fairly private about it. If he's been serious about anyone, he hasn't dated them around town. Not that I'd really know, but I think you've experienced the rumor mill around here enough to recognize that everyone in Destiny seems to want to learn, and discuss, all other residents' business."

"Yes," I said, "I've noticed."

"So both Ms. Tarzal and the Brownlings are on board with this proposal too?" Justin asked. "I thought they hated each others' guts and wouldn't agree on anything."

"That may be the good thing about all this," I said. "Maybe Lou's threats about repercussions if they didn't come to some kind of agreement got to them. I don't know. In fact, I'd love your official police assessment of what's going on."

"I'll try to figure it out," he said, "for the best interests of Destiny—like, are they all hiding their true feelings while deciding how to dispose of one another?" He paused. "Sorry. That's not funny at all, not in light of how the whole mess of the bookstore started."

"You're right," I said. "Though even if it's not funny, you authorities had better keep your eyes on them all, just in case."

Changing the subject a bit, I asked about the investigation of the tourist's death and also asked when—if—they were close to being able to rule it an accident. Justin said he still couldn't talk about it, that it remained under investigation.

"Does that mean it wasn't an accident?" I felt my insides tighten. Could there have been another murder in Destiny?

"No, we're fairly certain it was, but we still have some aspects … well, that's all I can say."

So they did consider it an accident but couldn't give the world a definitive statement yet. I got it. Sort of. But I also knew his department remained under a lot of pressure about it.

We soon began talking about what he'd heard about locals' reactions to my latest Destiny's "Black Dogs and Black Cats" superstitions presentation.

"Good, of course. Our residents like anything positive that promotes Destiny, its superstitions, and commerce. And people love their pets, so why not teach them about how their furry family members can help predict the weather?"

We shared a smile. By then, we had reached the Lucky Dog Boutique. I decided to stop in for a second, check with Jeri to see how things were going, and make sure she and Pluckie were getting along all right since I wanted to leave my dog there a little longer. That didn't take long—although I was pleased I had to wait a minute to get Jeri's attention since she was helping a raft of customers while I patted Pluckie. Jeri broke away briefly, and then Justin and I got on our way again.

By then, Gemma already seemed in charge of the Broken Mirror Bookstore. She was studying the main table in the front as she moved the somewhat sparse copies of *The Destiny of Superstitions* by Kenneth Tarzal into what appeared to me to be a more attractive array, fanning some out and stacking others with the titles in each row all aimed in one direction.

Stuart seemed to beam at her. The Brownlings looked both curious and tolerant.

The expression on Nancy's long face appeared skeptical.

"Hey, I like it," I told my friend, wanting to be utterly supportive of whatever she did, or didn't do, here.

"Do you? That's great. Of course the table is well situated to make sure anyone who comes in will see these particular books, so they especially need to stand out. I assume that the more books we can show off and sell, the better luck the Broken Mirror Bookstore will have. And I gather it could use some good luck now." She stepped back and glanced around the rest of the store, her brown eyes sparkling with fervor. "Those mirrors fortunately aren't broken." She pointed toward the farthest wall that appeared among the store's myriad tall bookshelves.

The mirrors actually had been broken not long ago, but I'd tell her that some other time—if I dared to talk about it. I'd also explain to her the significance of the five dollar bills hanging beside them in picture frames—which could turn around the seven years of bad luck for breaking a mirror.

"I'd like your professional opinion on how to arrange the rest of the books, too, including the luckiest way to display them," she continued.

"I can help a lot if they're dog or cat food, or toys," I said, then gave a little laugh at her suddenly grumpy expression. "Okay, I'll make some suggestions based on my extensive retail experience and my less extensive, but growing, knowledge of superstitions."

She smiled then, but only for a moment. As she looked over my shoulder, her face grew white and even fearful.

I turned. Frank Shorester had just stalked into the store. I had always considered him short and maybe even a little geeky as a male librarian, but right now I took a step back. The fury on his face was almost palpable, even from several feet away.

As I turned back toward Gemma, I saw that everyone else present had noticed. Nancy and the Brownlings appeared taken aback. Gemma herself now had a touch of anger in her scowl.

And Justin? He wore the only calm expression in the place. But though I didn't really know him very well, this looked like a cop assessment to me.

Frank finally broke the silence with a very loud question. "What's going on here, Gemma?" He took another step toward her, but she stood her ground.

I nearly interceded, then caught Justin's expression and stopped at the slight shake of his head.

"What do you mean?" Gemma's tone was ominously quiet.

"I ran into that public affairs guy when I was headed toward the library. He said I was too late, that you weren't there anymore. He looked so damned smug ... and told me to go home. That you and he were going to get to know each other better." Frank looked around the store with his lips curled in rage. "That you were going to run this bookshop and never, ever see me again. It's not true, is it? Gemma, come home with me."

Interesting that Lou would act so … well, sure of himself with Gemma. I knew he'd been flirting with her, but she'd seemed more interested in Stuart than in the p.a. director.

But that was up to her. And right now, Frank was the issue.

"I agree it's time for you to go home, Frank," Gemma said. "In fact, you should not have come here in the first place. But Lou was right, at least in part of what he said. I'm staying here and running this bookstore, at least for now." She'd apparently made up her mind, since she hadn't been certain while we were still at the library.

Or maybe her decisiveness was all for Frank's benefit.

"And as far as seeing you again?" she continued. "That I don't know, but it won't be as anything more than as friends."

I didn't move then. I didn't have to.

Justin took a few steps to plant himself beside Gemma. "And in case you have any hesitation about leaving town, Frank, you can be sure I'll be watching you. And I, as police chief of Destiny, can make sure you have nothing but bad luck if you stay here."

SEVEN

Fortunately, Frank left the Broken Mirror right after that. Would he listen and get out of town immediately?

Judging by the evil stares he leveled on each of us first, I suspected he wouldn't.

In case he somehow could impose bad luck on us, as I was sure he hoped to do, I crossed my fingers. In this group I probably should have hidden the gesture. Of all of them, only Justin was likely to question my motive since he didn't buy into superstitions any more than I did. And these strangers to Destiny might believe in luck even less than we did, despite hoping to make money from it off this store.

But just in case…"I hope he gets out of town without causing any problems," I said, showing my crossed fingers as if they would, in fact, ward off any bad karma.

"Me too," Gemma said fervently. To my delighted surprise, she imitated my gesture.

So did everyone else, even Justin—all showing different degrees of skepticism and amusement on their faces.

I laughed at myself and all of them, and that seemed to lighten the atmosphere a bit. "Anyhow," I said to Gemma, "I've got to get back to the Lucky Dog. I'm wishing you all the good luck possible for your first partial day managing this bookstore. And feel free to ask me anything." At my friend's smirk and shifting of her eyes from Justin to me, I felt myself flush. "Well, anything retail related," I amended.

She laughed. "Thanks. If you've got time, let's have dinner together. Otherwise, I'll see you back at the B&B later."

"Fine," I said. I'd ask her then if her decision to stay was final or still pending. And maybe she was mad enough at Frank to tell me at last what had happened between them. Her earlier frightened face had made it clear that there was more than a simple breakup involved.

The first thing I noticed as Justin and I walked out the door was that it was raining. Not hard, just a drizzle, but my mind shifted back through all the pet-related weather omens I'd spoken about at my superstition talk. For one thing, Pluckie had not acted sleepy at all, nor had she been scratching. She hadn't warned me.

On the other hand, as we started toward the Lucky Dog, I saw a black cat near the building. It didn't cross our path, or at least it didn't seem to. I saw, though, that I wasn't the only one around who'd noticed it. As always, despite the rain, there were a lot of tourists on the sidewalk along Destiny Boulevard. A bunch pointed toward the kitty. It was just stalking along now, not grooming itself with any of the motions that would have signified a change in the weather, and there wasn't a fireplace around for it to turn its back toward.

Maybe I was, after all, buying into this superstition stuff too much around here. But it was a good thing at least to know about it enough to discuss it with the tourists and anyone else.

Like Justin.

And the fact that the black cat was outside in the rain? Well, I already knew some of the omens that might mean. But poor cat. Did it like getting wet?

I'd thought again of when I particularly had reason to worry about Destiny's black cat—or one of them if they were plural. I'd seen it up on a mountain under less-than-desirable circumstances. Was this one it? Did it always survive? Which of its nine lives was it on?

I'd heard rumors of someone I might be able to ask, but she had turned out as elusive as the cats. I hadn't met her yet, if she existed. I assumed, from local residents' attitudes when I'd dared to ask, that it was probably considered bad luck to talk about her.

"So what do you think?" Justin asked as we reached the door to the Lucky Dog. We'd been walking relatively quickly, making our way through the crowd even though the rain wasn't particularly heavy. "Did your talk have anything to do with this unpredicted rainfall?"

"Was it unpredicted? I hadn't checked the news." Not even this week's issue of the *Destiny Star* that contained, along with its local news, a weekly weather prediction.

I had looked to make sure that one of its owners was at my talk, so I figured there would be a story about it in their next edition. I was sure they'd feel safe reporting about something so uncontroversial.

"I wasn't aware of it," Justin said, "and we always talk about potential changes in the weather each morning at the station."

"All right, then. Let's say that my talk, and descriptions of those pet-related superstitions, did cause this." My back toward the door to my shop, I gestured around. Justin laughed. I turned toward him.

There were too many people around for us to share a kiss goodbye. But…"Care to join Gemma and me for dinner tonight?" I asked.

"Absolutely."

Smiling, I turned—only to see the door to my shop open. I stepped back, expecting to see a customer come out.

No one did.

And when I stepped forward I saw no one near the door.

Justin hadn't taken off yet. I looked at him.

"Isn't there a superstition about doors that open by themselves?" I asked.

"You're more of an expert these days than I am," he said, "but yes. It's supposed to be a sign that you're going to get a visitor." Cop that he was, he stepped toward it and looked around inside but didn't seem particularly alarmed.

"Well, that's fine," I said as he turned to face me again. "That visitor will probably be another customer."

"Or not. The way I understand the superstition is that the person who'll show up is not someone you want to have around."

———

Our dinner that night at the Shamrock Steakhouse went well. Justin and I, and our dogs Pluckie and Killer, were joined on the crowded—and fortunately well-covered—patio by Gemma and her companion for the night, Stuart. The rain had lessened but a heavy mist still drifted downward.

We'd briefly thought of introducing Gemma to the Black Cat Inn's restaurant but immediately discarded the idea since that inn was where Frank was staying.

No use inviting bad luck. And we had no reason to believe that Frank had left town.

During our meal, we talked about Gemma's new potential career. "Yes, I'm staying for now," she said. "I even got my boss's okay to come back when I'm ready, just like you did." She grinned.

"Great!" I said, knowing I might never take advantage of that promise I'd received from the manager of the MegaPets store I'd worked at in L.A.

Later, Justin and Killer walked us back to the B&B. Gemma shot me an evil smile, and when Stuart strode inside the lobby, she followed him. I, in turn, aimed an amused smile at Justin as we both held our dogs' leashes. "I think my friend is encouraging us to share a good night kiss."

"I wouldn't want to disappoint her." Justin's voice was low and sexy, and he leaned down to comply with what we figured Gemma wanted. And I wanted. And clearly Justin wanted, too. And Killer and Pluckie? Justin's Doberman and my spaniel mix just sat tolerantly on the ground beside us, looking up.

The kiss certainly didn't disappoint me, but once again I was glad we were in public with other people around. I'd already acknowledged to myself that my attitude was softening, but I wasn't ready to jump into a new relationship ... yet.

Justin and Killer left then, and Pluckie and I went inside. Stuart must already have gone to his room since I didn't see him.

I braced for Gemma's teasing. Instead she just said, "It's nice that you've got a new relationship blossoming, Rory."

"Maybe, but you have a couple."

Before she could respond, our hostess and owner of the B&B, Serina Frye, joined us from the TV room off the side of the lobby. "Hi, ladies. Do you have everything you need for the night?"

Everything but Justin, I thought, then scolded myself internally for even harboring the idea. *Although …*

I did talk to Gemma in her room before we went to bed. She was ready at last to discuss her breakup with Frank. She spoke quite a lot, in fact, about how her quiet, sometimes insecure Frank had apparently decided they were more than an item and became verbally abusive about it at times. The end came because, just this past week, he had become physically threatening when Gemma talked to other men at the library where they'd both worked. "Even if I'd considered him my ultimate guy before, I definitely wouldn't after he started that," she said.

"Good girl," I applauded, and we soon said good night.

———

The next morning, I walked Pluckie first thing as always. I then joined Gemma to have breakfast in the B&B's dining area. "Stuart had a teleconference this morning," she told me. "He said he'd be on his phone for a while and to go ahead without him."

He didn't appear before we finished and left, walking toward our respective stores together with Pluckie accompanying us.

Gemma had already told me that Nancy was going to meet her at the Broken Mirror first thing to let her in and get her started for the day. "I won't be surprised if the Brownlings come, too, to make sure I also get their ideas and don't start playing favorites."

I laughed. Soon, we reached Destiny Boulevard. The Wish-on-a-Star children's shop was on the right. I ushered Gemma in that direction, pulling Pluckie's leash gently to get her to follow.

"I made a wish once on those falling stars," I said, pointing to the display in the store's window in which lights acted as moving stars burning day and night. Now, it was almost time for the shop to open, but I didn't want to take the time to introduce Gemma to the owner, Lorraine Nereida. Not yet. But I'd liked Lorraine when we'd talked before. "It came true," I finished.

It had been fairly unassuming. I'd merely asked to make the right decision about whether to stay in Destiny to run the Lucky Dog Boutique. My decision had sort of fallen around me like a soft sheet that had grown tauter, pulling me in and holding me here.

So far, I hadn't regretted it. Did it have anything to do with my wish?

Around here, I wouldn't be surprised.

"That's cool." Gemma's grin looked wistful. "Do you think I could try it?"

"Sure." I waited while, watching the display, she made her wish—which she of course didn't reveal to me. That would have assured it wouldn't come true.

Still avoiding cracks in the sidewalk, along with the window-shopping tourists and traffic on Destiny Boulevard, we crossed the street and reached the Broken Mirror Bookstore.

"I'll stop in later to see how you're doing," I told Gemma. "And feel free to call me anytime."

I gave her a quick, encouraging hug, then Pluckie and I headed next door to the Lucky Dog. It was around nine thirty, half an hour before we opened. I would be the only salesperson there for the first couple of hours that morning.

But Martha had come downstairs from her apartment above the store. Not only that, but her nephew Arlen, with whom she had a difficult relationship, was there too. Arlen Jallopia was a Destiny tour guide. In fact, I'd taken his tour and really enjoyed it. And now, partially thanks to my success in giving talks regarding pet superstitions, he had been able to add the Lucky Dog Boutique to his tour itinerary.

Arlen was a nice-looking guy who resembled a sitcom star, with spiky dark brown hair. As usual, he wore a red knit shirt with the Destiny's Luckiest Tours logo on the pocket.

Right now, aunt and nephew were at the side of the store near a display of superstition dog toys. Each had a cup of take-out coffee in their hands that I assumed Arlen had brought from the nearby Beware-of-Bubbles Coffee Shop. Yes, there were superstitions involving the formation and movement of bubbles in cups of coffee; I'd learned that soon after arriving here.

Whatever those bubbles were doing right now, I wanted to salute them. Aunt and nephew seemed to be getting along great ... for this moment.

Did I want them to get along permanently? That could lead to Martha hiring Arlen to run this shop, as he wanted.

Well, that would certainly make future decisions for me. I had even begun weighing the pros and cons of possibly asking to buy the place from Martha.

I chatted with them for a few minutes before taking the steps I needed to open the doors of the store. Arlen offered to help, and I took him up on it, at least as far as straightening some displays.

Soon after I opened the store I found myself waiting on customers, Pluckie at my side. It was fun sharing pet-related superstitions with the tourists who came in and asked questions about the products we sold. A few had been at my most recent presentation.

I really enjoyed this place. This store. The kinds of patrons who came in.

Maybe I would make that purchase offer to Martha someday. Not now, though. She hung around till Arlen had to leave for his job, then walked to the stairway that would take her up to her apartment.

"You okay to go up there on your own?" I asked her.

"Yes, I'm doing well this morning, dear. And if I trip going up the stairs—"

"Yes, I know, it's not as bad as when you go down the stairs." We'd talked about these superstitions before. The former meant a wedding in the family, while the latter meant bad luck.

She soon started up the steps, closing the door behind her.

Late morning, Millie came in. Once she got settled and started waiting on customers, I had time to go next door and check on Gemma.

Good thing I did. First thing I saw when I walked into the bookstore was that all three men who seemed interested in her were present. They stood around the table that harbored Tarzal's book on superstitions.

Glaring at each other.

Gemma quickly walked around them to join me at the door. "I have a feeling there's a lot of bad luck floating in the air around here," she whispered.

It was then I saw the black cat sitting calmly near the wall at the far corner of the store.

Same cat? A different one?

I wondered once more: How many black cats were there in Destiny?

Did I keep seeing only one? And though it—they?—never got too near, were they crossing my path?

Unfortunately, or fortunately, I'd left Pluckie next door with Millie, assuming I'd return to my store fairly quickly.

Now I wasn't so sure.

"We can fix that kind of bad luck," I told Gemma anyway. "Why don't you go check out the cash register or do something that looks official? I'll see what I can do about all your visitors."

"Thanks." Her tone was soft and grateful.

As to the first visitor I tried to approach, the cat must have had its own hidden access, since by the time I edged my way over toward where I'd seen it, it had disappeared.

By then, Gemma was behind the counter looking down at the computer that, unlike at the Lucky Dog, sat on the checkout counter all the time. I wondered if the screen was blank or if she'd gotten onto the Internet to see if there was some kind of superstitious ritual she could undertake to fix things around here.

In any event, she was avoiding the table with Tarzal's books. She nevertheless glanced that way now and then, and all three men—even Frank—aimed smiles at her.

Well, I wasn't the object of their unwanted attentions. And maybe some of those attentions were, in fact, appreciated by Gemma.

The only one I was sure wasn't welcome was Frank. But the public affairs director? The book editor?

All three were whispering to one another. Loudly.

Angrily at times, or so it sounded.

Each held a *Destiny of Superstitions* book in his hands. Their professions—a politico in his usual suit, a librarian dressed less formally but still sharp, and an editor in casual clothing—left each of their pairs of hands relatively smooth and sleek, not like those of a workman. Were there any superstitions relating to hands?

Maybe I was overreacting. Or maybe I just wanted an excuse to call Justin. But I did press his number into my phone—and only got one of his underling cops. I mentioned my name and her tone grew brighter. *Uh-oh.* I wasn't sure what it meant when cops started to know who you were, but I'd worry about that later.

Right now, I left Justin a quick message about a potentially looming altercation at the Broken Mirror. Then I hung up.

"So, fellows," I said as I drew near. "I assume you've read *The Destiny of Superstitions* many times, Stuart." I faced the editor, and he nodded.

"That's part of my job," he responded. With his height and athletic build, I suspected he'd win in a physical altercation with either of the others, but also figured, with his literary background, that he wouldn't take them on that way—not intentionally. "A very welcome part. I'm really glad to be here to help make sure this book remains readily available in this town."

"Fine, then." Frank's hazel-eyed glare at Stuart from beneath his glasses shot flames. He appeared unlikely to win a fist fight, but I suspected he was the most likely to start one. "You stay here. Run this shop. Sell some books. But stop whatever it is you're trying to convince Gemma to do. She doesn't belong here."

"Oh, but you're wrong about that," Lou said as smoothly as if he was discussing the town's attractions with tourists. Of all of them, I'd bet he would fare the worst in a battle of fisticuffs. But, also of all of them, I suspected he'd be best at worming his way out of it with words. He lifted the book he'd been thumbing through and pointed toward it. "The Broken Mirror needs someone in charge who knows books, and knows them well. Not just a few titles."

He shot a somewhat condescending look toward Stuart, suggesting that an editor only knew about those books he helped to get ready for publication. In this case, one of those books was definitely the most important anyway. I didn't particularly agree with the public affairs director but wanted to hear the rest of his spiel. And had he read any books lately besides *The Destiny of Superstitions*?

"As a librarian," Lou continued, looking at Frank, "you, of all people, must understand how marvelous the breadth of a librarian's knowledge of literature is."

"Then maybe I should stay here and run this place." Frank's growl elicited a worried frown on Lou's face.

"I don't think—"

"No, you don't," Frank cut in. "You don't think. Look, I'm not sure what's going on here, but I came to this ridiculous town to bring my girl back home. And the two of you are—"

"Oh, I don't think she's your girl," Lou interrupted, his voice raised. "In fact, I think she's the perfect person to run the Broken Mirror." He aimed a glorious smile in Gemma's direction, but she was still, wisely, working with the computer. Lou turned back toward Frank. "And I've definitely gotten the impression from Ms. Grayfield that she wants you to leave. Now." His tone had suddenly turned ominous.

Frank took a step closer to the director, not easy to do around the jutting table. Stuart appeared ready to intervene, and I wasn't sure of the potential outcome.

"Hey, fellows," I said, intervening myself. "I've already called the police chief. He's on his way."

I wasn't sure of that, but I certainly hoped so.

A group of customers walked in, chatting amiably. I knew Gemma had been watching—and listening. And sensibly staying away. But now, as at least today's manager in charge, she had to go meet the people who wanted to buy books.

All three men seemed to converge on her.

"Stay away from me," she all but hissed, then, shooting a panicked look toward me, turned her back on us and approached the customers.

"You know, guys," I said, "Gemma has been my friend for a long time. I suspect that acting this way will make her hate all of you."

"Oh, I don't think all of us," Lou said in his smooth voice again, irritating the heck out of me.

Before I could comment further, though, I considered giving a sigh of relief. The cavalry had arrived.

But not the help I'd hoped for. Instead of Justin, Detective Alice Numa strode through the door.

"I got word of a potential altercation," she said, walking toward us. "What's going on?"

Her eyes were on Lou Landorf, not me.

"So glad to see you, Detective," he said, smiling and holding out his hands as if he wanted to grasp hers.

Something in her gaze momentarily looked warm and pleased, but then she turned toward Frank. "I don't know you, sir, but I understand you're making threats against Ms. Grayfield, who is helping out at this store. Is that true?"

She glanced toward Gemma, who had left the customers near the table containing *The Destiny of Superstitions* and joined us.

"I'm afraid so," she said, then aimed a pleading glance toward Frank. "Please just go home. There's nothing for you here."

"We'll just see about that." He looked straight at Lou, pivoted to glare at Stuart, then at me and, at last, he strode from the shop.

I stared after him, then glanced toward Gemma. She looked beaten. The others must have thought so too. Stuart approached and took her hands sympathetically.

Lou intervened, putting an arm around her shoulders and giving a squeeze. "So sorry that man is making things difficult for you, my dear."

Alice just watched, her expression unreadable. "Well, at least things look better around here now," she said.

"Yes, thanks to you," Gemma said. "It's lucky that you came here. And right now I need to go back and help those customers." She didn't move right away, though.

"I'm a cop," Alice said, glaring at her. "Superstitions around here or not, I'm just doing my job."

That was when Justin walked in. "Everything all right here?" His head turned as he appeared to take in the entire shop.

"It is now, thanks to Detective Numa," I said, wanting to give her credit.

She nodded toward me in acknowledgment of my so-true compliment.

"Yes, Detective, you have helped out here tremendously," Lou said. He still stood right beside Gemma.

"Like I said, I'm just doing my job." Alice's gaze moved from Gemma's face to Lou's, then took in the rest of us one-by-one.

Then she, too, left the store.

EIGHT

I WASN'T SURE WHETHER there were any superstitions about life settling into a routine, but Gemma's and mine surprisingly seemed to do so over the next few days.

With Pluckie at my feet, I joined Gemma each night just before bedtime in her chintz-decorated and quaint room at the bed and breakfast to talk over the day. Our discussion after the meeting-slash-confrontation at the Broken Mirror was mostly about Gemma's combined excitement and trepidation. And, yes, we touched on her attitude about all three guys who were the men in her life for the moment.

She was worried about Frank and what he was up to since he hadn't left.

She was attracted to Stuart, both professionally and as a potential romantic interest.

And she was a bit bemused about Lou and his interest in her—and the fact she actually wanted to get to know him better too.

My opinion? Despite her denial, I suspected she'd previously been harboring a hope that Frank could be the one, so her emotions remained in disarray since she'd determined he wasn't. I had no idea if she'd develop an ongoing relationship with Stuart, or even Lou, but I was glad she had the distractions from Frank and his current nastiness.

Our discussions also focused on Justin and me at times. Yes, I really did think I was developing a relationship of sorts with the handsome, kind, and dedicated police chief, which meant I was finally reaching some degree of closure about losing Warren, even though I hadn't completely accepted whether his walking under a ladder had anything to do with it. Since I now lived in Destiny, I was perfectly willing to tell anyone who asked that of course the superstition had been involved. But inside? I remained skeptical, at least somewhat.

When we weren't on the subject of men, we discussed superstitions and Destiny and our shops and their relationship to the town. And how much we did—or mostly didn't—miss L.A.

After our discussions ended, Pluckie and I would go to our pretty much identical room and go to sleep. We'd all get up in the mornings and have a regular B&B breakfast with Stuart after I walked Pluckie. Then we would head to our shops.

Each day was, of course, somewhat different. The Lucky Dog Boutique nearly always seemed to be busy, which was a good thing. Tourists who'd been in town for a few days often mentioned my "Black Dogs and Black Cats" presentation, but even if they didn't, most of our customers came to Destiny with their dogs or their wistful tales of the pets who waited for them at home. They all bought a lot of superstition-related pet items, including the horseshoe-shaped dog treats we had just started carrying. I was also considering adding more to our inventory too.

When things slowed a bit and I had Millie or Jeri or both, and sometimes even Martha, to help out, I'd take Pluckie's leash and not only give her a quick walk outside to relieve herself but also visit the Broken Mirror Bookstore.

Gemma seemed to be getting used to it just fine. As with all shops in Destiny, the bookstore was filled with customers nearly all the time. And since the bookstore's primary book, *The Destiny of Superstitions*, seemed synonymous with the town, it was probably the busiest store around.

Gemma handled the busyness just fine. She slid from one customer to another, offering help and suggestions as well as, or even better than, I'd advised her to do. Plus, Stuart remained around and seemed to act as her assistant as much as Jeri and Millie acted as mine.

Non-customers also stopped in to visit at times, including when I was there. Some were other shopkeepers who wanted to introduce themselves or offer assistance, such as my buddy Carolyn Innes of the button store. Carolyn and I sometimes talked about adding a touch of each other's inventory to our stores but hadn't done so yet. As far as I knew, she hadn't suggested it to Gemma, but buttons and books might not go together as well as buttons and dog paraphernalia that included clothes.

Once, even Detective Alice Numa came in. She asked for a recommendation on a book about superstitions other than Tarzal's and bought the one Gemma suggested. Gemma seemed as surprised as I was, but of course the detective needed to know as much about superstitions as possible to do her job of solving crimes in this special town. I had to wonder, though, why she hadn't read that one before.

A couple of times when I was there, Frank Shoreston came in. Gemma told me that her sort-of ex visited at least a couple of times a day, and even, occasionally, bought a book. Mostly, he acted as if he was browsing or even sat on the floor reading while keeping a close watch on Gemma. It wasn't an overt threat, but neither did it make her feel good. Still, she told me not to call Justin or other cops as long as Frank continued to behave well and not cause disruptions other than simply being present.

Gemma also told me that city elders came in often to say hi to her patrons, make sure she felt comfortable there, and tell visitors how wonderful *The Destiny of Superstitions* was. Sometimes it was Mayor Bevin Dermot who came, and sometimes P.A. Director Lou Landorf, and sometimes both—but most often it was Lou who came in and encouraged her, by knocking on wood on her behalf and also complimenting her often on how she was handling the shop ... and he was flirting a lot too.

The store's owners encouraged her as well. Nancy Tarzal seemed to have been chosen by the others as their designated representative, but the Brownlings also visited often. They were all super encouraging, Gemma said; it was as if they wanted her to succeed so they could comfortably leave town. But there were days when Nancy hung out watching Gemma nearly all the time. Asking questions. Making Gemma uncomfortable, even while encouraging her.

"I understand," Gemma told me that busy Saturday afternoon as she took a quick break from waiting on a family of five looking at children's books on good luck and what it meant. "I stay calm and friendly and keep her aware that I'm learning more all the time, including about bookkeeping and inventory procedures, thanks to you and Stuart. She seems appreciative and even, sometimes, apologetic—like she can't wait to be able to stop."

"Then you're settling in here enough to agree to stay?" I didn't show her, but my fingers were crossed, both literally and figuratively. Having my good friend here had been really great so far, and I was sure it would only get better.

"That's still a little premature," she said, "but at this point I think the answer's yes."

She had agreed to go with me that night to the Destiny Welcome, the first to be held since she'd arrived in town. After closing our stores at seven that night we dashed back to the B&B to change clothes and so I could leave Pluckie up in my room. As much as Destiny loved dogs, especially lucky ones, and they were invited to other appropriate presentations at the Break-a-Leg Theater, they weren't necessarily welcome at the Welcome program. And although I sometimes left Pluckie with Serina, our hostess wasn't available that night.

Martha had decided not to come this time, so I didn't have to be concerned about her getting there and back.

There wasn't much time to eat but Gemma and I grabbed sandwiches from the Wishbones-to-Go shop and ate them on our way as we walked. We entered the theater with the rest of the huge crowd. We found seats at the end of a row on the far side of the auditorium and settled in, waiting for the Welcome to begin.

I listened a bit to the background music, especially when the song "Lucky Ladybug" began to play. I'd not been familiar with it until I'd come to Destiny, but I enjoyed how many superstitions it mentioned.

As always when I visited this theater, or nearly any other place in town, I also watched to see who else was there. Most looked like tourists, chattering and pointing at the theater's updated decor and, delightfully, carrying bags containing some of the superstition-related Destiny treasures they'd already bought. How did I know that? Well, some pulled things out of the bags to show them off to their friends. Others looked familiar to me—patrons of the Lucky Dog Boutique.

And, yes, I recognized some as having attended my talk here a few days ago.

It also wasn't surprising to me when some familiar people made their way through the door, including Carolyn Innes, who took a seat in the row ahead of us and turned so she could chat with us.

Much as I enjoyed Carolyn and her latest tales of dazzling her customers about button superstitions, I was even more interested when two men, who came in around the same time but separately, scanned the audience and let their gazes fall on us.

Rather, on Gemma.

One was Frank, and I held my breath and crossed my fingers that the few remaining seats around us would be filled faster than he could get here.

To my delight—and Gemma's even more, I was sure—Stuart, the other man who'd also come in, was faster than Frank and managed to maneuver to sit right beside Gemma.

They started talking, and although I continued my conversation with Carolyn, my eyes kept watch over the doorway.

I noticed Frank's scowl, but he didn't head in our direction. Instead, he walked down the steps and took a seat several rows in front of us.

I looked back at the door—and, sure enough, Justin soon entered, along with Alice Numa, a guy in a suit, and some other uniformed Destiny cops. Were they on duty tonight? It didn't matter. Just the sight of them should help to keep things under control here.

Of course things had always seemed relatively peaceful to me at Destiny Welcomes, except for the time when poor, now-deceased Tarzal had knocked over a bottle of milk, spilled it—definitely bad luck for him—and slipped on it.

The red plush curtains in front of us were rolled back to reveal the raised wooden stage, and the overhead lights facing it were turned on. "Welcome, welcome," shouted a voice from that stage. It was a little hard to hear since the speaker, Lou Landorf, wasn't using a microphone. He must have noticed it, too, since he yelled, "Sorry folks. Forgot something. I'll be right back." He knelt, knocked on the wooden stage, then walked off again.

"Isn't there a superstition about going somewhere but having to go back for something being bad luck?" Gemma had turned toward me, her soft brown eyes looking concerned. Like me, she was still dressed as she had been at her store that day—a nice button-down librarian pink shirt over beige slacks in her case, and a Lucky Dog T-shirt over jeans in mine.

"That's right," said Stuart from over her shoulder. "But maybe he took care of it by knocking on wood—like always." He, like Gemma, was dressed in business casual—and he'd have been a better candidate to answer her question in the first place. With his reading and editing, he was more of an expert on Destiny and its superstitions—although if the question had been pet-related I undoubtedly knew more.

I again looked toward the door and my eyes caught Justin's, but he looked away quickly as the cops who accompanied him pointed out some seats at the rear corner of the auditorium and they all started in that direction.

At least I should get an opportunity to say hello to him later.

Another minute went by, and then not only the p.a. director but Mayor Bevin Dermot, too, were back on the stage. Bevin now held the microphone and the house lights were turned down.

"Welcome, everyone," he said into it—and it was so loud at first that I cringed and figured everyone else there did too. But he fumbled with the gadget in his hand and his next words sounded just loud enough. "This is the Destiny Welcome, and we're all—everyone in Destiny, whether with us tonight or not—we're all delighted that you're here in our very special town."

"Hear, hear," said his companion Lou, leaning over to talk into the microphone too.

"Now, for those of you who've never been to a Destiny Welcome before, let me tell you a little about it as well as that special town of ours." Standing in the middle of the stage, his leprechaun personality demonstrated by his green suit and hat and air of mischievousness, Bevin began to talk about Destiny and the now-familiar description of its founding by the forty-niners who'd discovered a pot of gold at the end of a rainbow and decided to give homage to their luck by creating this town, dedicated to superstitions. They'd chosen this location thanks to seeing a second rainbow, but its end had been way up in the mountains overlooking this area. That place was the subject of many Destiny tours but it was too remote and craggy for this town to be located there.

No, Destiny's destiny had been developed here by its founders, in a nice, relatively flat area where tourists could easily visit.

Previously, the Welcome had been all but presided over by Kenneth Tarzal, the author of *The Destiny of Superstitions*, with assistance from his business partner Preston Kunningham, but now that they were gone it was mostly the mayor who led the meeting and any resulting discussion.

Other townsfolk had stepped in too. My buddy Carolyn Innes had taken charge once, and I'd also surprisingly enjoyed the local news angle described by Derek and Celia Vardox, the brother and sister who owned the town's newspaper, the *Destiny Star*.

They hadn't mentioned the fire they had at their offices, though, after their initial attempt to conduct interviews about what had happened in the investigation into Tarzal's murder and the evidence of the bad luck that would befall anyone who dared to violate the local command not to discuss it, let alone toss it into the media.

Tonight was the first time, other than at my own little talk, that I'd seen Lou on the stage, since he'd been traveling during all of the Welcomes I'd attended. In fact, I hadn't even known he existed till this week.

But now he clearly wanted to take charge. He remained in one spot while Bevin paced, watching him as if he were a cat preparing to pounce.

Or maybe that was just my impression since I enjoy animals. At least he didn't resemble a black cat. Lou wore a cream-colored suit that night, with a red shirt and busily decorated tie, although I was too far away to see what was depicted on it. His hair was light, and although it was thinning it had been combed up enough that if he resembled an actual cat at all, it would be a fuzzy golden one.

There was a small podium off to one side where Bevin went to get a swig of water from a bottle. As he headed there, Lou followed. As Bevin reached for the bottle Lou stood in front of him for an instant, then, when he turned, had the microphone in his hand.

"Hi again, everyone," he said into it. "I want to veer a little now from our standard welcome to particularly welcome a newcomer to Destiny. Her name is Gemma Grayfield." He swept his hand, holding the mike in the general direction of where we sat.

I glanced toward Gemma. If she'd been able to, I think she would have melted into her seat. Instead, as everyone looked toward us seeking her, she managed a graceful smile and wave.

"Gemma's a librarian," Lou continued. "Or at least she was one. Now that she's in Destiny, she's going to become our superstition go-to lady since she'll be managing the Broken Mirror Bookstore where the primary book on sale is *The Destiny of Superstitions*. Gemma, would you come up here, please?"

Her glance toward me appeared desperate. "It could help the store's sales," I said, quickly reminding her of the talks I'd been giving.

"But don't do it unless you want to," Stuart said from behind her. "In fact, if you want I'll go up there and talk about the store and the book."

"Come with me." Gemma turned to look toward Stuart. "If I say anything while I'm up there I'm not sure how it'll come out, and you can correct me."

Which I suspected my delightful, sure-of-herself friend would abhor if he actually did it. On the other hand, his presence might boost her confidence.

The two of them excused their way out of our row and walked side-by-side down the aisle to the right of us. The house lights were bright enough so they could see their way, and Gemma preceded Stuart at the end of the aisle up the steps onto the stage.

As she reached the top, Lou approached and gave her a big, public hug. "Thanks for joining us," he said in a friendly, loud stage voice. "Now, come over here and tell us about your background and what you're doing in Destiny."

He kept his arm around her back as he led her to center stage. It appeared to me that Gemma tried to hang back but Lou didn't let her. She turned her head once as if to see whether Stuart was behind her. He was, although I wasn't sure she could see him. I heard multiple footsteps on the wooden stage even from the middle of the audience, so I hoped she did too.

In moments, they'd stopped walking and Lou stood on one side of her. Bevin joined them and stood on Gemma's other side. Lou began interviewing her.

Yes, she was a librarian by background so she knew books. She was a friend of mine and had started researching superstitions to help me out with a question she fortunately did not specify. I still didn't talk much about what had happened to Warren. And, yes, she'd enjoyed learning about superstitions.

She had come here to Destiny to visit me, since I was staying. Wisely, she didn't mention her other personal reason that had brought her here a day earlier than planned—her breakup with Frank. I'd glanced toward him while Gemma was walking toward the stage and hadn't been able to see his face, so I'd no idea what Frank thought about what was going on now. I suspected he didn't like it, though, since it might seem to ensconce Gemma further into Destiny.

Then Lou started asking about the Broken Mirror Bookstore and what Gemma thought of it and how she was enjoying running the place. Her answers seemed spot-on to me, ones that could entice tourists to come visit and learn more about the books, including *The Destiny of Superstitions*.

When Bevin broke in and asked some questions about the book's contents, including superstitions regarding books, Gemma stumbled a little.

Stuart quickly stepped forward and offered some assistance. "I don't know too many superstitions regarding books, and there aren't a lot in *The Destiny of Superstitions*, either—but one is that college kids should respect their textbooks, which includes not reading them in the bathroom. If they do, it can bring them bad luck in their studies. Of course these days a lot of textbooks are in e-format like other kinds of books, so even though the superstitions are old and referred to print versions, we all could visualize the problems if a kid accidentally dropped his e-reader into the tub or toilet while in the bathroom. Bad luck? Yeah."

That garnered a lot of laughs, and then Stuart began talking about superstitions on travel, a good thing since a lot of the audience consisted of tourists. He described things like not turning back once you've set off on a journey, listening to grasshoppers since they portend good luck on a trip, and making sure to step onto a ship with your right foot first to ensure the best of luck. These all had been included in the book, even though I wondered whether Tarzal had made some of them up; but now they were in the most well-known superstition book so that gave them some credence—at least to those who believed in superstitions.

I noticed the less-than-happy looks Lou shot Stuart's way. Was he attempting to send the evil eye toward the man he seemed to consider a rival for Gemma's affections?

In a short while, Stuart handed the microphone back to Gemma after holding it away from both of them for an instant. Gemma's somewhat scared look dissolved into a happy smile. "You heard it right here," she said into it, "but that's only a smattering of what's included in *The Destiny of Superstitions*. Come visit me at the Broken Mirror Bookstore and buy a book, or many, to learn more."

That pretty much ended that night's Welcome. I was glad. I hadn't done a thing but watch and listen, yet I was exhausted.

Gemma soon returned to her seat, but only long enough to tell me that the night wasn't over yet. She'd agreed to join some of the townsfolk for drinks at the Clinking Glass again and wanted me to come along.

"I'm buying," she coaxed.

How could I refuse?

NINE

As I accompanied Gemma out of the auditorium into the theater's lobby, I looked around, wondering if I'd get a chance to say hi to Justin. Would I even see him? The room was crowded as everyone seemed to head slowly toward the exit. I felt the warmth of people jostling on all sides of me and attempted just to go with the flow, remaining as close as I could to Gemma.

I needn't have worried. Justin was near the farthest wall talking to the cops who'd come there with him. His gaze wasn't on them, though, but on the door I'd just exited. He had possibly been watching for me, as I was looking for him.

I smiled. He smiled.

"I'll meet you outside," I told Gemma.

"Tell your cop to come with us," she said, not even looking at me. Maybe it wasn't such a good idea for her to know me so well.

On the other hand, there wasn't really any harm in her recognizing my interest in Justin. And if she started teasing me about it, I could bounce it back at her threefold.

I determinedly made my way toward Justin and noticed that he was also edging his way through the crowd toward me.

"Need someone to walk you back to your B&B?" he asked as we finally met, looking down with a question in his gleaming blue eyes. He grasped my shoulder gently as if he thought I was off balance and needed some help. I was perfectly fine but didn't mind his touch.

"Maybe eventually," I answered, "but I'm heading now for the Clinking Glass Saloon with Gemma and some of her new friends. Like to join us?"

"I sure would, and since my companions here are now off duty, too, I'll get them to come along."

"Great," I said. Just then someone in the crowd behind me must have decided things were moving too slowly, and I was suddenly pushed in Justin's direction. I pressed against his chest, a nice, firm, muscular chest. I'd felt it before when we'd kissed now and then, and I was always appreciative of his law enforcer's physique. In fact, I was quite appreciative of a lot about Justin.

I was glad he'd be with me some more that evening.

But he didn't walk with me. Instead, he said he'd go with his gang since they had some things to discuss.

He didn't mention it, but I'd seen some not-so-cordial glances toward the cop contingent from the mayor and the p.a. director while they were up on the stage. No one mentioned it at the Welcome. It would have been highly unwelcoming. But I knew there was some potential scandal brewing because of the failure of the Destiny Police Department to declare the death of that tourist who'd fallen down the mountain an accident—or, if it wasn't an accident, to announce what had happened and solve any crime that had been committed. This would help Destiny's ability to reassure tourists that their welcome and safety wasn't affected.

I felt sure that Justin would handle the situation just fine. What I didn't know was when he'd reach a resolution, and that was apparently a problem.

I made my way outside and found Gemma standing with Stuart near the edge of the sidewalk. "Hope you don't mind me joining you for drinks," he said.

I stole a glance toward Gemma. She was beaming, even as her smooth complexion turned a shade rosier.

"I don't mind at all," I responded, and the three of us began negotiating the crowd along the sidewalk in the direction of the bar. Gemma and Stuart talked mostly about how things had gone during the Welcome, and how Gemma should feel flattered and not embarrassed.

By habit, I glanced down in the pale light from the lantern-shape street lamps to avoid stepping on sidewalk cracks. We soon neared the right block. As much as I'd have loved to go back to get Pluckie before the rest of the evening's festivities, the Clinking Glass was a lot closer than my B&B. And if Pluckie wasn't with me, I wouldn't have to insist on a table on the patio.

I worried about my dog, of course, but knew that tonight she would be just fine. But the thought had me crossing my fingers, just in case.

I headed for the dark, noisy inside area, along with Gemma and Stuart.

The high stools at the bar were nearly all occupied. A couple of grinning, busy bartenders were pouring drinks. Along the rear wall was a large mirror—unbroken, of course—over which were a couple of neon decorative lights in the shape of two round wineglasses with their stems crossed in an X.

The rest of the conversation-filled room was crowded with a variety of tables, mostly small round ones but also larger ones in oval and rectangular shapes to accommodate parties of any size. The chairs were somewhat uniform, though—all wooden with tall backs and seats of green faux leather held down by copper-colored bolts.

I had always sat outside on my previous visits here, such as after my dog and cat talks, and hadn't paid much attention to the inside area before. Now, I studied it as I stood at the door with Gemma and Stuart, looking around for an empty table.

There weren't many. But that didn't matter. Not with the town's most esteemed politicians there.

"Hey, Gemma, over here," shouted Lou Landorf. I wasn't surprised to see him, nor the mayor at the table beside him. This bar was a popular place to congregate for any reason, and especially after a Destiny Welcome—both by locals and by tourists. Not that I came here each time, but I'd heard that others did.

I gathered that the two politicians had had some underlings push a few tables together and save them. There were several vacant seats—in fact quite a few, considering how busy this place was—and those that were occupied became vacant quickly as the young occupants, maybe interns, stood and left as other people arrived.

Gemma, Stuart, and I joined them. So did Carolyn Innes, who had been sitting on the other side of the room from me at the Welcome with proprietors of a couple of other local shops. They all joined us now. The conversation turned immediately to the Welcome and the way Lou had focused on Gemma and the Broken Mirror Bookstore. None of the others seemed jealous. In fact, they appeared to welcome the attention, since that bookstore was always a draw to bring tourists to town. Thanks to Gemma, it still would be.

I noticed that Gemma and Stuart weren't able to engage in any private conversation; anytime they began speaking to one another Lou seemed to think of something vital to tell Gemma about how the Broken Mirror should be handled in the future. "I'll always be willing to speak up for you with the owners, if ever you have any dispute with them," he said at one point. "We don't need their … let's say, difficult relationship spilling over into this town. In fact, I'll knock on wood that it doesn't happen anymore." And knock he did.

With a big smile on her face, Gemma imitated what he'd done, which drew an even bigger smile from Lou.

Not so much from Stuart, though. It wasn't any surprise to me that he probably interpreted Lou's actions as being further flirtation with Gemma.

Some shop owners came and went. I hadn't seen what had happened to Frank Shorester after the Welcome, but I did notice when he joined us at the table—clearly uninvited, if Lou's glare was any indication.

But Mayor Bevin had drunk enough Irish beer that he didn't seem inclined to tell Frank he was unwelcome. And Lou appeared to defer to Bevin—although not without an unhappy look.

Frank didn't act like he wanted to talk to Gemma. Maybe he just wanted to try to call attention to himself by his presence. Perhaps he hoped to shame her into saying something to him. But other than an initial hi, she didn't pay much attention to him.

I was delighted when the law enforcement delegation arrived. I'd fortunately been successful in saving a seat beside me—or at least had Carolyn sit there and twisted her arm to stay until I suggested it was time for her to leave.

Her smile as she rose appeared as teasing as Gemma's, but I just gave her a small, grateful wave.

Justin sat down beside me. Alice took a seat at his other side. She'd taken off her suit jacket and now didn't look particularly like a detective. Beyond her was a young cop who'd been in uniform but was now in a T-shirt and jeans.

The timing wasn't perfect, though. Gemma and Lou had become locked into some kind of discussion, with Stuart attempting to break in now and then. From the little I overheard I had the impression that Lou was telling Gemma that she now owed him and should take absolute instructions from him for running the bookstore. "To attract more tourists," he said.

But I was quickly distracted by Justin's presence. I'd been sipping on a really good pinot noir supposedly handcrafted not far from here, in Santa Barbara. He ordered a locally brewed beer. And when he was served we—of course—clinked glasses.

We started talking about—well, I'm not sure what, just our day and the Welcome and other mundane things. We were kind of flirting.

And as I always did at such times with Justin, I gave a silent nod to my poor, lost Warren. I might not talk about him much, but I still thought about him a lot. Though he was why I was in Destiny, I was sure he would have wanted me to get on with my life without him.

Yet I'd never forget him nor his misfortune after walking under a ladder.

"Forget it!" That was Gemma's loud voice from behind me. I'd had my back toward her as I talked to Justin, and now I spun around in my seat and looked. She was standing, hands on her hips, facing

Lou. "If I'm going to be here running the bookstore, I have to do it the best way I can. I appreciate you introducing me before. And giving me suggestions. But I'll decide how I think things should be handled and run with it." She turned to look at Stuart beside her. He just shrugged his shoulders, apparently not wanting to get involved with whatever argument was going on.

I was aware when Justin stood up too. I glanced in his direction and saw that Alice and the other cop had also stood—peacekeepers even when off duty.

"You owe me," Lou yelled at her. "Just remember that, and make sure you listen to me, get it?"

"Let's keep things down," Justin said, a good idea since the underlying roar in the bar had been reduced to a hum as other patrons gawked at us. "If there's something you need to discuss, how about doing it later, when it won't be … enhanced by alcohol?"

"None of your business." Lou was standing now too. His complexion beneath his light, now-messy hair was beet red, and his glare looked designed to shoot someone. Not a good idea with cops, I thought.

"Oh, I think it is," Justin contradicted.

Alice maneuvered around so she was shoulder to shoulder with Justin, obviously offering support. "Please let's just calm down." Her tone was placating.

"Do your own jobs, and don't worry about me doing mine," Lou shouted. "In fact, you should be out there working on that case instead of drinking and trying to tell me what to do." His frown moved from Justin to Alice to their cohort. "You should be protecting tourists, that's what. Finding answers to that tourist's death. A *tourist's* death," he reiterated. "Not just someone who lives here. You're taking too damned long, and Destiny's continued success is at risk. It's a good thing the Destiny PD is adding a division to work solely with tourists so they'll know who to go to. But you—you want to keep your jobs? Or get promotions? If you have any ambitions for anything else, remember that you owe me, too—and you'd better fix things fast."

"I think it's time for this evening to end." Justin's gaze was moving beyond Lou toward the bar area, as if he was seeking the owner or manager or someone else who could gracefully kick Lou out.

"Not until—" Lou began. But then the redness of his face segued to absolute white. He was looking beyond Justin, up toward the ceiling of the room.

I turned to follow his gaze. That's when I saw that a pigeon had somehow flown into the saloon.

A pigeon? At this hour? What did that—

"A pigeon flying inside foreshadows doom," Stuart intoned from behind Gemma. He was standing now too. "That's what's in *The Destiny of Superstitions*."

"Not for me," Lou said in a voice so hoarse that I was sure he didn't believe what he said. "I'll knock on wood to ensure it." Which he did.

So did everyone else, after each saying something like they were knocking on wood as a precaution, to bring good luck.

Including me.

The pigeon apparently got the attention of the saloon's manager, whom I hadn't met. He had a broom and a large box in his hand.

Others inside helped him while standing on tables, shooing the bird into the box.

"Don't hurt him," I said, always the animal advocate.

"I just want to set him loose outside," the man said and wended his way out the front door.

But that event, after Lou's outburst, was enough to dampen everyone's party mood. Mayor Bevin and Director Lou both threw some bills down on the table and hurried out. So did most everyone else. Gemma and I also left, accompanied by Stuart...and Justin.

We had a nice, brisk walk to the B&B, where I left Justin in the lobby while I went upstairs to get Pluckie. Justin remained with us during Pluckie's good night walk.

Gemma and Stuart had gone upstairs, which was fine with me. That gave me a tiny bit of privacy to share a good night kiss with Justin outside the inn's door.

"Good thing neither of us believes in superstitions," I said.

"Yeah, or we might be worried about what that bird meant. Good night, Rory. Let's get together for coffee or something tomorrow."

"I'd love it," I said, then walked back inside with Pluckie.

Our hostess Serina was up late since she'd been to the Welcome too. "Everything okay, Rory?" My distress must have shown on my face.

But all I said was, "Everything's fine. Thanks for asking. See you in the morning at breakfast."

Then Pluckie and I went upstairs.

———

I had a hard time falling asleep that night. Pluckie, as usual, did just fine, snoring gently beside me as I lay there thinking.

The party at the Clinking Glass Saloon, such as it was, had turned weird. It had started off fine, but then there'd been Frank's appearance. And the strife between Gemma and Lou. Lou's miserable attitude toward others, too.

And then the appearance of that pigeon. Yes, I'd checked *The Destiny of Superstitions* when I'd gotten into my room, and pigeons—and other kinds of birds—flying inside could be an omen of death.

I pondered that. Would the statements made and knocking on wood somehow turn that around?

Heck, it was just a superstition. And I still didn't completely believe in superstitions.

Or at least I kept telling myself that.

So, I lay there in the near-complete darkness, with only a sliver of light coming through the draperies at the nearby window, thanks to the streetlights that stayed on all night.

I must have eventually fallen asleep since suddenly I startled awake. Pluckie was standing beside me on the bed, staring at that closed window. She gave a few muted woofs but didn't bark.

And then I knew what had awakened me and Pluckie.

I heard the sound of a howling dog somewhere in the distance outside.

The same kind of howl I'd heard a few times before.

And some of those times it had complied with the related superstition, as anticipated in the town of Destiny.

It had heralded a death.

This time too?

I found out the answer the next morning.

TEN

I WOKE UP BEFORE the alarm programmed into my phone went off—a good thing, since it indicated I'd fallen asleep. Somehow. Sometime, during that long night.

I realized right away what, besides my own uneasy mind, had awakened me. Pluckie was off the bed, standing with her back feet on the floor and her front ones on the mattress beside me, her nose pressing into my arm.

"What do you think, girl?" I asked a little groggily as I patted her. "Did that howl mean anything?"

She sat down and cocked her sweet black head, regarding me earnestly. If she'd known the answer and been able to communicate it to me, I was sure she would.

I sighed. "It's time to go find out."

I dressed quickly and snapped Pluckie's leash onto her collar. At the door to my unit I grasped the knob and took a deep breath. Just in case, I said, "I hope someone was just playing games, or we imagined it, or—whatever." I crossed my fingers hopefully.

I wasn't sure why some superstitions might trump others, and why some even seemed to be the entire opposite of others.

That only added to my many questions.

And no matter what I did that morning, if that howl had been a harbinger of death as the others had been, what I might try to do now to counter it wouldn't matter at all.

"Okay, girl," I said resignedly to Pluckie and opened the door.

There was no one in the hallway, so we headed downstairs. I'd take Pluckie out for a quick walk first, then go into the breakfast room, as usual.

I heard a lot of noise coming from the area where many of the B&B's roomers were undoubtedly eating. More than usual? Probably not. But I would be interested in finding out, when I joined them, if any others had heard that howl.

I didn't see Serina and figured she was in the room serving her guests, so I'd have to wait till later to ask her too. I opened the front door and walked beneath the horseshoe to the front yard of the B&B.

As I often did, I let Pluckie lead me in the direction she wanted to go. After all, she was the one with something to accomplish out here. She began sniffing the ground, heading along Fate Street in the opposite direction from downtown Destiny.

Some cars were parked along the street on both sides. It didn't matter since we stayed on the sidewalk. Pluckie squatted for the first time, then continued on as a compact white sedan drove by, followed by a green SUV.

Not a lot of traffic, but then, this wasn't Destiny Boulevard.

It was a pleasant day in September, with a clear sky and the air warm but not baking. I had no problem with Pluckie taking her time. I'd learn who heard the howl last night after we returned to the

B&B, and get the rundown of people's opinions about what it meant later. For now, we would just enjoy our walk.

As we reached the next street corner I saw a man and woman walking a Sheltie on the opposite side of the street. They didn't look familiar, so I assumed they were tourists.

It wouldn't hurt to be friendly to them—and maybe work into any conversation that they might enjoy bringing their pup to the Lucky Dog Boutique while they were in town.

"Come on, girl," I told Pluckie. But she had something to accomplish first, and this time, when she squatted, I had to clean up after her.

When I was finished, I checked and still saw the people and dog, a little farther down the street. They were walking in the opposite direction from Destiny Boulevard, which was fine since it was a lot quieter here where the street was lined with a few compact office buildings before the residential area started. In fact, I had the sense that the couple was headed toward the small park at the next street corner, a good place to walk dogs.

I checked to make sure no cars were coming then Pluckie and I crossed the street. "Let's hurry," I told her so we could catch up.

The dog was taking her time sniffing the sidewalk, and her people weren't hurrying her. We soon reached them.

"Hi," I said as Pluckie approached the dog. I held my breath for an instant, in case that dog didn't like others, but after they traded nose sniffs they seemed to become good buddies.

"Cute dog," the woman said. She was short and a little stout and smiling broadly. She wore a red knit shirt with buttons over beige Capri pants.

"Yours too."

We chatted for a minute, with the man joining in. They were the Plangers, Sue and Bill, from Tucson. Their dog was Pippin. And, yes, they'd heard of the Lucky Dog Boutique and planned to visit there today or tomorrow. They'd just arrived in town yesterday and had attended the Welcome last night.

They seemed pleased to have company on their walk. As we strolled with the dogs, I gave them a sketchy version of my background, only saying that I was fascinated by superstitions and that was what had drawn me here. Thanks to my lucky dog Pluckie, we'd found the ailing owner of the Lucky Dog and got help for her, then couldn't resist her request that we stay here and assist her with running the shop.

By the time I'd finished, we were at the park. A few more cars had passed by, but I saw no traffic, no more people walking dogs. This was a pleasant area, but it really didn't give a good sense of what busy Destiny was all about.

"You know," I said, "you might want to take a tour of Destiny. I did, and I found it fun and helpful for learning more about the place." I even mentioned Destiny's Luckiest Tours, the company that gave the tour I'd taken—where Martha's nephew Arlen was a guide.

"Good idea," Bill said.

The park was about a block and a half long, and it was surrounded on two sides by high ficus bushes that shielded it from the nearest houses. A small children's area with swings and a seesaw sat near the road.

The dogs stayed together as they sniffed and meandered and—

Pluckie suddenly stopped, her nose in the air. Then she barked—and began running. I was startled enough that I dropped her leash. And, in fact, when Pippin also barked and ran, Sue dropped the end of her leash too. Both dogs sprinted farther into the park area and toward the bushes, Pluckie in the lead.

"Pippin, no!" shouted Bill. "Wait."

"No, Pluckie," I also yelled.

My dog did stop when she reached the ficus, her face pressed into the bushes as if she was sniffing something. Some creature? I wasn't sure what kinds of small animals might frequent the park, but—

"Oh, my God," cried Bill, who'd caught up with both dogs. Pippin had already joined Pluckie. "Oh, no."

"What is it?" Sue called. She was behind us.

I quickly joined Bill and gasped too. A man's body lay on the ground beneath the bushes.

It was a man I recognized: Lou Landorf.

There was blood all around him, and no wonder. A large piece of wood, a stake of some sort, was protruding from his chest.

A sense of déjà vu hit me. I'd found another body like this, Kenneth Tarzal's, not long ago. He'd been dead, killed by a piece of broken mirror.

Was Lou dead? His face was white, and he wasn't moving. "I'm calling 911," Bill rasped, stepping back and drawing a phone from his pocket. "Sue, take Pippin and stay back."

I pushed Pluckie gently away and knelt in the dirt near Lou, touching his neck, checking for a pulse. I felt none.

My eyes focused on the stake that pierced him. It had a fist carved into the top. I'd seen similar ones at souvenir shops in town, encouraging people to knock on wood.

As Lou had always done. But I had a terrible feeling that it hadn't brought him good luck after all—and Lou would probably never knock on wood again.

ELEVEN

I STOOD UP, FEELING tears run down my face. For Lou? For myself? For all of us?

No matter. Bill stood a few feet away, bent forward and turned partly away from where Lou's body lay, clearly not looking at him. He held his phone to his ear.

I didn't wait to eavesdrop on his conversation with the 911 operator, although I did notice the pallor and fear on his middle-aged face as he held the side of his head while he talked.

I pulled my own phone from my pocket and pressed in Justin's number while holding much more tightly to Pluckie's leash. My little dog had sat down on the grass beside my feet, leaning against my leg. She obviously sensed my traumatized state of mind.

I'd no doubt Justin was awake already, maybe even heading for work. But it wouldn't have mattered if I'd awakened him. This was something he'd want to know about, and, even though he was bound to receive official notification via appropriate channels, I wanted to be the one to inform him of my own involvement.

No, not really involvement. I had nothing to do with what had happened to Lou. But my good luck dog Pluckie had led us both once more into a really bad luck situation.

Finding another murder victim.

"I want to report a dead body." Bill's voice was cracking in the background as I called Justin.

"Hi, Rory," he said. "Good morning. It's early, so ... what's wrong?"

I'd have laughed if I wasn't so upset. My voice shook as I said, "Why does there have to be something wrong for me to ... never mind. You're right. It's so horrible. Pluckie has led me to another body." I swallowed hard.

Silence for a second while Bill's voice continued in the background, describing where we were.

"One like Martha?" Justin finally asked. "Or like—"

"Like Tarzal," I blurted. Thanks to Pluckie, Martha had been found alive, but it had been too late for Tarzal. "In case you're wondering, a couple of tourists and their dog were with us. The man's called 911."

"And I'm getting another call now too. I'll take it, then call you right back."

"Fine. But Justin, you should know that the victim is Lou Landorf."

———

Justin did call me back within a couple of minutes. "I'm on my way," he said, "but others will get there first. I hate to say it, but I'm sure you know the drill."

I nodded even though he couldn't see it. "Stay here. Touch nothing. Make sure any other witnesses hang around, too, and also don't disturb any possible evidence."

"Close enough. See you shortly. And … Rory?"

"Yes." The word came out shrill enough for Pluckie to look up at me. "Yes," I repeated.

"I'm sorry you had to see something like that again."

"Me too."

When I hung up, I knelt to hug Pluckie. Needing even more reassurance, I picked her up. When I looked around to start doing as Justin wanted me to, I didn't immediately see Bill and my heart rate sped up in panic. At least I knew his name and his wife's and dog's if I needed to give the information to the cops to go find them. Would their fleeing be an indication of their involvement with the killing?

But they'd seemed so calm till we found the body. And, as it turned out, Bill hadn't gone far. Sue had walked a distance away with Pippin and just stood there near the street, her back toward us. Her shoulders were hunched beneath her red shirt. Bill was striding toward her, and I heard sirens in the distance.

Putting Pluckie down again and holding onto her leash, I hurried to join them. "Thanks for calling the authorities," I told Bill. "I just spoke with Destiny's police chief. He said we need to stay here to give our statements." And answer whatever questions might be leveled against us—like, did any of us decide to stab Lou last night after the Destiny Welcome?

The Destiny Welcome. Had it turned unlucky? Pluckie and I had also found Tarzal's body after a Welcome … although there'd been other presentations in the weeks between them. Not all of them resulted in a murder, thank heavens.

Surely the killings couldn't be related to the Welcome. Yet, in Destiny, some superstition mavens were likely to recall the same thing as I had—and start spouting how unlucky those events had become.

That would be horrible for Destiny. The Welcomes were part of the town's culture, designed to introduce tourists to what Destiny was all about.

I'd have to think about how to turn it around. What about these two particular Welcomes could be described differently—and avoided forevermore in the future?

It wouldn't really be up to me, even if I could come up with something—and I was far from a superstition expert. But maybe Gemma, the librarian and knowledgeable researcher, could find something...

Gemma. She had been flirting with Lou, or at least not reacting unfavorably to his apparent interest.

Until last night.

She'd argued with him then. Surely the situation wouldn't turn into another battle on my part to save a friend from suspicion of being a murderer.

Surely Justin and the other cops would have a much better suspect to glom onto.

Though preferably not me.

"Are you okay?" That was Bill, yelling over the approaching siren. He stood with one arm around his wife, staring at me. I must have looked spaced out or confused or, worse, anxious and nervous. I felt all of those things but didn't really want anyone else to know.

The couple were both on a path close to the road that abutted the park, with Pippin at their feet. I didn't have time to respond and reassure them I was fine before a police car slammed on its brakes beside us.

A couple of uniformed officers jumped out. "Did one of you call to report finding an injured person?"

"I did, officer," Bill said. "And I think he's more than just injured."

I definitely agreed, although, for now, I kept silent, kneeling to hold Pluckie close.

Another car screeched to a halt behind the first one. Two other cops got out and hurried toward us, while the first two accompanied Bill back toward Lou's body. I rose, holding Pluckie in my arms, and started to follow them.

"Wait here, please, ma'am," said a young female cop from the second car. She looked vaguely familiar, but I didn't recall talking with her before. I might just have seen her at the police station when I'd been there visiting Justin, or at a Welcome, or who knew?

"Okay," I said. "But I wanted to tell them who the victim is before—" I heard a shout emanate from back near where the trees began. "I suspect they know now." I sucked in my lips, shaking my head both in sorrow and in wry amusement at the reaction.

"Who is it?" That was Sue. She was now, like I'd been, kneeling on the ground beside her dog. The Sheltie was probably too large for her to pick up easily, the way I still held Pluckie.

"Please don't say anything, ma'am," the lady cop said to me. Her nametag identified her as Officer Sweelen. I suspected she had started her law enforcement career recently considering how young she looked, with absolutely smooth facial skin and pale, glossed lips beneath golden hair pulled back into a clip.

Her partner, who'd joined her, looked even more familiar. He had been one of those who'd first appeared at the Lucky Dog Boutique when I'd called for help after Pluckie discovered Martha in the backroom in distress. I couldn't check the officer's nametag because of the angle at which he stood in the now-increasing sunlight. "We'll need for you to answer a few questions," he said.

I nodded. I knew the drill. "How long do you think it will be before—"

I didn't need to finish since I saw Justin striding down the path beside the police cars, dressed as usual while on duty. He must have parked his vehicle behind the second one.

I restrained myself from running to him and into his arms for a comforting hug. I already had Pluckie with me for comfort. And as much as I'd begun to appreciate Justin, we were still not really in that kind of relationship—if any relationship at all.

This wasn't a time to think of my poor lost Warren, but of course I did.

There weren't any ladders leaning against trees here, so that hadn't contributed to Lou's death. Those trees looked mostly like conifers—pines, maybe.

What superstitions were affiliated with them, if any? I'd no doubt there were some. In fact, I'd seen some reference to them in *The Destiny of Superstitions* but they hadn't registered in my mind as being of any importance so I couldn't recall them now. Or maybe I wouldn't be able to remember anything at the moment.

But now maybe tree superstitions were important. I'd have to check them out.

I recalled then that a pigeon had flown into the Clinking Glass Saloon last night. Had it presaged Lou's death? He'd knocked on wood then. But he had still died.

I realized that my mind was going off on all kinds of tangents now, possibly to avoid thinking of the reality of what had happened here.

I didn't recall getting this upset after finding Tarzal. Maybe I was more in shock then.

Or maybe the reality that Pluckie might be less than lucky when it came to discovering ill, or dead, people was sinking in. Not that I'd love her any less. But I hoped that, if this kind of thing ever happened again, it would be more along the Martha situation than the other ones.

Suddenly I did find myself in Justin's arms, even though I still held my dog. "Rory, are you okay?" he asked softly. Pluckie squirmed and tried to lick Justin's face.

"I ... guess so." But it was all I could do to keep myself from breaking down. Instead, I made myself smile a little and squash Pluckie against Justin so I could stretch up and kiss his cheek. Then I pulled away. Speaking quietly, I said, "I suspect superstitions are involved—surprise, surprise—but the murder weapon appears to be a stylized carved fist on a stake that represents knocking on wood."

Justin's expression also turned wry. "As you said, surprise, surprise—especially with it being that particular superstition and Lou. But of course we'll have to see what our forensics experts come back with."

"Justin?" That was a familiar voice from over his shoulder. Detective Alice Numa stood there looking grim. Despite the deep tone to her skin, she almost appeared pale. "I heard on our radio. Is it— Is Director Landorf the victim?"

I nodded. Justin hadn't gone to see the body yet, but I'd no doubts at all.

"I believe so," was what he said. "Are you okay to conduct some of the witness interviews, Alice? Richard's on his way too." He glanced toward me. "That's Detective Richard Choye. I don't know if you've met him yet, but he might be the one who'll question you."

"No, I haven't," I said, voicing no preference even assuming I had a choice of whom. The idea of being questioned either by Alice, or by a stranger—well, I knew it was coming but would have preferred not to answer anything, no matter who asked.

"I can handle it," Alice said. "All or a few of them, whatever." She seemed to straighten herself within her dark pantsuit and reassume her professional demeanor as she looked at me. "I take it that you're a witness again, Rory?" Her tone sounded cool, and yet her expressionless stare seemed to accuse me. Of what? Finding another body?

Murdering him?

I made myself relax and not take umbrage. At least not yet. "Pluckie and I were walking here, then joined up with the tourists who are still around, too, the Plangers. Pluckie and their dog scented … the body."

"Then I guess you are, in fact, a witness again. I'll check out the others and we'll work out the details for an interview of each of you." She looked me over as though checking to see if I had any blood stains on me. My fingerprints were already on record after last time. Yes, I did know the drill—at least somewhat.

Then Alice turned and strode toward where a couple of uniforms stood near the Plangers and their Pippin.

I saw that two men in what looked like hazmat outfits had arrived. They carried a gurney in the direction of where Lou lay, followed by a guy in a suit.

I hadn't seen anything exactly like this when we'd discovered Tarzal's body, but that had been indoors, in his shop, and Pluckie and I had been ushered into the other room while this kind of thing was being done.

"That's our medical examiner," Justin said. "I'd better go talk to him. Are you okay waiting here?"

"Sure," I said, not positive that I meant it. But as long as I didn't go far I'd be able to walk Pluckie around a little.

We strode down the path along the road, away from the rest of the park and closer to where the buildings began. Pluckie seemed quite interested in sniffing, which slowed me down—a good thing, since I had an urge to run away.

Not that I wouldn't be found later when Alice, or whoever, was ready to bombard me with questions.

But the only answer they'd really be looking for were those I wanted to know too.

Who had killed Lou Landorf, and why?

———

I hadn't noticed the picnic tables inside the park area before. Maybe because they were near where the trees began, yet also adjacent to the rear yards of the closest buildings.

I saw them now, though. That was where Alice directed the Plangers to go. She sat now at one of the tables with Bill, while a man in a gray suit sat at another table with Sue and Pippin—Detective Choye, I presumed.

I'd probably be next, but I couldn't tell which detective would take my statement.

Too bad I couldn't just give it to Justin, but I felt sure he would have concerns about it being a conflict of interest. Or at least looking that way. We hadn't attempted to keep it secret in Destiny that we sometimes shared meals or went out for drinks. People could interpret that as if we were in a relationship.

And I couldn't say, with a straight face, that we weren't headed that way.

Sorry, Warren.

I continued to stand there with Pluckie as a light wind picked up. Realizing that the morning was growing later, I called my assistant Millie, who was due in first that day, to tell her that something had come up and I would be late.

I didn't elaborate, and she, fortunately, didn't ask.

I also watched what was happening at the crime scene from as far away as I could get and yet stay in this small park, while also observing what I assumed were the first official interrogations.

I supposed it would be best to talk to someone I knew, but I wasn't that friendly with Alice. Would I be better off speaking with Detective Choye? I didn't think so.

Why couldn't Justin act as a detective here? I knew he'd help to calm my frayed nerves, make me feel better—at least as much as possible under these difficult circumstances.

But he'd joined the first group around where we'd found Lou Landorf's body, which I assumed was still there since I hadn't seen it carted off toward the official vehicles parked along the nearby road.

Pluckie was being her usual good self, sniffing the grass and pulling a bit to continue walking, although she obeyed each time I told her "sit." As we stood there, I felt a tickling at my neck and reached to rub it.

Fortunately, it must have been my below-shoulder-length blond hair tickling my skin in the breeze and not—thank heavens for many reasons—a spider, which had been my first thought. As I'd touched the area I remembered a superstition I'd heard sometime after arriving here in Destiny, although I didn't recall the source. I'd been thinking about Justin. And the superstition said that if you have a spider on your neck, you'll also have a lover.

If that ever happened between us, I certainly didn't want it to have anything to do with a creepy, crawly insect's intrusion.

I nevertheless kept watching the area where Justin had gone— mostly because I was hoping somehow that I'd been wrong, that Lou Landorf had been wounded, yes, but not killed.

Although if there'd been any hope, EMTs would undoubtedly have arrived by now. And Justin had mentioned that one of the men who'd arrived before was the medical examiner ...

No, I shouldn't bother to hope. Yet—

"Rory? Do you know what happened?"

I was startled at the voice from behind me. Pluckie wasn't surprised, though. She'd been pulling in that direction on her leash, and I'd just assumed she was still on sniff-and-piddle patrol.

I turned, knowing who it was.

And knowing, too, that I didn't really want to talk to reporter Celia Vardox.

TWELVE

"Oh, hi, Celia," I said, not responding to her question. To avoid it even longer, I continued, "What brings you here? You don't have Charlotte with you." Then, inspired by my implied scolding of her for not having her sweet black Lab along, I did answer what she'd asked. "I'm here because I took Pluckie to this park for her morning walk."

"I figured," she acknowledged, glancing down at Pluckie and then back up again. "But what did you find here?" Her brown eyes studied me with her usual journalistic inquisitiveness. She was about my age but shorter than me, with curly hair, a strong brow and a wide, contemplative mouth.

"Find?" My voice sounded too shrill, and that changed her curious expression into something that appeared victorious.

"I heard sirens in town and followed them. They led here—which shouldn't surprise you." She gestured toward all the police and other emergency vehicles along the curb. "So, what's going on here?"

I took a deep breath. She'd hear about it anyway, so it shouldn't hurt for me to talk to her about what—who—Pluckie and Pippin had found, and in what condition he was.

Except—"If I say anything to you, I don't want to be quoted or mentioned in any way, not even as an anonymous source. Not me, and not my dog. Okay?"

I'd gotten into a predicament before, thanks to the *Destiny Star* and its owners, the Vardoxes, who'd written an article that featured me—and called too much attention to me having moved to Destiny and why. It had led to trouble, to a danger I hadn't anticipated. It perhaps had helped garner a resolution, but I didn't want to go through anything like that again. Ever.

Celia hesitated, but only for a moment. "Okay," she said. "I'm sure I'll find other, more cooperative sources once I know what I'm looking for." She raised her brows as if she believed that I'd roll over and let her quote me rather than let others get the credit for what I was about to tell her.

"Fine. So I do have your promise?"

She nodded and held up her right hand, her little finger bent. "Pinky swear," she said. "And that's a stronger vow than a handshake. Superstition has it that if you violate a promise made with a pinky swear you're supposed to cut off that finger to avoid bad luck."

"Ugh," I said and didn't link my pinky with hers. "I'll take your word for it."

"So," she prompted. "What happened?"

If anyone would leap to combine the situation here with what Pluckie had discovered before, it would be Celia. I therefore decided to tone down my dog's involvement if I had to mention her at all. I simply said, "An apparent murder victim was found in the park this morning."

Celia's staring eyes grew shrewd and excited. She had a large shoulder bag and I could see her restrain herself from reaching for it, perhaps to draw out pen and paper to take notes ... for now. I figured she would eventually. A camera too.

As long as Pluckie and I were not featured in either I didn't care.

"And it is—?" she prompted.

I swallowed, then blurted, "Public Affairs Director Lou Landorf."

Her expression looked almost delighted. Did she hate Lou that much, or did she just love the idea that the news would interest a whole lot of people, both in Destiny and elsewhere?

They must not have been close friends, or surely her reaction would have been different.

"Really? Lou? How was he killed? Is a suspect in custody?"

"That's all I'm going to tell you, Celia," I said firmly. "Partly because I don't know much more than that. But also because it's bad luck to talk about such things. You should know that. Your offices burned after you tried to interview people about ... that situation before, after we were all warned about how much bad luck there'd be, that we shouldn't talk at all about what had happened, or what we speculated had happened." I didn't really have to remind her of that. The *Destiny Star's* office wasn't totally decimated after her brother's attempt to dig into information involving a superstition that had supposedly come true, but it had taken the entire Destiny Fire Department to put out the blaze.

The Vardoxes were still finishing the restoration of their building and its contents.

"Who said it was bad luck to talk about this situation?" Celia countered. "Or about any murder or whatever? If that was really true, there'd never be anything in the media anywhere about death or war or anything terrible like that because anyone who talked about it would suffer, maybe like the victim. Is that what you're saying? And don't blame it on superstition being the cause. People can claim that regarding anything that happens."

What she said made sense, but I wouldn't admit it. And who knew—yet—if talking about what had happened to Lou involved a superstition, or whether discussing it would be bad luck?

"You, of all people, should know better," I said. I wanted to walk away. Alice Numa or the other detective would be able to find me. Maybe they could question me later, somewhere else.

In any event, I didn't want to continue this debate with Celia.

But when I glanced toward the picnic tables, both detectives were now seated there together with Sue and Bill Planger. Neither was ready for me. And when I pivoted slightly to look over Celia's shoulder I saw that Justin was following some people pushing a gurney toward the street. A lump covered with a white sheet was on top. Lou, no doubt.

Maybe I should just point there and sic Celia on them. But I didn't. She'd jump on them soon enough.

"What I'm saying is that things are different in Destiny. But you know that. And—"

My expression must have said something my words didn't. She looked over her own shoulder, then raised her hand and said, "Thanks, Rory. We'll talk again later. All off the record." And she hurried to catch up with the procession.

I watched her dash up to Justin and begin talking to him. What would he say? Would he be more forthcoming than I?

I doubted it. I figured the official line would be either "no comment" or "that's still under investigation."

And, evidently, I was under investigation, too, because I saw the two detectives rise, as did the Plangers, who started walking off with their dog. Then Alice Numa seemed to scan the area with a determined gaze that soon settled on me. She beckoned me to join her.

I knew I needed to obey.

———

The interrogation went well, I thought. I was becoming a pro at this. Or at least my prior experience seemed to kick in and help me respond to Alice's questions this time.

She was slightly overweight, clad in a dark, official-looking suit, including a jacket, even outdoors here in the park. She had a cop's utility belt on too. I didn't see her weapon but I knew it was there. Her dark eyes were alert and seemed studiedly blank as she asked her questions—most of the time.

She was taking notes again, as she had before. Plus, she was once more recording what I said.

I kept Pluckie's leash looped over my arm, and my dog seemed fine with lying down on the grass beneath the table.

At Alice's behest, I described minute by minute what I'd done that morning till Pluckie and I helped to find the body, including our partial walk with the Plangers and their dog Pippin. No, I didn't see anyone else at the park when we got here. It was early.

No, I didn't see any vehicle peeling out of the area along the road, or anything else that appeared suspicious.

Why had I come to this particular park this morning? She leveled her now narrow-eyed stare at me, as if she expected me to reveal something important that she'd draw out of me.

I didn't. "It wasn't the first time," I said, although Pluckie and I had always stayed at the park's fringes before. "It's not far from the Rainbow B&B where we're staying. I just happened to notice the Plangers walking with their dog and thought that Pluckie and I could say hi, invite them to visit the Lucky Dog, that kind of thing." Why? Was she insinuating that I knew what we'd find here?

"Okay," she said. "Now, let's go back to last night. You were all there together at the Clinking Glass Saloon, right? Did you hear or see anything that appeared suspicious, any threats leveled at Director Landorf, that kind of thing?"

I'd already been pondering that. Lou hadn't been on his best behavior. He seemed to have drunk too much. He'd sniped at a number of different people, including Gemma, but I wasn't going to mention her.

Instead, I could mention his other targets of nastiness and generate Alice's irritation without appearing to point any fingers. "Well, he was criticizing the Destiny Police Department," I reminded her.

"Yeah, I know," she said glumly. "But I assume you're not accusing Chief Halbertson or me of killing the director to shut him up." Her dark eyes stared at me as if challenging me to do just that.

I didn't. "Of course not."

Speaking of the Destiny PD, I noticed that Justin had broken away from Celia and was walking toward us. I forced myself not to smile. He wouldn't necessarily rescue me from this interrogation. In fact, he might have questions of his own to toss at me.

When he reached us, Pluckie stood and wagged her tail, then stood on her hind legs to put her forepaws on Justin's legs, a happy greeting if I'd ever seen one.

I couldn't exactly tell her to back off, that this man who seemed to be our friend might be here to do more stuff I didn't really want to deal with.

But Justin just said hi to Alice and me, then asked, "How are we doing here? Did you have anything useful for us, Rory?"

"I doubt it," I said. "I didn't see anything or anyone that would solve it for you—unless there was something I didn't focus on but told you, Alice?" My voice rose, turning what I said into a question.

Her answer was to shake her head in the negative. "Not that I heard," she told Justin. "But like with the rest of it, I'll listen again and put it into a report, Chief."

"Great," he said. "Are there any more questions you need to ask?"

"No, I think we're done here."

I let my breath out in a sigh of relief. I hadn't noticed, but my breathing had gotten shallow out of nervousness, and now I could let it go.

For now.

But I still had some questions of my own, none that I'd reveal to either of these cops. I'd get the answers in my own way.

"I take it that neither of you have had breakfast," Justin said. "Care to join me? It'll have to be fast food."

"I need to get back to the station with this, Chief," Alice said. "Thanks anyway."

"And I need to get to the Lucky Dog," I said. But then I relented. "No sense showing up there hungry, though. I can feed Pluckie at the shop, but I can join you for a quick bite on the way."

114

I was delighted to see the breadth of the smile on Justin's handsome face.

————

I hurried back to the B&B for my car. Justin and I each drove since we'd have our own destinations after we were done.

The closest fast food place wasn't far out of town—none right inside Destiny, though. If there were any superstitions applicable to fast food I didn't know them, and none of the major chains had apparently tried to find some to justify inserting their presence here.

Our breakfast was brief, but Justin and I managed to sit at a table on an outside patio so Pluckie could join us. I shouldn't have, but I needed something to revitalize my energy, so I chose hotcakes and coffee. Justin ordered a biscuit sandwich with egg, bacon, and cheese.

And when we were seated, he looked me straight in the eyes. "Are you okay, Rory?"

"As okay as I can be after finding a dead body. A second dead body." I closed my eyes and shook my head. "That never happened to me before, and I don't like it now."

I hadn't been near my Warren when he'd died...

"I'm concerned that Destiny is unlucky for you," Justin agreed. "We need to find some ways besides your amulet to send good luck your way. I've got some ideas of people to ask, but with Tarzal, who really knew superstitions, gone..."

He didn't finish. Didn't have to. And Tarzal might not have been appropriate to ask even if he were still alive, since he'd been shifting his position on the reliability of superstitions before he died.

"I know," I said. "Let me know if you come up with any ideas, either of people I should talk with or good luck charms or whatever that can help turn things around. Or," I amended, "that true believers would think could turn things around."

He laughed. "Unlike us," he said.

"Unlike us," I agreed, smiling at him. Catching his eyes with mine. Seeing some interest there beyond cop concern and even just friendship.

Which made me smile a bit more. Maybe I was looking right at what—who—could bring me good luck.

And I did know of someone I could talk to about superstitions and changing my luck. I'd talk to Gemma a little later to see if her knowledge of superstitions in books could help.

That wasn't all I intended to talk to her about.

THIRTEEN

Foam coffee cup in hand, I said goodbye to Justin in the fast food restaurant's parking lot. We exchanged a brief kiss and he promised to call me later, which was good. I'd have questions about anything the DPD learned about Lou's death.

Not that I really thought Justin would let me know everything, but he might be able to fill me in on what they intended to tell the public before anyone else heard about it.

That might even include what superstitions they planned to feed to people as the cause of Lou's bad luck. Considering how often the city's head public relations guy had knocked on wood, at least when other people were around, it had to be something pretty terrible to counter the supposed good luck he was preserving for himself.

Or maybe superstitions had nothing to do with it—as if people in Destiny would ever buy into that.

As I drove to the Lucky Dog with Pluckie I listened for sirens as a matter of habit, but figured all the urgency was gone. There was no life left to rescue, no occurring crime to halt.

I wondered where the Plangers were now. Hightailing it out of Destiny as fast as they could go? Or had they been told their ordeal in the town of superstitions was not yet over and they had to remain in case anyone had more questions—like, did one or both of you kill the p.a. director?

Or were they hanging out here to see if superstitions helped to solve this heinous crime?

I parked my car, a medium-sized dark blue sedan, back at the B&B so Pluckie and I could walk the few blocks to the store. I still had a little coffee to sip on, so I brought it along too. The sidewalks were fairly empty on Fate Street until we got closer to Destiny Boulevard, where the usual crowds appeared. Not surprising. It was mid-morning now.

We crossed the street and walked by the Broken Mirror Bookstore as we neared the Lucky Dog. I peeked in. It looked crowded. Gemma was talking to a group of people I presumed were customers.

I thought about going in right then to vent to her and see her reaction to the news, assuming she hadn't already heard. But why disturb her in the middle of what looked like possible sales?

Plus, I needed to make sure all was well in the shop I managed first.

Which it was. I was glad to see a crowd there too. Lots of tourists, many with dogs, were in our aisles examining our pet food and toys and accessories. Millie was clearly busy, but she had help. Martha was downstairs, too, and she looked fairly energetic as she also waited on customers.

"Hi, Rory," Martha said with a big smile on her aging but happy face as she saw me. She wore a hot pink Lucky Dog Boutique T-shirt over her slacks. Millie's was green, and mine, today, was purple. I hadn't even paid much attention to that with all that had gone on earlier, but it didn't matter. Everyone I'd talked to that morning, except for the Plangers, knew who I was and where I worked. And I'd invited them fairly quickly to come visit this shop with Pippin.

Maybe I wasn't needed here at the moment, but I nevertheless put my purse away in the rear storeroom, threw my empty coffee cup away, and came out with Pluckie, ready to answer questions and make some sales.

Which I did, for about ten minutes after fastening Pluckie's leash to the counter so I wouldn't worry about her following anyone outside.

Then, as things slowed down, I saw Martha's customers leave with a couple of large plastic bags in hand and I approached her.

She was standing behind the glass case containing superstition amulets that could be attached to collars—or human necklaces— that had smiling animal faces. "You may not have heard, but another terrible event occurred in Destiny last night."

Her soft hazel eyes, already flanked by creases, narrowed even more as her wizened lips frowned. Her voice came out as a cracking whisper. "Is someone else... dead?"

I nodded briefly and said very softly, "Director Landorf."

She grabbed the counter. "Lou? What happened?" She put up her hands. "No. Don't tell me... unless I'm going to be accused of doing something to him too?" Poor Martha had been considered a major suspect when Tarzal was murdered since she had argued with him.

I wasn't aware of any disagreement she had with Lou, so all I said was, "Not as far as I know." But I didn't really know who might be genuine persons of interest in this latest murder.

Millie had finished waiting on her customers, who bought some cans of food. She must have heard what I'd said. Her youthful face appeared stricken. "That was why you were late," she said, and it wasn't a question. "What happened?"

"I don't want to go into the—literally—gory details, but it looked like he was killed intentionally." That was all I needed to say. I was sure they'd hear more about it soon. "Right now, I want to go next door and talk to Gemma. She's been studying superstitions, including those in Tarzal's book, so I'd like to find out if she has ideas about any that could have led to what happened."

That wasn't the only reason I wanted to talk to her. Lou had been flirting with her. She hadn't seemed extremely interested, but neither had she completely shrugged him off.

Plus, they had shared some not-so-pleasant words last night. Not that the minor encounter would have been enough to make her a murder suspect … I hoped. But I at least wanted her to know what had happened and to prepare her for a possible interrogation too.

Maybe I should have done that immediately when I'd gotten into this area. But interrupting her for something like this hadn't felt like a great idea. And distracting myself, even for a short while, had definitely improved my state of mind, at least for the moment.

I loosened Pluckie's leash so she could accompany me next door.

As we arrived there, I considered again that it might have been better if we'd stopped in before. If so, I might not have had to tell its current owners what had happened. But Nancy Tarzal and Brandon and Edie Brownling were all there, standing together near a tall set of bookshelves watching Gemma wait on two couples who were pondering how many copies of *The Destiny of Superstitions* to buy.

The two factions might not have been especially fond of one another, but they all managed to scowl as a unit toward Pluckie, then me. So they didn't like dogs, or just didn't like one in their shop? No matter. That drove them down even more levels in my estimation.

Gemma must have seen their glares. She sidled away from her middle-aged customers and approached us, beaming first down at Pluckie, then up at me. Loud enough for everyone to hear, she said, "How wonderful! A black and white dog visiting the Broken Mirror Bookstore. And since we're conducting the business of book selling and buying here, we're all bound to have some good luck!" She aimed her smile toward the visitors and picked up a book from the table near them. "Let me find it here for you." She thumbed through the volume, then pointed toward a page. "Yes, here it is. A black and white dog is considered to be good luck, especially if you see one around a business meeting."

That was one of the first superstitions I'd heard here in Destiny, of course, thanks to Pluckie's discovering an ailing Martha.

"That's wonderful!" one of the women exclaimed. In the next couple of minutes she and the others bought half a dozen copies of the book, for themselves and to bring luck home to their adult kids, they said. They finished their transaction and left the store.

With no other tourists there, it was time for me to speak. I pondered the best way to approach the subject then realized there wasn't really a good or subtle way to do it.

Before I did, though, Nancy said to Gemma, "That was a good save. Like we told you before, it's not enough just to answer questions. You need to encourage shoppers to buy, get into the whole good luck angle even more, make them feel as if it's bad luck if they don't spend a lot of money here." She stood there, tall and slim and nasty-looking in the tight beige dress she wore that day.

"That's right," Brandon added, hands on his wide, jeans-clad hips. He might have been decades older than Nancy, but his attitude seemed just as spiteful.

If I were Gemma, would I confront them all and quit? But my friend wasn't a quitter. And she'd gotten the results they wanted, even if they chose to give her a hard time about how she might act at other times.

I wondered where Stuart was. Since he seemed fond of Gemma, the editor's attitude might have softened the blow the store owners levied on their new manager.

Although Gemma scowled briefly, she didn't look toward the owners and instead seemed to shrug off her irritation. She came over to where Pluckie and I stood, across the shop from her bosses but near another set of bookshelves. "Great to see you two here, Rory! And I'm delighted you helped me make a sale. Both of you are welcome here any time." I was sure that was intended as a possible slap in the faces of the store owners, a challenge for them to say otherwise and potentially lose her as a manager—not to mention the bad luck sending away a lucky dog might have on this place.

A smile lit up her pretty face, and her cinnamon-shade eyes sparkled as she silently thanked me for intervening here. As always, she had dressed like a professional librarian, nice, soft, light pink button-down shirt and black slacks.

But my return look must have told her I wasn't here only because I was her friend. A worried frown appeared beneath her dark bangs, and she gnawed slightly at her glossy lips. "Is something wrong, Rory?" she asked softly.

Before I responded, Stuart appeared, walking in from the doorway to the rear storeroom. "I've finished unpacking those two boxes of children's books on superstitions," he said, looking from Gemma to the others, and then to me. "Hi, Rory." He paused then and asked no one in particular, "What's wrong?"

"Not a thing," Gemma said, approaching him, although her expression appeared dubious as she glanced back toward me.

I considered picking up Pluckie to hug while I gave them the bad news. Instead, since my wonderful little dog was sitting calmly by my feet on the wooden showroom floor, I decided to leave her where she was. Still clutching her leash, though, I crossed my arms. Clearing my throat, I said, "Actually, there is something wrong and you'll all hear more about it soon, I'm sure." Maybe I should just have blurted out that Lou Landorf had been found murdered, but it was easier for me to tell them my morning story, keeping it somewhat brief, at least.

"Lou's dead?" Gemma interrupted when I got to the part where Pluckie and Pippin had led Bill Planger and me to his stabbed body.

I nodded, feeling my eyes well up partially in sympathy for her, since as soon as I'd responded in the positive Gemma began to cry.

"I'm so sorry," she said. "He was—well, he was basically a nice person. He didn't deserve that."

I considered pulling my phone from my pocket and taking her picture. One thing about her reaction was that it told me she couldn't possibly have had anything to do with Lou's killing.

But would the police agree with that—or might they assume that she regretted now what she'd done, and that was why she had become teary?

Well, if questioned, there would be five of us who could summarize her reaction. Just in case, I also moved my gaze from Stuart's sympathetic look as he took Gemma into his arms, to Nancy Tarzal's apparent wide-eyed shock, to Brandon Brownling's gaping mouth to his wife Edie's long, slow shake of her head as if in denial.

None of them were admitting to anything, either, by their expressions. Neither was Stuart.

Did that mean none was guilty? Not hardly. But I didn't know them, or Lou, well enough to determine if anyone in this room had had a motive to kill him.

I'd heard him giving Gemma orders, too, about how to run this place. Did those orders conflict with the owners'?

Even if they did, that would be a pretty flimsy reason for them to kill him—unless there'd been more to it than that.

Worse, Gemma had argued with Lou. But he'd had no business telling her what to do, unlike the store's owners.

And the fact that he had ... did their argument make her a murder suspect?

"Are you okay, Gemma?" Stuart asked her.

She didn't look okay, but my friend started to nod bravely.

I wanted to talk with her—now, if possible. "I'm not doing so well about it," I said. "After all, I found ... Look, could you watch this place for a little while, Stuart? I'd like to go grab a cup of coffee with Gemma and cry on her shoulder a bit."

I'd be adding to my caffeine high, but I knew that, if I slowed down even for a short while, my thoughts would focus even more on all that had happened today. How Lou had looked when I'd seen him ...

And even more than I wanted to talk to Gemma for my own sake, I wanted to talk to her for *hers*. Did she want to vent? How did she really feel? Was she pondering applicable superstitions she'd read about?

How had she really felt about Lou and how had she gotten along with him?

"I'd like that too," Gemma said softly. "Would you mind, Stuart?"

I suspected Stuart would have preferred having the owners take over so he could be the one whose shoulder Gemma would cry on, but he said, "Not at all." He aimed a glance toward Nancy Tarzal and the Brownlings, almost as if challenging them to say no. They didn't.

"Thanks," Gemma said huskily to Stuart. "I won't be long. Would you like for me to bring coffee back for any of you?"

Before they could answer, a wave of tourists entered the shop through the front door—a family with three teenage kids.

"No, we'll be fine," Nancy Tarzal said. She aimed a quick look at Stuart that seemed to say, *You said you'd handle the store for a while, so handle it.*

As he hurried toward the new customers, I touched Gemma's arm and, as I hung onto Pluckie's leash, we all exited through the storeroom. I assumed Gemma wanted to grab her purse, which she did from beneath a backroom bookshelf.

I just wanted us out of there.

FOURTEEN

GEMMA HELD PLUCKIE'S LEASH while she waited outside for me in the alley behind the Lucky Dog. I went inside through the back entrance to grab my purse. Fortunately, Millie and Martha remained out front so it was easy for me to sneak back out again.

We all then returned to the sidewalk in front of the store and headed in the direction of the Beware-of-Bubbles Coffee Shop, which was pretty close to the Lucky Dog Boutique along Destiny Boulevard. It nevertheless took a few minutes since we had to synchronize our walk with all the tourists who were also on the sidewalk, some with dogs who traded sniffs with Pluckie. Also, it was fun watching the visitors point toward some of the stores, excitedly talking about the names and the superstitions they represented.

But though I enjoyed that kind of thing most of the time, today I preferred talking with Gemma.

As we reached the coffee shop, she said, "I just want to walk for now. Is that okay?"

"As long as you also want to talk," I replied. I had a feeling, from how my friend was acting, that Lou's murder had shocked her in many ways, and not just because I'd hinted at his terrible condition when I'd found him.

I glanced sideways toward her when she didn't respond immediately. As a matter of habit on the busy sidewalk, I'd not only been watching the tourists, but had also automatically started looking down to avoid stepping on cracks. With so many people around I doubted I'd spot any heads-up pennies that hadn't already been picked up, even if some of the shopkeepers had seeded the walkway earlier.

Right now, though, I shut out all the people around us and didn't look down toward my feet. Instead, I turned to look straight at Gemma.

I always considered her a pretty lady, but at the moment her pallor and grim expression seemed to limit her good looks. And that worried me.

"What's wrong?" I asked, realizing how ridiculous that sounded. Someone we'd both met, spent a little time with, spoken with, had died last night under mysterious and terrible circumstances.

I nevertheless believed there was more to Gemma's reaction than mere horror and sorrow at an acquaintance's death.

I was right.

"Do you promise not to tell anyone what I'm about to say?" she asked so quietly that I had to strain to hear her among all the conversations surrounding us. Her question ignited my curiosity even further.

"I wish I could promise that," I told her. "But as I said, I've already been interrogated about Lou's death, and how Pluckie and I and some tourists found him. I could be faced with more questions, and it's not like there's any kind of privilege between us that I could invoke if I'm asked something about what you've told me." I hesitated. "But I hope you'll trust me enough to tell me anyway. Whatever it is, I won't just volunteer it."

But I crossed my fingers on the hand on my far side from where Gemma stood beside me, the one that held Pluckie's leash. If she was about to confess to Lou's murder, I didn't think I'd be able to hold back on telling Justin. It would depend on the circumstances of why she'd done it.

"All right." She shot me a grim smile. "I was thinking we should go somewhere quiet and private, but the only park I'm aware of in town is where..."

She didn't have to finish. The only nearby one I could think of, too, was the one where I'd been that morning with Pluckie. Where Lou had been.

I was a little surprised that Gemma knew about it, though. Which made me wonder how.

"Have you been to that park?" I asked her as casually as I could muster, bending down as if to straighten Pluckie's leash.

"No." Gemma's tone was brusque, and when I stood up again I could see the hurt in her eyes. "You do suspect me, don't you, Rory?"

I glanced around, but no one appeared to be paying any attention to us, which was a good thing.

"Let's get off Destiny Boulevard, at least," I said without really giving her an answer. I hadn't suspected her of anything at first, but her behavior now made me wonder a bit.

What was she driving at?

Could she have killed Lou?

But why?

We were walking slowly among the crowd and had reached the front of the Heads-Up Penny gift shop. A narrow alleyway beside it led to California Street, where some apartments, doctors' offices, and a hospital were located.

Fewer people would be hanging out there, so I led Gemma down the alley.

"Okay," I told her when we reached the nearly empty sidewalk on that side. "Tell me what's on your mind." I led her in the opposite direction from how we'd been walking, since if we continued that way we would eventually reach the town's civic center—which included not only the Break-a-Leg Theater and City Hall, but also the police station.

Not that Justin or anyone else would care that I was taking a walk with my friend Gemma. But if seeing me with her now somehow triggered questions … not a good idea.

She stopped walking and looked at me, tears shimmering in her brown eyes—another reason that it would be better not to be seen by someone who knew me.

"Lou called me after I got back to the B&B with Stuart and you," Gemma began. "He said he wanted to apologize and invited me to go for a ride with him. I told him we could talk again, but not that night. He—well, you heard how he was earlier. He kept his tone softer over the phone, and not as commanding. But he still tried to convince me that he would be the best one to help me learn to run the Broken Mirror so it would make money and I'd be invited to stay permanently in Destiny. I didn't want to talk about it, not then, so I just told him good night, that we'd discuss it soon, although my intention was to keep putting him off forever. He seemed a nice enough guy when he wasn't telling me what to do, but…"

Her voice trailed off, and the look she leveled on me seemed to be asking for my reaction.

"I understand," was all I said. I smiled at her. I knew it wasn't the brightest, friendliest, most understanding smile. But I couldn't help thinking there was more she wasn't telling me.

"No, I don't think you do." Her tone sounded dejected and she turned away. When she pivoted back toward me, she said, "The police will probably learn about that conversation if they check Lou's phone, or mine, or both. Not that they'll know what we talked about. And… Rory?"

She stopped and looked down at the ordinary, well-paved sidewalk along this less-traveled street.

"What?" I prompted.

She sighed deeply as she raised her gaze back to my face. "This they won't know at all unless I tell them—or you do."

"Know what?" And did I really want to hear it?

"I was all keyed up after that call. I didn't think I'd be able to sleep, or at least not right away."

I was afraid I knew what she was about to tell me. "So what did you do?"

"I decided to take a walk. I didn't see anyone in the B&B as I left, or on Fate Street while I was outside. But I did walk a block or two north, then back again. Not as far as the park, but—"

"But you might have been outside near there at the same time as someone stabbed Lou Landorf to death," I finished.

———

I held Gemma for a while after that as she cried and whispered over and over, "I didn't do it. Honest, Rory. I didn't."

But did my friend protest too much? She didn't really have a motive, at least not one she had told me about, but had their argument led to more?

Maybe I didn't want to know.

When she settled down a bit, I suggested that we start walking back toward our respective stores.

"I need to stop somewhere to freshen up," she said. She was a pretty enough lady that she didn't look too bad despite her crying, but I could understand her need to check that out herself. Rather than trying to find someplace private on Destiny Boulevard, we walked into a building containing some doctors' offices. Fortunately, there were no security guards visible, and we found a ladies room at the end of the downstairs hallway.

We didn't stay long, since it didn't take Gemma much time to put water on her face and smooth her makeup a bit. Soon we were back on Destiny Boulevard among all the tourists.

"I assume the news about what happened to Lou will be everywhere soon," Gemma said so softly that I could hardly hear her.

"Probably." I told her about having seen one of the owners of the *Destiny Star* by the murder site earlier. "I reminded Celia Vardox about what bad luck it can be to talk about some situations, but she's a media person, and she's not the only one. And as far as I know so far, no one has proclaimed that talking about Lou's death will bring bad luck." I'd informed Gemma about everyone had been instructed not to talk about how, due to superstition, Tarzal's murder had resulted in his partner's death, or how that situation had been solved.

I'd also told her how the media-oriented Vardoxes had violated that ban—and about the fire in their offices that had resulted from it. Maybe. At least if one happened to be a believer.

"Well, I'm not going to talk about it," Gemma proclaimed as we passed the Lucky Dog and I walked her to the Broken Mirror Bookstore next door.

"Good idea," I said, but I didn't say that I wouldn't, either.

In fact, I wondered what Justin would think if he knew Gemma had been out and about possibly at the same time Lou had been stabbed. I wouldn't tell him—unless something came up where I felt I had to.

I really didn't think Gemma was the murderer, any more than I'd believed Martha had been Tarzal's killer.

I'd had to fight to prove Martha innocent.

Was I going to have to do that for my bff Gemma too?

FIFTEEN

UNDER THE CIRCUMSTANCES, I decided it would be most prudent not to contact Justin again that day, at least not while I pondered how best to deal with what Gemma had told me—and what kind of involvement I might need to undertake.

Even so, I kept my phone in my pocket when I returned to the store and kept checking it to make sure I hadn't missed hearing any calls or texts.

I thought Gemma might call to remind me to stay quiet—and to describe her own feelings more. To cry on my shoulder via electronics rather than in person. But she didn't, and I hoped that was an indication that, having told me what she had, she'd been able to shelve it in her mind as nothing to worry about. At least not much.

But what about Justin? Not that I had any urge to tell him what I now knew about where Gemma had been yesterday evening. Still, I'd have enjoyed hearing from him, letting him vent about what was going on—at least as much as he could talk about it.

The Lucky Dog remained busy that day, so I waited on a lot of customers seeking a variety of superstition-related paraphernalia for their pets. Martha had gone back upstairs and Jeri came in for a while to help Millie and me, but even the three of us seemed always to be talking to, or waiting on, tourists with questions and credit cards.

That was all a good thing. It helped me focus on something other than what Bill Planger, Pluckie, Pippin, and I had nearly tripped over this morning—and how Gemma might have tripped over it, or worse, last night.

No. I needed to remind myself that, since we didn't know who had murdered Lou or why, I should be even more concerned that Gemma might have been very lucky last night. She'd possibly been in the neighborhood where a murder was committed, and yet she wasn't harmed.

What superstitions could have been involved in that?

As I helped a tourist pick out a few hematite charms to put on his dog's collar, as well as to bring back as gifts for his dog-owning friends, I wondered if Gemma had any hematite jewelry. I knew my own dog-faced pendant might bring me good luck. But what about my friend?

I doubted she'd found any heads-up pennies on the walk she'd taken to settle her nerves last night, so they were an unlikely source of good luck. A rainbow? But she had walked out of the Rainbow B&B. A horseshoe or wishbone? Maybe.

Had she crossed her fingers? Just knocking on wood probably wouldn't have protected her.

It hadn't protected Lou …

At lunchtime, I decided to leave Pluckie at the shop and head for the Wishbones-to-Go eatery down Destiny Boulevard. There, I ordered several sandwiches that I intended to distribute among Martha and my employees—and Gemma. I also got the requisite number of wishbones that they passed out at this place, depending on the size of one's order.

This was a restaurant frequented more by townsfolk than visitors, but I didn't see my usual contingent here—not Evonne Albing, the owner of Destiny's Luckiest Tours, where Martha's nephew Arlen Jallopia worked, nor her manager Mike Eberhart, nor my friend Carolyn Innes. I did see each of them often in this place.

I'd also run into one or the other of the Vardoxes here now and then, and I was just as glad not to see one of the town's media experts right now.

Bringing lunch back in a couple of large plastic bags gave me a good excuse to stop into the Broken Mirror to hand a sandwich to Gemma. I supposed I could also have brought one for Stuart, at least, although not necessarily for the store owners.

As it turned out, I was both glad and sorry when I got to the Broken Mirror. Gemma was there. So, fortunately, was Stuart. He was the one waiting on customers.

Less fortunately, Frank Shorester was there too. Dressed in jeans and a T-shirt that read UCLA—nothing to do with Destiny, I noted—he stood in a corner leafing through a book and glancing up now and then. The expression he aimed on Stuart was less than cordial.

Had he disposed of one of the men who'd been flirting with Gemma? Was he waiting now for a good time to deal with the second?

I didn't see Gemma at first but heard murmuring from the tiny office that jutted into the rear of the showroom. Stuart, dressed a lot more nattily than Frank in a beige button-down shirt and light brown slacks, nodded a greeting at me before returning his attention to his customers.

I decided I could just poke my nose through the office door to say hi to whoever was there, and leave a sandwich if it happened to be Gemma.

It was, and unsurprisingly, considering I'd heard voices, she wasn't alone. But I'd anticipated seeing Nancy Tarzal or the Brownlings with her.

Instead, it was Detective Alice Numa, dressed in the same dark suit I'd seen her in hours earlier at the park.

Her presence here couldn't be good news for Gemma. Were Alice and that other detective simply interviewing everyone who'd been in contact at all with Lou yesterday? Or was there more to it than that?

Good thing I was carrying lunch. It gave me a good excuse to intrude and find out.

"Hi," I said with a large smile as I pushed open the door. "I didn't expect to see you here, Detective. I brought lunch from Wishbones-to-Go for my buddy Gemma." I lifted the bags in my hands and approached Gemma, who sat at the chair behind the small desk. "I know you're in the mood for smoked turkey with provolone."

She nodded, and her smile was about as fragile as I'd ever seen it. The pallor I'd seen on her cheeks before was rosy compared with how white she looked now.

I put the bags on the antique wooden desk and rifled through them. "Ah, here we are." I pulled out a wrapped sandwich and a wishbone. "I'll bet this would be a good time to make a wish, wouldn't it?"

She nodded. "But I doubt I'd get the bigger half anyway." So she believed her luck at the moment to be bad. Not surprising.

"I assume you're here because of the investigation into what happened to poor Lou Landorf," I said, turning to face Alice, who sat on the compact chair facing the desk on which she'd placed her phone, undoubtedly for recording her interrogation of Gemma. "But you surely don't think the small disagreement he had with Gemma yesterday makes her a suspect."

"You know I can't discuss particulars of an investigation with you, Ms. Chasen."

Alice's tone was bland, her glance solemn. Plus, I was "Ms. Chasen" and not Rory. This was official and, apparently, serious.

She surely didn't know about Gemma's walk, did she? Had someone seen Gemma? She wouldn't have mentioned it her-self... would she?

No, the more likely scenario was that the cops had found Gem-ma's number on Lou's phone. But I didn't want to bring that up. No need for Alice to know that Gemma and I had discussed any of what had happened.

"Yes, I know that, Alice," I agreed. "And I also know you're just doing your job. But in case you need any kind of character reference for Gemma, you should know we've been friends for a long time. She'd never hurt anyone or anything—although I do admit I've seen her swat mosquitoes off a couple of kids visiting her library this summer."

Alice's eyes rolled briefly toward the ceiling in apparent disgust, but she didn't say anything.

"Hey, you know, Gemma's been researching a lot of superstitions. She started for me before I came here, and that's also the reason she's been hired to run the Broken Mirror. Maybe she can help you. Just let her know who some of the persons of interest are in Lou's murder and why, and maybe she can help you come up with superstitions that might help prove or disprove their guilt."

"I think it would be better if you just left Ms. Grayfield's lunch here and went back to your shop," Alice said.

"Let's see," I continued. "Are there any people who got irritated by how often Lou knocked on wood?"

"Besides me, you mean?" Hey, did Alice Numa have a sense of humor after all? She didn't smile, but was that a little twinkle in her deep brown eyes?

"Aha! Is someone interrogating you about whether you killed the p.a. director?" I demanded, keeping my tone light.

A look I couldn't interpret shot across her face that time. Irritation? Anger? A different hint of amusement? Whatever it was, it ended quickly and she once again projected her usual impassive and unreadable expression.

"I'm the interrogator around here," she said, "and I think it's about time you left so I can complete this session." When she aimed her eyes at me this time, impassivity had given way to command.

I glanced at Gemma's face. She looked both accepting and frightened.

"I understand you need to do your job, Detective," I said. "But Gemma doesn't really need to answer your questions. In fact, I could give her the information about a lawyer I've met here in Destiny." Emily Rasmuten had been the attorney Martha used to draw up her will—and she'd also advised Martha when she was a suspect in Tarzal's murder.

"No need, at least not now. But we will be looking deeper into that matter I asked you about before, Ms. Grayfield." Alice rose. "And I'm sure I'll be back with more questions."

She picked up a notebook and phone she'd rested on the desk, then left the room.

I looked at Gemma. "Care to talk about it?"

"She meant my phone call with Lou," Gemma whispered. Since she said nothing else, I assumed the detective didn't know about Gemma's late-night walk after that call. "I was honest about it, that Lou and I weren't getting along very well before that conversation and didn't really resolve anything as we talked."

"But you weren't getting along badly enough for you to kill him." I didn't keep my voice as low as hers. If someone heard that, it might be a good thing—especially if it was Alice Numa. Then, very quietly, I asked, "I assume you know Frank's here. Have you talked to him? Do you know where he was last night?" Since he'd wanted Gemma back, I'd already considered that he might have done something to Lou to keep him from flirting with her any more.

But that seemed to me like a pretty flimsy motive for murder, too.

Gemma shook her head no. "I said hi to him but not much more. That was when the detective got here, so he said he'd hang around, see me later."

We were both silent for a moment, just looking at each other. "Anyhow," I finally said, "I hope you enjoy your sandwich. And—well, you might want to break that wishbone, but I don't think I want to be the one to work with you on it."

"Because you think I'll win the good luck, larger half?" she asked, smiling slightly.

"That's right," I said. But it was more because I was worried she wouldn't.

———

All continued to go well at the Lucky Dog after I returned. Pluckie was glad to see me, and so were my assistants and Martha, for whom I'd brought lunch.

I did break a wishbone with Martha, who was upstairs in her apartment for the rest of that day. I always tried to let her win the larger half, and if she didn't I made sure to wish something favorable to her as well as to me.

Today she won, which was fine. I'd considered wishing something more beneficial to Gemma than Martha for this day only but didn't get that opportunity. I hoped I wouldn't need it.

But I did dig up attorney Emily Rasmuten's information, just in case...

Time went quickly, as usual, after I returned downstairs and waited on customers, talking about our products relating to pets and superstitions. I was learning more about them all the time, plus, when our visitors were few and Jeri and Millie could work with them to help them find what they wanted, I pulled out the laptop computer from under the cash register and looked for more items I could order.

It was surprising how many dog toys there were, for example, that were shaped like horseshoes and other lucky forms.

And, as with any other day, our closing time of seven o'clock eventually approached.

During all that time, I'd tried not to think—much—about Lou Landorf's death. I didn't check out any media for news, not even when I was on the computer.

Not that it ever completely left my mind. I also sort of wondered, since Detective Alice Numa had been in this neighborhood asking questions, where the other detective who'd been at the crime scene—

Choye—was, and who he was interrogating. Were other detectives on this case, too? What persons of interest were they digging up?

I also wondered where Justin was, and whether he, too, was attempting to find answers.

Whatever he was up to, it didn't include me. That meant I couldn't cry on his shoulder any longer about having been one of those who'd found poor Lou.

The good thing was that I also didn't have to worry about somehow inadvertently saying something that would let Justin know of Gemma's ill-timed walk last night. She felt badly enough about the whole situation, and she was already under interrogation for having spoken to—and argued with—the man before he died.

If the authorities had reason to believe she'd been in the vicinity when he'd been murdered ... well, they weren't going to learn it from me.

But I thought about it. And instead of having Justin to soothe me, I just hugged Pluckie a lot. For her sake as well as mine. She'd been the one who'd really found Lou, after all, although she'd also had the help of the Plangers' dog, Pippin.

Eventually, both Jeri and Millie said good night. Jeri would come in first thing the next morning, and Millie had that day off.

I soon followed my usual routine of closing things down, checking cash drawers and locks, calling Martha to say good night—then leaving, with Pluckie, to go home to the Rainbow B&B.

Maybe now that I'd helped to find Lou Landorf's body so close to the bed and breakfast, I'd finally get serious about locating at least an apartment to rent—one where it would be easier to get meals together than in the B&B. I hadn't discussed my longevity here in Destiny with Martha for a while, and I was enjoying my job and my life in this quirky little town—or I had been until last night. Despite the dead bodies, I wasn't ready to move away.

I did call Gemma before I left to see if she was heading back to the B&B soon, too, and wanted to walk with us. But she said she'd just sent Frank on his way.

I didn't ask if he'd admitted anything to her. She sounded calm enough that I figured their encounter hadn't been a big deal.

If I'd spent more time with Frank, I'd have asked if he'd been questioned by the DPD yet. Maybe I could find that out another way.

In any event, Gemma said that Stuart and she were going to return to their lodgings later that night, after dinner. The implication was that she would be with him for a while—and then she would remain in her room for the rest of the evening. With Stuart? I wasn't about to ask.

As usual, the sidewalks of Destiny Boulevard remained busy despite how late the evening was growing. But when Pluckie and I got onto Fate Street, fewer people were around.

How many had there been when Gemma had walked this street late last night? Any? Had she been seen by someone who would report it to the police?

I gathered it hadn't happened yet, but that didn't mean it wouldn't.

Rather than strolling along thinking about Gemma's presence outside the B&B last night, or who else might have been around—the murderer, of course, but anyone else?—I all but jogged with Pluckie to our destination.

We stopped at the 7-Eleven on the way so I could grab a premade small salad from their refrigerator case for dinner.

At the B&B, Serina was in the lobby at the desk talking to several guests. About the murder? Reassuring them that all here was fine?

I didn't stay to find out. I went into the breakfast room to eat—alone.

I headed upstairs quickly when I was done. There, I fed Pluckie. A short while later, I took her back downstairs for what would be her last walk of the night.

That was when my phone rang. I pulled it from my pocket.

Justin.

I drew in my breath as I answered, glad to hear from him, yet concerned.

"Hi," I said, throwing cheerfulness into my tone. "How are you doing, Justin?" Like, are you being driven crazy by your investigation?

Or have you found the murderer—and it's not Gemma?

"Okay," he said. "Rory, Killer and I are nearly at your B&B. Would you and Pluckie care to go for a walk with us?"

"Sure," I said without thinking. But I did mean it.

Maybe he could tell me something I'd like to hear.

And I didn't have to tell him anything I didn't want to.

SIXTEEN

When I opened the B&B's front door, Justin was waiting on the sidewalk along Fate Street right outside, with Killer on his leash beside him sniffing at the curb.

Pluckie seemed as happy to see Killer as I was to see Justin, since she immediately pulled on her leash to join them. I gladly followed.

The two dogs traded sniffs as Justin and I traded smiles. That made me feel a bit more comfortable meeting him out here on this night at this hour, but I still wanted to know what he was up to.

"Hi, Rory. Glad you could join me." His voice was soft, his tone warm and sincere.

"Me too." I didn't want to start questioning him yet, so I decided to keep things friendly and general. "Nice night. I can tell it's September. The air is a little cooler than it's been at this hour for a while." Which was just after nine o'clock.

"Yes. It's very pleasant." So was the sound of his voice, including the touch of humor in it that suggested he knew I wanted to keep things impersonal.

I was pleased but a bit surprised when Justin took me into his arms, right under one of the lights. When we kissed, anyone on this side of the B&B, or anyone who happened to be in any nearby building—although most were businesses closed at night—might be able to see us.

I wasn't a murder suspect, thank heavens, but I'd gotten a reputation in the earlier murder investigation, however briefly, of sticking my nose where it didn't belong—a reason for the chief of police not to act overly friendly with me in public, especially with another murder investigation pending. An investigation involving a second body I'd helped to discover. That discovery could also lead to me intruding into this investigation.

Although I hoped not. Maybe, by kissing me out here, Justin, too, was demonstrating that he hoped I would stay remote from his official duties.

Of course Justin might not have considered any of this as he held me tightly against his delightfully hard body.

We started to walk slowly north, taking time for the dogs to sniff out their paths along the sidewalk.

The sky was dark, but Fate Street, as always at nighttime, was illuminated by lights on poles—regular streetlights here, not the mock gaslights along Destiny Boulevard. But a glow emanated from old-fashioned lanterns mounted on either side of the horseshoe above the Rainbow B&B's door.

Thanks to those lights, when Gemma took her walk from here last night, or at least when she started off, she wouldn't have been concerned about strolling in the dark. But strolling alone … I shuddered at the idea, especially considering what had actually transpired near here.

She should have at least called me. I'd have talked her out of it—or come along.

If the latter, we both might be sweating what was going to happen next as Lou Landorf's murder was investigated.

As I strode slowly with Justin and the dogs, I wondered if any superstitions involved being out in the night air with a highly attractive man. Did it matter that I was still seeking answers about the reality of superstitions?

No ladders leaning against any buildings here. And the stars in the night sky weren't overly visible with all the streetlights on around us.

I knew there were superstitions about wandering spirits that roamed the skies and earth in darkness, which was why it was always a good thing to keep lights on at least somewhere.

Not to mention the fact that real, genuinely evil people might hesitate to show themselves in the light, where they might be seen.

I didn't talk about that, though. I followed Justin's lead and described how well things seemed to be going at the Lucky Dog Boutique while I managed it. I was working on another "Black Dog and Black Cat" superstition presentation that I'd give sometime next week.

I tossed into the discussion that I was glad the Broken Mirror Bookstore remained in business and seemed to be doing well. I didn't mention Gemma, or Lou Landorf's interest in her and how she was running the shop, or anything related that came to mind.

Neither did Justin. Nor did he talk about the Destiny Police Department or how he enjoyed his job or anything related to important things in his life.

So what were we doing here?

Eventually, after we'd walked a couple of blocks and drew nearer to the park, I had to ask. "It's really good to see you this evening," I began.

"But you want to know what I'm doing here," he finished.

He stopped walking and so did I, feeling Pluckie's tug on the leash with its handle around my wrist. She'd kept going at first, and so did Killer. I watched as the dogs turned to stare at us with sadly accusatory gazes. They must both have been enjoying their amble.

"Is there a superstition about reading minds?" I asked lightly.

"Probably. There is about everything else." His grin was so wry that I had an urge to kiss it.

Hey. I was getting too hung up on this man and his moods and how they helped me manage my own moods. I gently pulled Pluckie back toward me and started walking again.

"So do you want to know why I decided to take a walk with you here tonight?" Justin was beside me again, keeping up at the brisk pace I'd undertaken.

"If you want to tell me," I replied noncommittally, not stating the truth, because I really wanted to hear it.

I gathered our walk wasn't just because he wanted to see me. Which was fine. Sort of.

"Well, you're my cover for tonight."

I stopped and looked at him. "I'm a cop's cover?" I shook my head. "How odd is that?"

"Pretty odd. But the thing is I wanted to see what this neighborhood was like at night. I don't know what time Lou Landorf might have come here after our impromptu party at the Clinking Glass Saloon, and our medical examiners are saying he probably died a little while after that."

"So we're looking for a murderer?"

"No. Whoever did it isn't likely to show up again here tonight. If they do, I've got it covered—my guys know where I am and I wouldn't have to do much to get them here pronto. But mostly I just wanted a sense of the atmosphere."

"That sounds a bit woo-woo for the chief of police," I said, once more starting to walk, but this time a lot more slowly. I, too, was thinking about the atmosphere here. Nighttime. A scent of fir trees in the air as we approached the park. No other people around, and no cars—because of last night's murder? Was everyone keeping away? I hadn't walked this way at this hour before, so I didn't know.

There was someone I could ask … but I wasn't about to mention that to Justin. Not now, at least.

"Not so woo-woo," he said. "I've generally found that it helps to get to know the area around a crime scene. It talks to me, but not supernaturally or superstitiously or anything like that. I already have a sense of stuff in town, although I did spend a bit more time around your shop and the Broken Mirror after Tarzal died—not that I disliked being there. You know what I think of Martha."

"Yes, I do." But did he think of me, too, while spending time around there?

And why was my mind going in that direction so much? I'd already decided I liked this man, and when—if—I ever was ready for a relationship after Warren, I might pursue something with Justin. But I wasn't there yet.

Was I?

This wasn't the night to decide. Justin said, "This is far enough, Rory. I don't want us to actually enter the park area. The crime scene techs are finished with it so we wouldn't mess anything up, but I don't want to put you through that, especially now, just one night after the killing occurred. Besides, there's more to it than that. I wanted to get my mind around the situation as well as the location."

I wasn't sure what he was driving at. "Around it how?"

"I've gone over your statement and those of the others, including the ones taken from people who'd been at the party last night, especially if they'd argued with Lou, or even had a little tiff."

"Like you?" I inquired with a smile.

"Well, he was giving my department a hard time."

Justin, and Detective Numa, and more? I'd heard him snap at them, but they weren't the only ones.

"And a lot of other people," I said, without naming any. Gemma, yes. But Lou also hadn't been getting along with the others who'd been flirting with her: Frank and Stuart.

He'd also snapped a bit at the servers at the bar. And what about his boss, the mayor?

I had to ask. "As I think about it, I'd imagine you have a whole list of potential persons of interest, including yourself. But are you zeroing in on any of them as prime suspects? Like, were there fingerprints on the murder weapon or any other obvious evidence, like who owned that stake?"

"That's another reason I wanted to take this walk." His tone sounded exasperated. "I know it's early in the investigation, but the answer to your question is no, there's no evidence like fingerprints or a purchase receipt that makes the solution easy. And at the moment I don't have any suspects standing out as being most likely."

"Then—"

"I will, though. Very soon."

I wondered, then, what he'd thought of the public affairs director. I hesitated, looking up to where clouds above the trees obscured any stars in the night sky. "How did you meet Lou?" I asked.

"When I came here to interview for the police chief position," he said, also looking around us. "I learned about it online and sent my resume. I think I mentioned to you before that, at the time, I was deputy chief in a larger town north of here. I was invited to visit here to talk to a group of local administrators, including Bevin and Lou. We had dinner at the Shamrock Steakhouse, which was a selling point." He grinned.

"You must have impressed them," I said.

"I guess so. I was so impressed with them that I knocked on wood and crossed my fingers after our meetings." He grinned. He'd told me that before and I hadn't been sure whether he was serious— and I wasn't sure now, either. "Bevin called several days later with a job offer, and I came back. Lou was there, too, and I was introduced to some of the people who would be reporting to me."

"That's great!"

"I thought so, although Lou took me aside and warned me that some people here thought the job should have gone to a local member of the PD. It wasn't long after I moved here that I heard Lou, who liked to give orders, had insisted on hiring me and Bevin had given in, this one time, at least. But then Bevin turned the tables on Lou and gave him some orders—like, he was to really act like the public relations guy he was supposed to be and travel a lot to tell the world about Destiny. He apparently didn't fight it. It kept him away from the people who'd apparently not been thrilled that I'd been brought in."

I hesitated again. "Do you think now that Lou was back in town, anyone who wasn't thrilled about your hiring might have—"

"That was two years ago," Justin said, looking down at me with a wry grin on his face. "Lou has made a lot of folks mad since then. He didn't stay completely away. He came back here a lot, in fact. But kill him? We're still checking into who happens to be mad at him now."

He soon changed the subject. He sort of had to, since Killer squatted and required a clean-up. Pluckie was very interested in it, but she'd relieved herself well before I'd headed into the B&B with her for what I'd imagined would be the last time that night.

We started walking again, back toward the B&B. I couldn't help asking Justin, "I don't suppose you or your staff have found a loose wolf or anything that could have let out that howl we heard last night, have you?"

We'd learned where some of the howls that had heralded deaths or strong endangerment had come from during the Tarzal death and investigation, but not all of them.

He replied the way I figured he would. "No, but this is Destiny. And, yes, we have seen a black cat prowling through the park."

"Of course."

A car went by, followed by another—the apparent extent of night-time traffic on Fate Street.

Soon, we were back outside my lodging. "Well, thanks for the walk," I told Justin.

"Thank you for joining me." And before I could turn to unlock the door, he pulled me into his arms.

The kiss was breathtaking. The feeling of being this close to him was more than welcome.

Warren? my mind called, but this time I didn't sense any kind of manufactured response, the way I often had before—not even a "go ahead and live your life" kind that I'd figured he'd have told me by now, if he could.

And with that I realized that I had reached a kind of closure over losing my wonderful former fiancé.

Did that mean I'd develop a real romantic relationship with Justin? Who knew?

But at least now I'd—probably—be open to it.

The walk this night had been more than a crime scene investigation involving a death.

It had also involved life.

SEVENTEEN

PLUCKIE AND I SLEPT alone that night in our cozy and charming room. That was as it should be. But I did lie awake on the canopy-covered bed a lot longer than I'd hoped to.

On one level, I listened again for a howling dog, presaging a death. Fortunately, I didn't hear one, and neither did Pluckie, who slept deeply.

I also went over in my thoughts how someone had attacked Lou Landorf and killed him not far from here.

But that wasn't all that was on my mind. I needed to learn if there were any truly effective superstitions to determine whether someone a person found attractive was appropriate to form a relationship with. Assuming I'd believe in those superstitions even if I learned them.

Besides, that presupposed Justin was actually as interested in me as he appeared to be.

Sure, I knew a few romance-related superstitions. I wondered if the Bouquet of Roses flower shop also carried daisies. If so, I could perform the age-old ritual of pulling off one petal at a time and chanting with each, "He loves me. He loves me not." If the last remaining petal was on "He loves me," then I'd have a theoretical answer of what was on Justin's mind.

But that wouldn't necessarily tell me whether pursuing a relationship with him was supposedly good for me.

I pondered doing some research the next day. Gemma might be gaining the reputation of being the person around here who knew the most about all superstitions, with her librarian and now Broken Mirror Bookstore manager background. But there were a lot of reasons I didn't want to bring this up to her.

One was that she knew me so well. She already was aware of my interest in Justin and his possible interest in me. But I didn't want her to know I was considering ramping up the situation.

She'd also known Warren and my relationship with him.

So who…? Then it came to me. Before Gemma had arrived, I'd been developing more of a friendship with Carolyn Innes, the button shop lady. She'd lived in Destiny a long time, maybe her entire life. She knew superstitions.

She might be curious about my research into additional ones involving relationships, but she wasn't likely to judge me, at least not like Gemma might. Although I'd need to be discreet. She would probably guess who was the subject of my superstitious inquiries, but I'd try not to admit it.

Gemma had major issues of her own to deal with—but why not ask her along, if I was careful? This kind of diversion might be exactly what she needed.

Maybe tomorrow I'd meet with both of my best friends in this town and see what came of it—but be cautious what I asked in front of Gemma.

That must have been the key. I realized, when I awoke the next morning, that I must have fallen asleep soon after making that decision.

———

But things didn't turn out that easy.

Gemma and Stuart joined me for breakfast in the busy dining room at the B&B after I'd taken Pluckie for her first outing of the day. We soon walked together along Fate Street, then Destiny Boulevard, toward our shops.

On the way, after chatting with Gemma without giving her particulars of what I hoped to gain from a conversation, I called Carolyn. She, too, was in her shop early. She loved the idea of getting together later that day with both of us. Tea time sounded best for her—midafternoon, even though there were no tea shops in Destiny.

What—no superstitions about tea? There had to be. And if so, that might be a great theme for an enterprising entrepreneur to use for a new shop here someday.

We decided to meet at the Beware-of-Bubbles Coffee Shop. They served tea there too.

And rude as it might have been, I didn't invite Stuart. After all, he'd need to stay at the Broken Mirror and run the bookshop.

I said goodbye to Gemma and Stuart outside the door to the bookstore, and Pluckie and I continued to the Lucky Dog. As I arrived, I got a call from Martha. She asked us to stop upstairs before I opened the shop.

Everything was pretty much in order in the store and on the shelves, so I complied right away. As always when I went up to visit her, I considered yet again the superstitions she'd told me about slipping while going upstairs versus going downstairs. Downstairs was bad luck, and so was turning on the stairway, but tripping while going upstairs would mean there'd be a wedding in the family.

I was very cautious on my way up. I had no intention of tripping, let alone thinking about weddings, even if I wanted to see if any superstitions could advise me on how to deal with Justin.

Far as I could tell, Martha was just a little lonesome and hadn't wanted to go downstairs too early, before the shop was open. But fortunately she seemed to be feeling well.

I sat in her quaint and small living room on one of her plush, ornate chairs that matched the sofa, where she positioned herself. We chatted for ten minutes or so with Pluckie lying protectively on the floor near her feet. Martha's questions revolved around her shop, but I also discerned some subtle references to the Broken Mirror Bookstore and how it was doing post-Tarzal. I assured her that so far all seemed to be going well there, and that my friend Gemma was a good choice for managing it.

I didn't attempt to refer to the men who'd been flirting with her —and especially not the public affairs director.

Soon, I looked at my watch. "I think I'd better head back so we can open on time. Will you be coming downstairs today?"

"Of course."

I suggested that she try to make it mid-afternoon since I'd made some plans then. She could supervise Millie and Jeri, and maybe even run the place if she was feeling up to it.

We both rose at the same time, and so did Pluckie. Impulsively, I crossed to where Martha stood and gave her a hug. "See you later," I told her with a smile. "But don't ever hesitate to call if you need anything."

She gave me a second hug. "Thank you, Rory."

———

I didn't trip going downstairs, and neither did Pluckie. It was about nine fifty-five, which meant I'd unlock the doors in five minutes.

I bustled around, making sure everything was ready for a hopefully huge crowd to visit the store. Lucky plush dog toys arranged on shelves beamed down on us. I tethered Pluckie to the counter, not that she was the kind of pup who'd hurl herself out the door when it opened, but I felt better knowing where she was.

I checked the time on my phone and did the countdown so that, at exactly ten a.m., I went to the front of the shop and unlocked the glass door.

There was, in fact, a crowd on the sidewalk outside. Not a huge crowd, but respectable. None of the people looked familiar, so I assumed they were tourists, and a few had leashed dogs at their sides—everything from a jumping, golden Yorkie to a sleek and well-behaved Weimaraner.

We were open for business!

I had fun answering customers' questions, including letting those who asked know that I'd be presenting another of my pet superstition discussions next week at the Break-a-Leg Theater. Apparently word was getting around, and my talks might actually be achieving what I'd hoped they would: drawing tourists into the

Lucky Dog to check out our superstition-related animal products. Being included in Arlen's tour, too, didn't hurt.

Jeri arrived around ten thirty, as scheduled. The shirt she wore today was another from her family's store, the Heads-Up Penny gift shop, which was fine. I didn't mind her promoting them too. And I knew she sometimes wore Lucky Dog Boutique shirts when she headed there. Her black hair was getting a little long and swung around her shoulders. She looked very pretty.

Her presence took a lot of pressure off me handling our visitors, but I still managed to keep busy with them, not only answering questions but also making a substantial amount of sales.

I was delighted. It felt good.

Good enough for me to do something about my idea of settling in Destiny? I'd initially planned to go home to the job in the Mega-Pets store where I'd worked as assistant manager before coming to Destiny to learn about superstitions. This visit was supposed to have been temporary.

But now I was leaning toward staying. I was putting down roots of sorts.

Despite running into multiple murders. Ugh.

But whatever I learned about Justin and whether any superstitions leaned toward my staying to see how that progressed—well, I'd have to decide if I'd become enough of a believer to pay attention.

I was leaning over the glass counter containing lucky amulets when I noticed a man in a suit come through our door. It was Detective Richard Choye, whom I'd seen at the crime scene.

I pretended not to see him, although I did manage to peek around the shoulders of the young couple I was waiting on. Choye was of moderate height with wide shoulders and an otherwise slim build. He was good looking with thick but short black hair. His gaze moved from one part of the shop to another, as if he was seeing its contents for the first time, which was possible. I didn't recall seeing him here before.

I wished he weren't here now. If he was a local resident who hadn't been here previously, he might not have come because he had a pet for whom he wanted to buy a cute, superstition surprise today.

But surely, if the authorities had any further questions for me, they'd have sent Alice Numa, who'd talked with me before.

Better yet, Justin.

The customers I'd been helping decided on amulets in the shapes of four-leaf clovers and a horseshoe. I removed them from the display case, and placed them into small boxes. We then moved over to the cash counter where I swiped their credit card.

When I'd given them their bag and receipt, they took their time leaving, heading toward the display of collars and leashes decorated with pictures or rhinestones depicting symbols of superstitions. I smiled, ready to go after them if they had further questions—like, which of the collars would go best with their new amulets.

"Ms. Chasen?" The voice from off to one side was a strong tenor. I looked that way and wasn't surprised to see Detective Choye standing there.

"I'm Rory," I said with a smile. "What kind of superstition items involving pets are you interested in today?"

"I'm interested in totally different kinds of superstitions," he replied. He pulled open his jacket to reveal a badge fastened on the pocket of his white shirt. "I've got some questions to ask you regarding the investigation into the death of Public Affairs Director Landorf."

I didn't want to play games any more. "I've already given my statement to Detective Numa and answered her questions. Now, if you'll excuse me, I need to go help those customers." I nodded toward the couple I'd sold the items to previously. Did they need my help now? I doubted it, but Jeri was waiting on the only other customers, an apparent family with two dogs, and I really had no interest in answering any further questions.

Unless, of course, Justin wanted me to.

"I understand that," Choye said. "Detective Numa would have come here herself to follow up but she was assigned questioning someone else today. The Plangers, in fact—the people you were with. They intend to go home today, so we needed to ask them a few more questions first. And this shouldn't take long. I need to know whatever information you have on Frank Shorester."

Frank? Were they now zeroing in on him as a major suspect? That could be good. If he was it, then Gemma wasn't, and I wouldn't have to worry about her any more, late-night walk or not.

Obviously the Plangers weren't on their suspect list or they probably wouldn't be permitted to leave so quickly. I hadn't seen them here at my pet shop with Pippin. I suspected they just wanted to leave Destiny as soon as possible.

"All right." I knew I sounded more reluctant than I suddenly felt. Glancing around, I said, "Let's go into the backroom where we can have some privacy."

"Great."

He followed me through the door behind the mesh drapery into the storeroom, and I motioned for him to sit on one of the chairs at the card table in the center.

I considered offering him a refreshment, even just a bottle of water, but decided against it. I didn't want him to feel welcome. Nor did I want him to stay an instant over however long it took for him to ask his questions—and for me to decide whether or not to answer.

"Okay, Rory." He apparently decided to accept my former friendliness, although I might prefer retracting it now. He pulled out his phone and pressed some buttons. "I'm going to record our conversation." Not a question but a statement. I didn't object, though. "Here's what you might be able to help us with."

Did that half smile mean he knew I might have a reason to want to help them—like, the fact I knew Justin?

"What's that?" I kept my tone noncommittal.

"Have you known Frank Shorester long?"

"A while." If he was going to ask for something more specific, the best I'd be able to do was that it had most likely been for about a year. I thought that was how long Gemma had been dating him.

Choye did ask, and I told him, although since he was a cop and what I said might not be entirely accurate, I let him know that the year was only a guesstimate.

"How well do you know him?"

This was getting slow and boring. "Not well at all."

"Then how do you know him?"

I'd considered volunteering that before but didn't really want to volunteer anything now. Even so, I responded with more than a short sentence. "You may be aware that Gemma Grayfield, who's currently running the bookstore next door, is a good friend of mine. We all lived in L.A. when I met Frank, and he still does live there, as far as I know. He and Gemma were dating then, but she's broken up with him."

"So you didn't know him independently of her?"

"No, not at all."

He pursed his lips as if that wasn't the answer he'd hoped for. "Let me ask this, then," he finally continued. "Do you know him well enough to either trust, or mistrust, something he says?"

What was he driving at? Had Frank admitted to something involving Lou's death, enough so the cops were trying to determine if his statement could be trusted, that he might, in fact, be guilty?

It struck me, though, that the opposite was more likely to be true. Maybe, in anger against Gemma—or because Frank had, in fact, murdered Lou—Frank was pointing toward his ex-girlfriend as the guilty party.

That would unfortunately make sense from his perspective.

But this was sheer speculation on my part. What Choye was asking could be for an entirely different reason. And I doubted he would answer my questions, even though he wanted me to answer his.

Just in case, I tried to cover my own butt and Gemma's too.

"Detective, all I can tell you is that, whether or not I'd have trusted what Frank said before, I'm not sure I would now. It would depend on what it was, for one thing. He came here supposedly trying to win Gemma back, and he's been unsuccessful. To me, he's seemed pretty angry since he's arrived. Maybe that would lead him to tell the truth if he felt he could get revenge on Gemma or someone else he considered a rival for her affection. Or maybe he'd feel he could get a better result by producing lies. But all you can get from me is speculation, and I know that kind of thing isn't evidence, which I assume is what you're after, right?"

He didn't exactly respond. Instead, he leveled a really nice, wide smile at me that suggested I'd said exactly what he'd hoped for.

How odd, I thought.

"Thanks for your help, Rory," he finally said. "I'm sure we'll have more questions for you, and I hope it's me who gets to ask them."

And then he left, leaving me even more puzzled than I'd been about his questions.

EIGHTEEN

I CONSIDERED HURRYING NEXT door to talk to Gemma to get her take on what this was about.

To ask if she knew where Frank was—and what he'd been saying about Lou's murder. And to whom.

And whether she had heard anyone claim superstitions were involved.

But I'd be seeing her this afternoon and could ask those same questions more subtly.

Still standing near the trinket counter, I glanced at Pluckie, who was tethered nearby. She hadn't barked or jumped at the detective but had sat there observing him, as if trying to figure out what he really wanted.

I knew I was projecting my own feelings onto my dog, but sometimes Pluckie seemed so attuned to the people around her I figured she had some kind of psychic connections with humans, or at least with me.

And if I could potentially accept that, why couldn't I accept superstitions as real?

Were there any superstitions about psychic animals?

Another party of tourists walked in, which served to emphasize that I'd made the right decision about staying here, at least for now. I got busy helping them.

When Millie arrived a while later, she brought in lunch for all of us, including Martha, so I didn't have to worry about taking a break before I had to leave. I repaid her for everyone's meals, as I did often with my helpers, despite not committing to do so all the time.

Soon, it was near the time Gemma and Carolyn had chosen for tea. Martha had come downstairs by then so there were three people eagerly waiting on customers when Pluckie and I departed for our afternoon get-together.

We made our way through the usual noisy and excited crowd and stopped first at the Broken Mirror next door to get Gemma, even though that shop was slightly in the other direction from where we were going.

Then, walking west on the sidewalk along Destiny Boulevard, the three of us headed toward the Buttons of Fortune shop, about halfway between the Lucky Dog and Destiny's Civic Center. We actually passed the Beware-of-Bubbles Coffee Shop on the way, but I'd arranged with Carolyn for us to drop by at her Buttons of Fortune shop so I could show it off to Gemma. Then we'd return to get our refreshments.

On the way, I asked Gemma about Frank. Was he still hanging around the bookstore?

"More than I like," she said. We exchanged glances, and she continued. "He usually stays for an hour or so at a time, thumbing through books and not buying any. But he's mostly quiet so I don't really want to start a nasty conversation by telling him to leave."

"Then he isn't talking much?" Like telling lies, as Detective Choye intimated? Or telling truths that perhaps Gemma didn't want to hear?

But her answer was, "Mostly, if he finds a superstition he particularly likes he'll tell me about it. Or if he eavesdrops on a conversation with some customers, he'll sometimes point them to a place in Tarzal's book, or a different book, where they might find answers. It's strange, but when he does that he actually seems to be helping me— and contributing toward my staying here. Why do you ask?"

Choye hadn't told me to avoid talking to Gemma. Even if he had, I wasn't under any official obligation, and the detective certainly wasn't a friend of mine. Gemma was. So was Justin, but he hadn't been part of this except as Choye's superior. I related to Gemma my odd conversation where Choye seemed to want to know how much I trusted Frank.

"I let him know that, at the moment, I don't have a good reason to trust him, but he'd seemed okay to me before, when we all were in L.A. together."

"Good answer. I guess. But do you know what the cop wanted that information for?"

"No," I said. "Anyway, we're here."

We had reached Buttons of Fortune. The store was housed in a delightful two-story beige brick building that, like so many other structures in Destiny, was reminiscent of the architecture of the Gold Rush era. It might even have been built way back then, although if so it had been kept up well.

An ornate white wooden canopy jutted to become a patio for the second floor, forming shade over part of the sidewalk below. Upstairs was a row of tall windows emphasized by stone trim. Below, the windows were wider, holding displays of clothing with unique rows of buttons, as well as jewelry boxes containing lots of other buttons of many shapes and sizes.

"Charming place," Gemma breathed as I found a spot on the sidewalk that gave us the best view, then blocked some of the strollers so my friend could get a better look at the store. I made sure Pluckie was in front of me and unlikely to get stepped on.

"Agreed," I said. In many ways it resembled the store she managed from the outside, although the Broken Mirror Bookstore was built of red brick. The Lucky Dog Boutique was clearly constructed to fit the same era, but its exterior was entirely of wood.

Inside, the button store was even more appealing and dramatic. Carolyn had multiple wooden cabinets open at the front that also appeared to be from the 1800s, and in them were shelves tilted to show off rows of buttons displayed mostly on velvet backings. Many buttons were of metal resembling gold and silver, although I suspected few, if any, were truly made of precious metals. Some were carved wood. Others were plastic; some of neutral colors of white or ecru, but many more in bright hues like magenta and royal blue.

Sizes varied. So did shapes: oval, round, square, even triangular. The number of holes was also diverse.

There were bolts of fabric and spools of thread on shelves near the back walls, in case customers wanted to buy everything at the same place for a new outfit they were about to sew.

What made this place all Destiny, though, were the rows of posters in pseudo-gilt frames, each proclaiming a superstition about buttons. One said, "Finding a button is good luck." Another provided, "It's bad luck to button your buttons wrong. The fix? Remove your garment and put it on again." Yet another said, "If you find a button on the street, you're about to enter a new friendship." Plus, there were several more.

The one with the largest frame and most prominent position said, "Giving buttons as a gift is good luck." That made perfect sense in a button store.

"Hi, you two." Carolyn emerged from behind one of the tall cabinets and approached us. "No, three." She looked down at Pluckie, who sat like a good girl on the floor at my feet. "Need any buttons today?"

She, too, had a couple of assistants, which was a good thing since there were several customers oohing and aahing over the multiple button collections.

"Hi yourself." Gemma's smile was huge. "I wish I did need some. What a delightful place. I happen to love buttons—and I've come to love button superstitions, too."

I'd worn one of my usual outfits for managing my shop, a gold-colored T-shirt with the Lucky Dog Boutique logo on the front. My jeans were nice ones, but they had snaps, not buttons.

Gemma, on the other hand, was dressed in one of her usual librarian-like outfits, a professional-looking beige shirt tucked into deep brown slacks. Yes, her shirt had buttons, small white ones with two holes each. As far as I could tell, she had fastened them correctly. None of the superstitions on the walls would appear to apply to her—unless, of course, she sought good luck by giving some buttons as gifts.

Then there was Carolyn. Although she sometimes wore T-shirts displaying black cats or rabbits or other animals with button eyes, today she had on a frilly blue shirt that matched the shade of her eyes. It hung loosely over her navy slacks. The shirt had obvious gold buttons with a diameter of about an inch. They, too, all appeared to be fastened in the appropriate holes.

Carolyn was in her mid-thirties, like me. A brunette whose mid-length hair was highlighted here and there with deep auburn streaks, she was a couple of inches taller than me, and quite slim. She had lived in Destiny for about ten years. Despite my revealing my reason for coming here—Warren—she had never explained the draw of this place to her, nor why she had glommed onto buttons as her superstitious calling. I hoped someday to get her to reveal it, but her mystery was just another reason to stay in this unique town.

"Let me check in with my helpers, and then we can go." Carolyn headed toward where her customers were being waited on. Gemma and I looked over the nearest shelves of buttons till Carolyn returned a couple of minutes later. "Okay," she said and led us out the door.

As we walked back in the direction from which Gemma, Pluckie, and I had come a short while earlier, Gemma, in the middle, started asking the kinds of questions whose answers I hadn't learned, like what had drawn Carolyn here. I couldn't hear her well in the crowd, and I especially strained to hear the answer.

"Just a fascination with superstitions," was all Carolyn said on that topic. "And you? I know what brought you to visit Destiny, that you're Rory's friend. But I want to hear all about what convinced you to stay."

They chatted a bit about Gemma's arrival here and her interest in the library—and how that had somehow led to her being asked, thanks to her strong background in books, to manage the Broken Mirror.

We reached Beware-of-Bubbles. Pluckie and I snagged one of the larger outside tables on the patio along the sidewalk, and Gemma and Carolyn, still chatting, went inside to get their refreshments. When they returned, I let them watch Pluckie for me while I did the same.

The patio wasn't overly crowded, although there were other tables occupied and a hum of conversation in the background. The temperature was comfortably cool and no precipitation seemed to threaten, but I figured there were a lot more things for tourists to do at teatime besides sitting down and drinking coffee or tea.

When we were all seated, with Pluckie lying at my feet, I said to Carolyn, "I've been learning about superstitions a bit since I got here, especially those involving animals. Gemma has studied them in books. But you've been here long enough to know a lot more than we do. I was hoping, on this outing, that you'd tell us a few. And since Gemma has had interest expressed in her by some men lately, maybe you could describe some that involve relationships."

There. I put it onto my friend. Sure, I'd be interested, but I didn't have to mention Justin or my mixed emotions about getting involved with him. Or remind Carolyn of why I'd come here: to obtain closure about my poor, lost Warren.

Three men appeared to clamor after Gemma. One was not going to follow her any longer—not Lou. But Frank was still here. So was Stuart, and Gemma seemed at least somewhat interested in him.

I took a sip of latte. I'd chosen not to drink tea but elected not to have straight coffee, either.

Carolyn's gaze roved from me to Gemma. "I can get into that," she said. "But I actually have information about superstitions and Destiny that I'd wanted to tell you two about, and now seems a perfect time." She took a drink from her cup, watching us. The teabag hanging over the side informed me that she had decided to take full advantage of our teatime outing.

"What's that?" Gemma sounded enthused, as if, now that she had taken on the role of superstition maven at the bookstore, she wanted to hear everything.

I did, too—but something about Carolyn's tone and the wryness in her smile made me hesitate. What was she up to?

"We may have a theme here in Destiny, but it's somewhat like a lot of other small towns. People here interact, communicate with each other in lots of ways. We learn who's thinking what, that kind of thing." Carolyn glanced at me, and I nodded. I'd learned how much people could connect on things like the *Destiny Star's* website when I was trying to learn what had happened to Tarzal. "A lot of email has been going back and forth the last couple of days."

Those emails hadn't included me, although I was on a local town loop and also checked the *Destiny Star* website nearly daily to see what the Vardoxes considered to be new and pertinent.

I did receive general emails about town events and such but I was sure that wasn't what she was talking about. Maybe I hadn't lived here long enough to be included—or my reputation for finding bodies made me *persona non grata* when it came to these discussions. Whatever they were.

"I take it that you believe we'd find it interesting," I said. If not, why mention it?

"I'd say so. You won't be surprised to know it involves superstitions."

I gave a brief laugh. "Not hardly. Which ones?"

Gemma, who looked troubled, moved her gaze between us, her glass of iced tea at her lips.

"For one thing, the people referencing them are trying to justify someone like Lou Landorf, who always knocked on wood, failing to have the good luck that superstition signifies."

Gemma nodded slightly and set her glass back on the table. "I'd wondered what people who really believe in superstitions would think about that too. I checked some of our books in the store, Tarzal's and others, to see if knocking on wood had any bad connotations but I found nothing that seemed to fit."

"You're right about that—mostly." Carolyn's look grew contemplative as she drank more tea. "The thing is, that particular superstition has a lot of possible derivations, but a lot of them involve invoking the favorable spirits that supposedly dwell in trees."

"So knocking on wood is good luck if those spirits who may live in wood are pleased by it," I interpreted.

"Exactly. But … well, here's what some of our town gurus are wondering. A reason to invoke those spirits was to show gratitude for all they then gave to you. But maybe, if someone doesn't act grateful enough, or lets his ego run away with him and tell other people how to act or what to do …"

"Then knocking on wood might only anger those spirits?" Gemma finished.

"That's the speculation," Carolyn agreed. "Those of us who don't exactly buy into all we hear about superstitions aren't so sure, but that's at least an explanation to believers."

"So for Lou to be knocking on wood that much, he should have been more reserved about the power he believed he had as one of this town's leaders? And he shouldn't have been so quick to give orders, like he was trying to do about the book shop?" And had apparently done before, in other situations. But skeptical me shook my head. "A pigeon flew into the Clinking Glass Saloon when we were there, but even if it indicated someone would die it wouldn't have been the cause of death. I guess that interpretation of knocking on wood lets those who want an explanation besides finding out who the murderer is to think Lou brought his death on himself."

She didn't deny it. "Which brings me to the other point. People have been trying to find more superstitions regarding books and libraries. As you know, both deaths appeared to have some connection with the Broken Mirror Bookstore."

"Libraries? And librarians?" Gemma's voice was sharp. "Are there any superstitions about them?"

"I don't know. The stuff about books seems to have been made up to get kids who are students interested in superstitions, like you should sleep with a book under your pillow opened to the right chapter so you can be sure of learning your lesson."

I took another sip of my latte, then placed my glass carefully on the table, watching it instead of Carolyn. "So what's the point of all this?" I asked. "You said you wanted to talk to us about town chatter, right? So far all I've heard is that gossip says Lou might have brought this on himself."

"People are also speculating on who might have killed him," Carolyn said softly. Her gaze seemed to take in the space around our table to make sure no one was close enough to listen in.

"We're all doing that," I retorted, not reminding her about how I helped to resolve what had happened to Tarzal. I was sure I didn't have to. And I didn't particularly want to do it this time, but I felt myself being drawn in.

"Okay, Rory. Here's the scoop, sort of. For one thing, they're speculating that you're bad luck, and that things happen in threes.

You and Pluckie have found two dead bodies. Maybe you should leave town before there's a third."

I stared at her. My heart rate had escalated. Anger? Fear? Both? I took a deep breath. "You can tell anyone who mentions it that Pluckie has already found three bodies. The first one, Martha, fortunately still happened to be alive."

"You're right. I'm championing you, by the way, and letting people know you're good luck, if anything. Just ask Martha."

"Thanks," I told her.

"Besides that," she continued, "I've seen some responses to claims that the Destiny Welcome is now cursed since both murders occurred the night after one of the Welcomes. But the majority of people in town love the Welcomes and don't want to accept that, so they're not giving it much credence."

"Good," I said. "I assume whoever is supporting the Welcomes is also reminding everyone about the ones that were held in between, with no ill effects."

"Exactly. The thing is ... well, they're also talking about you, Gemma. Apparently your friend Frank—your boyfriend? He's going around telling people how much bad luck your relationship has brought him and suggesting that you also imposed it on Lou Landorf. Frank is here, he says, to research superstitions and learn about how to draw lots of good luck to himself, but he's intimating that in some ways—maybe the worst ways—you're the one who brought death to Lou."

NINETEEN

I NOW HAD AN explanation for Detective Choye's nasty inquiries. But I needed more information. Like, what was the DPD thinking?

Was Frank actually accusing Gemma, or was he just playing a game in retribution for her dumping him?

Had he been the one who'd murdered Lou?

Step one seemed to be that I should talk to Justin again. I knew he wouldn't, couldn't, say much, but I still wanted to let him know what had been happening and my perspective on it—and see what his reaction was.

All of that passed through my mind as Carolyn and Gemma continued talking, Gemma nearly in tears as Carolyn acknowledged that there were those in Destiny who believed what Frank said and consequently thought that his ex had become a killer. Bad luck to think otherwise, maybe. At least that was apparently what Frank was trying to get everyone to believe.

"You know," Carolyn eventually said, "I'd better get back to my shop—and I imagine both of you should do the same."

I nodded and, taking a final swig of my latte, I stood. So did Pluckie.

Carolyn's store was the opposite direction from Gemma's and mine so we split up right there. "Do you have any lucky buttons you'd like for us to 'lose' on the sidewalk on our way?" I asked Carolyn.

"I sure do." She reached into her purse and pulled out a zipped plastic bag containing buttons about three-quarters of an inch in diameter that just happened to say Buttons-of-Fortune—Destiny. They were too small to have the Destiny Boulevard address on them, but the tourists who found them and picked them up for luck would undoubtedly locate the button shop if they were interested. And, hopefully, a lot would be.

I, on the other hand, didn't want to run into Carolyn for a while. Not till I'd processed all she'd said and made up my mind how to deal with it. I wanted to use my local friend as a resource for communicating reality, at least the way I saw it, to her Destiny contacts, but I wasn't sure what that ongoing reality would be.

I had some planning to do.

I nevertheless hugged Carolyn goodbye and smiled as she hugged Gemma and bent to pat Pluckie.

"Take care of yourselves. Both of you." Standing again, Carolyn moved her gaze from Gemma to me. She reached up then and I saw her fingers were crossed. "I'm just hoping that, whatever happened to Lou and whoever it was who killed him, the local authorities figure it out soon." Her stare lingered for a few seconds on Gemma as if attempting to read her mind and learn there whether the new bookstore manager was guilty. Then she turned, her hand in the air in a wave, and entered the crowd walking toward her store.

"Does she think it was me?" Gemma's voice was low but squeaking as we started off in the other direction.

"I think she's just not sure it wasn't you." While holding the bag Carolyn had given us, I raised my chin and began looking around as if oblivious as the buttons began spilling from my fingers to the sidewalk. This was a lot easier than seeding the area with pennies, since the coins had to be left heads-up or they wouldn't be as lucky.

"But—" The conversations around us now were louder as the crowd grew thicker, but I still heard the indignation in Gemma's voice.

"We just have to make sure the real culprit is found soon," I said.

I just hoped I was right—and that real culprit actually wasn't Gemma.

———

Pluckie and I walked with Gemma past the Lucky Dog to the Broken Mirror. She didn't ask why I continued with her, but if she did I'd merely tell her I'd had enough fun not to want our brief outing to end.

That was true. But it wasn't the only reason.

I wanted to see if Frank happened to be in the bookstore.

If he was, I didn't know what I'd say to him, but I'd figure something out—now, or when I next saw him.

Which wasn't to be this afternoon. At least not now. Stuart was there, and I fortunately didn't see either set of owners. The editor grinned as he talked to what looked like a large group of tourists. A copy of *The Destiny of Superstitions* was in his hands, open to a page in the middle. He looked busy and happy, both good things. And now Gemma was back to help him.

I quickly said my goodbyes to her at the door. "Let's talk at the B&B this evening," I told her, then Pluckie and I left.

On the short walk back to the pet boutique I pulled my phone from my pocket and called Justin. It went directly into his voicemail, which told me he was probably in some kind of meeting and had shut his phone off. Otherwise, he usually left it on vibrate if he was unable to speak. I left a short message asking him to call me.

The Lucky Dog was delightfully crowded. Martha looked a little overwhelmed, but the two assistants seemed to have things under control. My presence, and Pluckie's, would make things even better. We wended our way through the visitors and I hooked my dog up to the counter as usual to make sure she didn't follow anyone out the door. Then, standing not far from her, I got to work.

I'd learned a lot since first arriving here, which was a good thing. Many of our visitors wanted to find out the significance of each of the stuffed toys for dogs and cats. Some meanings were fairly obvious, like the black cats, although I did point out to these customers as I did with many others that the superstition is that it's bad luck for a black cat to cross your path. Otherwise, black cats don't have a bad reputation. In fact, they're considered lucky in some countries.

Some of the toys were big red apples, well-sewn stems included. Why? Well an apple a day keeps the doctor away, quite possibly the vet too.

Stuffed horseshoes and rabbits' feet were obvious, but frogs were less so. I told them that if a frog entered your home, it was considered good luck. Some members of my audience grimaced at that, though.

"Is it true you give a talk on animals and superstitions?" asked a pretty woman who appeared college age. She stood with a guy who held a stuffed black and white dog that vaguely resembled Pluckie. I'd already mentioned that my pup, and those who looked like her, were definitely good luck.

"Yes, I do." I grinned and gave the particulars of the one scheduled for the upcoming week.

Before I started on another batch of plush toys my cell phone rang. I glanced at it and excused myself.

It was Justin. "Hi, Rory. Everything okay?"

Strange questions, which could mean he knew the reason I might consider things less than okay. I didn't respond directly. "Thanks for returning my call. I was just hoping we could get together again soon. I've got some things I want to run by you."

"This afternoon might work. I'm at the park meeting with some of my guys near the crime scene, but I don't have to stay in the thick of things. If you're too busy to come, though—"

I glanced around. Our crowd had thinned a bit, and most people I'd been talking to were now in the checkout line, staffed by Martha, to buy some of the stuffed toys.

"Pluckie and I will be there soon," I said.

———

The last time I'd taken this walk beyond my B&B had been with Justin. Had that helped him learn anything about the case? I doubted it. Fate Street was a little busier than it had been that night, but now it was still daytime, even if it was nearly evening.

Pluckie seemed fine with her usual strolling and sniffs, even without Killer as company. And me?

Well, I was thinking about Justin, but not romantically—at least not much.

Instead, I thought about who he really was, the Chief of Police of Destiny. He'd been the chief for a while now. He was in charge. He surely knew about how Choye had questioned me. And about Frank Shoreston's apparent attitude against Gemma, real or assumed for reasons of his own.

Who did he think was the murderer? Surely not the person Frank was pointing to.

We soon reached the park. It was late enough in the day that kids were out of school and parents were there observing them play on swings and seesaws. That was on the nearest part, in an area where the ground was sand.

Farther away, I could see the members of the PD who were here grouped together, but I wasn't able to tell if they were conducting any further crime scene investigation or just having a party. I doubted the latter, though. They might only be having a meeting to discuss the status of their investigation.

Pluckie pulled on her leash toward where kids were shrieking and laughing and apparently having a good time in the play area. That wasn't where I wanted to go, but I doubted I'd be welcome in the other location. I let Pluckie lead me into the park and I stopped in between the two areas, ostensibly to let my dog sniff. I kept my attention directed toward the police group.

Justin must have been watching for me since I saw him emerge from the middle of his gang. Dressed in his standard blue shirt and dark pants, he walked toward me. I wondered if he was sliding at all on the grass with his black slip-on shoes, but I figured by now that they must have good, thick tread since I'd never seen Justin's stride falter.

As I observed him approach, I glanced past him. The group was thick and not particularly close but I saw Alice Numa and Choye among them.

Justin raised one strong hand as he got near me—to say hi, or to tell me to back off? I didn't move except to copy his wave. Pluckie, on the other hand, recognized him and pulled on her leash, wagging her black and white tail eagerly.

When he was close enough, Pluckie stood up and leaned on his legs. He greeted her with enthusiastic pats, then drew closer to me.

"Hi, Rory," he said. "Are you okay?" He studied me with his incisive blue eyes. "You sounded a bit upset on the phone."

Upset? I'd thought I'd kept my tone quite level and pleasant. Maybe he was reading into it the mood he figured I'd be in.

"I'm fine, but curious about how things are going. I also have some scenarios I'd like to run by you." Like your detectives are taking much too seriously a suspect who's trying to level suspicion on someone else. "Any possibility of getting together later for a chat? Maybe we could grab a drink."

"Tell you what," he said. "We'll be wrapping up here within the next hour. I was planning to bring dinner home from the Shamrock Steakhouse. I could make it for two. It'd be more private there for us to talk."

Without anyone eavesdropping was what I heard by implication, not words. Which was fine with me.

I'd also get to see where Justin lived. I actually knew what area it was in but hadn't been there before.

"Sounds good," I said. He gave me his address, and we decided that Pluckie and I would arrive around seven thirty.

———

Were there any superstitions about going to a prospective guy friend's house? There were supposed omens that someone was about to visit you, but how about that you were going to visit someone else?

I'd heard that if you walked into a person's home with your left foot first, you could bring evil onto the homeowner, although you could reverse that by walking out once more, then reentering with your right foot.

I would pay attention to that and enter Justin's house using my right foot first. But would protecting him that way theoretically be good for me too?

Pluckie and I drove there since it was getting late, and it would be quite a walk back to the B&B from Justin's home. We crossed California Street, where doctors' offices and the local hospital were located—not places where tourists were likely to go, fortunately. Farther down were apartment buildings for residents of Destiny. Beyond California Street, south of Destiny Boulevard, was a very nice residential area containing homes where locals lived. Justin's was among them.

I parked on Quail Street in front of his house. This area had been built up long after Gold Rush days, and the homes appeared more like typical modern structures of Southern California.

Justin's was a single-story home on a nice, wide lot. It was built of white stucco with a red Spanish tile roof. "Here we are," I told Pluckie.

As I held her leash, I let her climb over my lap to get out of the car. When we were both on the sidewalk, I took my time so she could decide whether to relieve herself. While she did, I looked at the other residences. This was an eclectic area, with some structures of brick or siding, some multiple stories and others also single story. All had driveways and garages, and there was plenty of street parking.

I suspected that, if the chief of police lived here, any houses that came on the market would be out of my price range—assuming I decided to purchase a home in Destiny. Surely there were more affordable condos somewhere. I'd check that out if I decided to say.

I couldn't tell if Justin was home since presumably he'd parked in his garage. I felt sure, though, that if he was going to be late, or changed his mind, he'd have called me.

Just in case I hadn't heard him, I pulled my phone from my pocket. No missed texts or calls.

I gave Pluckie a gentle tug on her leash and we went up the front path.

I noticed a neighbor doing some yard work a few houses down. Did she see me too? If so, would Destiny gossip channels begin to describe how the police chief had a visitor that night?

Not my problem. And I was sure Justin could deal with it.

I reached the wide wooden door and pushed the doorbell button. I heard a chime inside. In moments, the door opened.

Justin looked more casual than usual, in a gray Ojai T-shirt and jeans. They looked good on him, especially since the shirt hugged his upper body and emphasized his muscular physique. No five o'clock shadow on his handsome, angular face—or going-on eight o'clock shadow, considering the actual time. Had he shaved in anticipation of me joining him?

"Hi, Rory. Come in." He stepped back, although our entrance was partially blocked by Killer, who stood wiggling his behind and wagging his tail.

"Hi, boy." I hugged the Dobie to my legs while patting his head.

Justin pushed Killer gently and the larger dog moved, giving Pluckie room to enter and trade nose sniffs. I laughed and followed my dog.

"Ready for dinner?" Justin asked. "I picked it up on the way home and have everything set up in my kitchen."

I followed him down a wide, bright hallway, peering into a neat living room with sparse furnishing. The kitchen was large and inviting, with a butcher block table in the middle. Not surprisingly, the table was set. The flatware was simple, and the plates were red pottery. An aroma of cooked meat permeated the room.

"Go ahead and sit down," Justin said. "Is red wine okay with you? I have a cabernet I'm told is pretty good stuff."

I smiled. "Sounds fine. Can I help with anything?"

"No, it's all ready."

I did help him put the wine glasses on the table, followed by the side dishes for the steak dinner. Then we sat down to eat.

We started out talking about how I'd made it a point of using my right foot to enter his home and graduated into a few other superstitions that neither of us really believed in.

The dogs sat at our feet begging pieces of steak. We both obliged, at least a little. It was delicious, after all.

So was the company.

But I'd wanted to see Justin not to simply enjoy myself. I wanted to ask him why Choye had been sent to interview me—and what was going on with their investigation into Lou Landorf's murder. What would he tell me? Anything?

I took a long sip of wine, looking him straight in his eyes before I began.

But he intercepted the moment. He was the one to speak first.

"I figure you want to know what's going on in our attempt to determine what happened to Lou, right?"

I nodded. "Yes, but I realize you can't tell me everything. Just let me know what you can." I figured that was good and rational and designed to get him to say at least something.

"I will in a moment," he said, nodding. That made me smile. Until he spoke again. "First, I want to know exactly what you're hiding to protect Gemma."

TWENTY

"Nothing," I responded, trying to keep anger out of my voice. I didn't stand but leaned back in my chair to get farther away from him, not attempting to hide my scowl. Pluckie, at my side, must have read my change in mood since she sat up and looked at me, head cocked. "I'm not hiding anything. And I don't like your accusation. Why would you ask me something like that?"

Even as I said it, my mind scrambled. Was there something I knew that would lead to evidence against my good friend? Not that I could think of.

The fact that she happened to have walked toward the park where Lou was found dead a while later didn't mean Gemma had killed him.

And surely Justin didn't know about Gemma's walk—or my knowledge of it.

So where had his allegation come from?

"To see your reaction," he responded a bit too mildly. I didn't believe him.

"Did your colleague Detective Choye point a finger at me? I answered his questions. They were strange, anyway. He mostly asked me whether I believed anything Frank Shoreston said."

Which might be the answer. I was somewhat equivocal in my response but it had mostly been negative.

"No. He gave me his report on your conversation and it sounded reasonable. But I'll admit I'm getting frustrated. I know Gemma is your good friend. I also know Lou and she had talked to one another a lot in the short time since she'd gotten here. Maybe there was even mutual attraction there." When I opened my mouth to comment, Justin held up his hand. "Or not. In any event, there was apparently some ill will between them when he was killed."

"Arguing with someone isn't proof of murdering them," I said.

"No, but it could be a factor. A motive. Now, can we change the subject?"

"You brought it up," I retorted. "And since you did, I'd like to know more about what Detective Choye said. Has he spoken with Frank?"

"This isn't something I want you to repeat, but a lot of people are aware of it anyway." Justin leaned back, too, his arms folded. "Frank has come to our department several times. He claims he is worried since the p.a. director had expressed an interest in Gemma, and then he was killed. Everyone knows, Frank says, that he and Gemma had been an item. He's worried that something will happen to him, too."

"That's bull pucky," I said. "Who does he suspect? Stuart Chanick? Gemma herself? I'd be more likely to bet on Frank being the killer."

"Don't worry, we're considering that possibility, too." Justin shifted again, this time leaning toward me. His expression now appeared softer. Apologetic? If so, he didn't say it aloud—not exactly. "Like I said, Rory, I wanted to see your reaction. You've known both Gemma and Frank for a while, longer than any of us around here. It isn't evidence, of course, but I'll keep in mind that you're more inclined to believe Frank could have killed Lou Landorf than Gemma."

"You're damned right." Now my arms were crossed.

But Justin stood. "Have you finished eating? If so, I'd like to give you a tour of my house."

Talk about changing the subject quickly. I considered just telling him no, saying that Pluckie and I had to get back to the B&B right away since we had to get up early the next morning, whatever.

Instead I rose without saying anything. He gestured for me to head toward the kitchen doorway, and I complied. Then he led me down the hall, followed by both dogs.

Justin's home was larger than it had appeared from the outside since it extended farther back on its lot than had been evident. It had three bedrooms, one clearly used as an office and another containing a large bed and other furnishings delineating it as the master bedroom. Its decor was plain and masculine, with a dark comforter and matching pillow shams on the bed and a huge TV hung on the wall. The third was apparently a guest room.

I wouldn't say that Justin was a great decorator, nor had he appeared to have hired a designer. But the place was pleasant and relatively neat ... and I wondered why he had wanted to show it to me.

To end our sort-of disagreement?

Or because he was hoping, as we got to his room, I'd grab his hand and lead him to the bed?

Were there superstitions relating to that—a guest seducing a homeowner? A woman versus a man? I didn't know offhand, but the thought of crossing my fingers to try to make sure I didn't somehow invoke bad luck passed through my mind.

Plus, I did consider quickly what it might be like to make love with this man. But it wasn't going to happen this night, if ever. Not after the somewhat adversarial exchange we'd just had.

And so, I didn't have to apologize mentally to Warren—other than for having the thought cross my mind. Even at that, I'd already somewhat acknowledged to myself that I was approaching some degree of closure in my loss of him.

"What do you think?" Justin asked as he led me through a back door into a garden. It mostly contained a lawn surrounded by low bushes, all wrapped behind a tall, natural wooden fence—again, nice and masculine and not particularly decorative.

"I like it," I said, meaning it.

Night had pretty well fallen, and there was just a dim light projected from some lamps attached to the house. The air was cool, and I caught a faint floral scent from somewhere nearby without seeing any flowers.

Pluckie and Killer explored the yard, perhaps with a goal of elimination in mind. Justin and I stood on a small paved patio near the door, watching them. At first.

I turned to my host. "How long have you lived here?" I asked.

"Around two years, since about a month after I moved to Destiny to become the police chief. I was lucky to find this place not long after I arrived."

"That's for sure."

"Why? Are you starting to look for a place to live?"

I felt my face redden a little. "You know I haven't decided how long I'll be staying."

"No, but I've got a feeling you're putting down some roots. I know Martha's hopeful you'll be around for a long time. I've talked to her about it."

I already knew Justin was like a son to her. His enthusiasm and perseverance were definitely factors in my agreeing to stay here to help her out after Pluckie discovered her when she was ill.

Sure, I had been considering finding someplace to live other than the B&B. But I wasn't ready to admit that to anyone else except maybe Gemma, but especially not Justin.

"I've got a lot to consider," I equivocated.

"Like the superstitions involved about moving? I was fed a lot of them around here when I found this house, but the ones I learned are more about what to do as you move in to make sure you stay lucky. None involved whether or not to move from another place. I'd already made my decision about that."

Maybe I should ask my new superstition guru Gemma about the pros and cons of me deciding to stay here. I felt sure she'd try to convince me it was lucky, as long as she, too, chose to move to Destiny for good.

On the other hand, maybe she was ready to flee by now, considering everything that had happened. If she could. She was, after all, a possible murder suspect.

"I do like your home," I said. "But even if I decide to stay here and find a place to live, I doubt I'd be able to afford this neighborhood. An apartment that accepts dogs should be fine, right, Pluckie?" I bent to pat my little friend, who'd returned to stand at my feet. Her wagging tail suggested she agreed. Or maybe she was just reacting to the fact I was talking to her.

Killer, too, had returned to be with the humans. He stood beside Justin but was watching Pluckie.

"This isn't that expensive of an area," Justin said. "An apartment, condo, or house—it's your choice, of course. But you'll make someone very happy when you make that decision and settle in here."

"Martha's a very sweet person," I said, turning to smile up at Justin under the patio light.

"She is," he replied. "But I wasn't talking about her."

He reached over and took me into his arms before I could react—positively or negatively. It clearly was the former, though, as I put my arms around him, too.

At first our kiss was inquisitive, as if we were trying to decide whether it was a good idea here and now. But the longer I stayed in his arms, his lips on mine, and mine reciprocating, I didn't have any questions about appropriateness any longer.

It felt good. And right.

And unnerving. But even recognizing that didn't make me pull away.

His body was strong and hard against mine. I tossed out of my brain any comparisons with Warren's physique. He was gone. I was here. And I was very glad to be here.

After a very pleasant while, I pulled away. Smiling up at Justin, I said, "You do have an excellent way of trying to convince someone to stay in your adoptive town."

He laughed. "Yeah, it's how I work on all women I think will be an asset to this place—not." He didn't release me entirely but led me back into the house. "Now, if you've any interest in me trying even more to convince you, this wouldn't be a bad time." He aimed a very sexy and suggestive look in my direction.

"Rain check," I said, "even though the weather in Destiny seems quite nice." That way, I wasn't saying no exactly, but despite my interest and definite enjoyment, sharing a kiss was a lot easier to justify in my mind than anything more.

For now.

I insisted on helping him clear the table, although he said he'd be glad to take care of putting our plates into the dishwasher. He soon walked Pluckie and me out to my car, leaving Killer in the house.

"Thanks for dinner," I told him. "The best way I can reciprocate is to invite you out one of these days. Or to bring in food when the Lucky Dog is closed."

"Until you decide on that apartment, condo, or house." He grinned.

I smiled back. "Yes, until I decide."

Once again, he seemed inclined to help with that decision. After I unlocked my car door and got Pluckie to jump inside, I prepared to sit down too.

But before I did, I was once more in Justin's arms. Right here, in his own neighborhood without a fence shielding us from prying eyes, he kissed me. Again.

"Give me a call when you get to the B&B," he said. "So I can feel okay that I didn't accompany you home."

This hadn't exactly been a date, and I appreciated that he was a gentleman.

That wasn't all I appreciated about him.

"I will," I told him.

"We can also talk then about when and where we'll meet tomorrow."

I felt my eyes widen. Yes, I was interested in getting to know him better, but I didn't want him to take over my life here in Destiny.

"To talk more about how we can try to clear Gemma," he continued.

Surprised, I smiled.

"Assuming," he went on, "that she really is innocent."

"Good assumption," I said, planting one more quick kiss on his mouth and sliding into my car.

TWENTY-ONE

I TALKED TO PLUCKIE a lot on the way to our B&B. I intended to keep my mind away from Justin and the murder investigation ... and those kisses. As it turned out, I did discuss them a bit with my alert dog, who sat in her harness in the seat beside me staring and panting a little, as if she was eager to contribute to the conversation.

All I got from her, though, was her concern for my increasingly bad mood, which I definitely would not take out on her.

Were there superstitions about how things you didn't want to think about took up every square centimeter of your brain? If so, were there any cures—touching a steering wheel or talking to your dog or whatever?

Guess I was tired as well as frustrated. Otherwise, I wouldn't be having such weird thoughts.

I parked in the lot beside the B&B and let Pluckie take her time as we headed toward the building. This would be her last outing for the night and I didn't want to rush her.

She soon took care of business, and I led her around to the front so we could enter under the horseshoe. Would that insert some good luck into my life? Who knew?

I used the key I'd been given to enter the building. Inside, the lobby was still lit although more dimly than if it had been earlier in the evening. I headed for the stairway.

"Rory? Are you okay?"

Startled, I turned right, toward the sound of the voice, and saw Gemma standing at the open door to the room where the inn's owner Serina often relaxed and watched TV. Gemma wore a comfortable-looking print shirt dress and a large frown.

"I'm fine—or at least I was. What are you doing down here?"

"Waiting for you. I tried knocking on your door and you didn't answer, and you didn't respond to your phone, either. I was worried." She came into the lobby, followed by Stuart. That was interesting. On the other hand, he was staying here, too, so maybe it would be natural for her to ask a friend to keep her company while she fretted about something.

I pulled my phone from my pocket. It wasn't turned on, which was unusual for me, but when I pushed the button I realized it was out of power. I mustn't have gotten it fully charged last night. Not a wise move. What if I'd really needed to call someone?

Like I did now, in fact. I promised Justin I'd let him know when I got here.

The charger was in my room so I could call him when I plugged the phone in. I considered asking Gemma to join me so I could have her say good night to Justin, too—and reassure him he was right to try to clear her from suspicion and assume she was innocent. But that could wait for another time.

Preferably when Stuart wasn't standing beside her, an arm comfortingly over her shoulders. He was clad in a yellow knit shirt and long khaki shorts. Maybe he, too, would be proven innocent. Maybe not.

But whichever, it wasn't going to happen that night. I approached and gave Gemma a hug of my own. "It's sweet of you to be concerned," I said. I whispered into her ear, "I had my car along so I wasn't … walking." As she had been on that fateful night.

She pulled back and smiled at me. "That's a good thing. Anyhow, I'm glad you're okay. Did you hear, by the way, that the town is going to hold a memorial for Lou?"

"No, I didn't." Did Justin know? If so, had he purposely avoided telling me? Or had he simply not thought I'd be interested in attending? "When and where?" I asked.

"They're still deciding," Stuart said. "Probably this weekend, though."

"Sounds like a nice gesture," I said without really stating an opinion. I wasn't sure I had one at that moment. I was too exhausted to decide if I liked the idea. "I'm going to bed."

"Me too," Gemma said.

"That's all of us," Stuart added. The editor did look tired. His light brown eyes drooped beneath his thick blond brows.

Of course, I'd no doubt he'd perk up if Gemma suggested that they not go to bed alone. Maybe she already had, but I wasn't about to ask.

"Including Pluckie," I said, bending to pick up my dog. "Good night, all." Hearing the others behind us, we headed up to our room.

I plugged my phone in and called Justin immediately. I noted from numbers on the screen that he'd apparently tried calling me before.

He answered quickly. "Rory, are you okay?"

I explained that my phone had been out of juice, and I was fine. "Good."

I asked if he'd heard about the probable upcoming memorial for the deputy mayor. "I just learned about it," he said. "I checked my email after you left. I assume I can't talk you out of going."

"Good assumption." I didn't try to hide the smile from my tone. He was learning that I didn't take orders well, even if they were meant to be helpful.

"I'll see you in the morning at the Lucky Dog," Justin said after a few seconds. "I'll be checking out some things in town and can stop in. Okay?"

"Fine." I had a feeling that the things he was going to check out in town involved mostly me. Was he getting overly interested, overly protective?

Maybe so, but I still had a smile on my face when Pluckie and I settled into bed twenty minutes later.

———

Justin did, in fact, show up at the Lucky Dog Boutique fairly early the next morning. Jeri and I had just opened and already had a few customers checking out decorative collars and superstition-related amulets when I happened to look toward the entrance.

There he was, Destiny's police chief, his posture perfect, his wide shoulders filling the doorway.

Pluckie saw him too. She started to pull at her leash, which was attached to one of the counters. When I glanced at her, she seemed to be smiling.

I knew Justin left Killer at home while he went to work, but he also had a dog walker stop in mid-afternoon to take his dog for a walk and to play with him.

My customers, a senior couple, were engaged in a debate about which collar to buy the little Yorkie they'd brought along who sat in the woman's purse, so I excused myself and went over to greet Justin.

"All okay here?" he asked.

"All's fine here. And far as I know it's fine next door at the Broken Mirror too. Gemma, Stuart, and I walked here together after breakfast and I waited a few minutes while they opened up."

We'd talked about the pending memorial for Lou. We'd also discussed that Stuart needed to return to New York within the next week or so to check in with his publishing house. He seemed inclined to return here as soon as he could, but that remained uncertain.

I didn't mention any of that to Justin, though. I was much too glad that he'd done as promised and stopped in.

He didn't stay long, though, which wasn't a surprise.

"Hope you catch Lou's killer today," I whispered to him with a smile as I saw him on his way.

"I could always stop next door to do that," he said, but since he, too, was smiling I felt somewhat relieved to think that was meant to be a joke.

He looked over my shoulder and bent down to kiss me quickly on the lips. And then he was gone.

Which I found myself regretting sorely about an hour later.

―――――

It had been a while since I'd had Pluckie out for a walk, and Millie had just arrived at the store. She and Jeri planned to go out for one of their coffee outings, an event I encouraged to keep them happy.

Martha hadn't come downstairs yet that day, but I'd gone up briefly to see her and she was doing well.

I told my assistants that Pluckie and I would be back in a few minutes, and they could leave on our return. I unhooked my sweet dog's leash from the counter, greeted some customers whom I left to Jeri and Millie to help, and headed out with Pluckie.

The sidewalk, as always, was filled with tourists on this Friday morning. I joined them, telling a few randomly the town's edict that they had to be careful as they walked. "Step on a crack, break your mother's back." That old saying was taken seriously here in Destiny, even though I'd never heard of any mother's back being injured. My own mom had passed away a long time ago, so at least I didn't have to worry about her.

Most of the strangers I mentioned it to smiled and made a point of saying how fun it was to visit Destiny. A couple appeared shocked, and I wondered how they ultimately would enjoy their trip here if they really believed in this superstition.

Someone, probably one of the shop owners, had apparently seeded the sidewalk with a few heads-up pennies that morning, so I had the fun of describing the good luck that would bring to those who found them: "Find a penny, pick it up, and all the day you'll have good luck." I saw no buttons, though, so I didn't have the opportunity to mention that finding one also portended good luck.

I didn't spend much time on greeting the tourists, though. I started walking with Pluckie toward the Broken Mirror Bookstore.

And saw Frank Shorester stride through the front door.

Some of the nearby visitors started asking me questions about shops and superstitions, since I'd already made myself appear to be knowledgeable. I answered a couple briefly, but started gently bull-dozing my way with Pluckie toward the neighboring shop.

What was Frank doing there? Was he going to be nice or nasty to Gemma?

Was he going to accuse her directly of murder, as he apparently was now suggesting to the cops?

I doubted he had gone in there to admit he was the killer—but could I somehow get him to admit it anyway?

Maybe I was worrying too much since he'd already been there so often. That was before his most recent conversation with Detective Choye, though. Was he going to do something to make Gemma appear more dangerous—like a murderer—now that he'd made his allegations to the cops? Was he going to attack her now and allege self-defense?

Just in case, I pulled my phone from my pocket and called Justin, who'd only left this area an hour or so ago.

"Something wrong, Rory?" he asked after saying hello.

I'd stopped right outside the door into the bookstore and peered in. "Probably not, but—"

"But? What's up?"

I told him. "There are customers in there, but I don't see Frank or Gemma through the window. Or even Stuart. Everything is probably fine, but—" There was that word again.

"You're most likely right," Justin said. "But just in case, wait outside for now. I'll get someone over there to check things out in just a few minutes."

"Don't bother," I said. "I'm sure I'm overreacting. I'm still look-ing through the window and don't even see anyone frowning."

"That's what I'm figuring, but wait out there anyway."

We hung up, and then I stared for a second at my phone.

Everything was fine. And I still wasn't overly excited about fol-lowing Justin's orders.

"Let's go in," I told Pluckie. And then I opened the door.

TWENTY-TWO

EVERYTHING WAS FINE. STUART had a group of college-age kids in a corner, talking to them about the reality—or not—of superstitions, as described in Tarzal's book.

Though Tarzal had started, before his death, to question superstitions a lot, his book reported them as real.

I looked around for Gemma and Frank. They were together along one of the other walls of the store, behind a tall bookcase. Frank sat on the floor, with a book, maybe Tarzal's, open on his lap. His knees were up so he could rest the book against them, and he leaned enough forward that his curly dark hair, despite his receding hairline, poofed over his forehead.

Gemma stood near him, possibly out of his sight since another bookcase was between them.

Was she observing him? Or stalking him? The latter seemed okay to me, since just by being here he was stalking her.

But as I tightened Pluckie's leash so she was right beside me and drew closer, I saw Frank look up as if my movement had gotten his attention. He look startled, rising immediately to his feet. It was Gemma he stared at as if in horror, though, as he rose and seemed to cringe. "How long were you standing there?" he demanded.

What nonsense. He must have realized she, or at least someone, was there even before I arrived.

"Only for a minute. And don't pretend, now that someone's listening, that you weren't aware I was watching you."

"I was really into the book." He gestured toward us both with it. "And you were out of my line of sight anyway." He seemed to straighten his shoulders, glaring down at her. "Were you plotting your next murder, how you were going to kill me?"

The sudden pallor of Gemma's face was emphasized by the darkness of her short, black hair. "What a horrible thing to say," she said hoarsely. "At least you stopped threatening me, but you don't need to try to get back at me just because I don't want the kind of relationship you do."

"I'm glad you don't," he said. "Right now, I see you for who you are: a killer."

"Then why are you still here?" I broke in, stepping forward with my hands on my hips. Pluckie fortunately kept up with me. "If you think it's dangerous to be around Gemma, why don't you leave?"

His eyes seemed to catch on something behind me, and I realized from footsteps and whispers that we weren't alone in this part of the store. We probably had an audience of tourists, and Frank was milking that for all he could.

"Because this is Destiny," he responded in a hushed tone. "Curses might already have been placed on me that will bring me bad luck even if I leave. I need to figure out what they are, turn them around into good luck, before I dare go home. That's what I was researching here." He lifted the book. "I still haven't found any answers that'll help me."

"If you've been cursed, you brought it on yourself," I countered. "Maybe by your threatening behavior before toward Gemma—and certainly your behavior now. Stalking someone surely can't bring on good stuff. Neither can murdering someone."

"Me?" His tone squeaked, as if I had struck him where it really hurt his masculinity and more. "Gemma's wrong. I never threatened her. And I didn't murder Lou Landorf."

"You had as much motive to kill him as Gemma. Probably a bigger one. She'd had a mini-argument with him over nothing. You, on the other hand, saw him as a rival for the woman you cared about." I was getting into this much more than I should have. I knew it. But I continued facing Frank, knowing I was potentially riling him enough to come after me.

Well, let him—here and now, with all these people around. That would provide some proof as to his state of mind—and any tendency to physically attack someone he was angry with.

But if he didn't do anything immediately, and that certainly was likely in this group, I'd have to start watching my back even more.

"Not me. Him." Frank pointed past me, and I turned to see Stuart now watching this argument. "I knew Gemma's interest in me was less than it had been, but that guy had more reason than I did to get rid of potential competitors."

"You're a bitter jerk," Stuart nearly yelled. He moved forward around the shelves toward Frank, and I could see his fists flexing at his sides.

"Stop it!" That was Gemma. She inserted herself between them without looking at either. "I just can't live with the idea that Lou might have gotten killed because he showed some interest in me." Tears ran down her cheeks, and I immediately regretted getting involved in this argument.

"I hope that doesn't mean you're about to commit suicide," said a droll voice from somewhere behind me. The crowd parted enough so I could see Detective Alice Numa coming toward us. "Although if you do, please be sure to leave some kind of viable evidence, a note or whatever, so the DPD doesn't have to get involved trying to find a murderer like we are now."

What an attitude. Maybe I should have asked Justin, if he couldn't come, to send Choye in his stead. But then, I hadn't liked that other detective much, either.

No, it would have been much better for many reasons if Justin were here.

"Joking aside, Detective," I said, picking Pluckie up so she wouldn't get stomped on by the growing crowd, "I understand there are some questions about Mr. Shorester's attitude toward Gemma—such as, notwithstanding his showing up at this shop to supposedly just research superstitions, he's using the opportunity to make allegations against Gemma to you and to others."

"I can't comment on that." Alice stepped forward to join the group consisting now of Gemma, the two men courting her, and me. Alice's customary official-looking pantsuit today was of deep green, her expression suggesting amusement as well as officiousness. "Looks as if it's a good thing I'm here. Which of you is attempting to get the others to attack you? Ms. Chasen, I'd vote for you first, maybe Mr. Shoreston second. But you're definitely a close third, Ms. Grayfield. And I'm not ruling you out, Mr. Chanick." She pivoted quickly to face Stuart. "In fact, I suspect that you pose the most immediate threat. Care to comment?"

Stuart appeared to decisively pull back his rage. "Sorry," he muttered. "I should know better than to react to that man's obvious attempts to goad me and everyone else around him—undoubtedly to make us all appear guilty, when he's clearly the killer."

This time it was Frank who clenched fists, but his were still holding the superstitions book. "Oh, I think the killer is in this room, all right." He glared from Stuart toward Gemma and back again.

"I wouldn't be at all surprised if the murderer is with us here," Alice Numa said, looking at me with a Cheshire cat grin. "Care to comment, Rory? You seem to enjoy trying to solve murders since you've arrived in Destiny."

"My only comment is to hope that the police zero in on the right person, and fast."

"I suspect we will." Now her gaze focused on Gemma for a few long seconds. Then she reached into the black bag over her shoulder and pulled out a pad of paper with printed sheets. "I think I have enough reason to ticket Mr. Shoreston for disturbing the peace. Shall I give him one and order him never to return to this shop?"

She once more looked at Gemma, this time questioningly instead of accusingly.

"No, please don't. Frank, as far as I'm concerned you can come back here. But please stop telling people you suspect I'm the killer, okay?"

"As long as you do the same and stop accusing me. You too, Rory."

This was turning into a silly game—which was better than the nasty alternative.

"I don't think we have a problem here any longer, Detective," I said to Alice. "And if the killer is here, he's not going to admit it." I purposely used the masculine gender, since I knew it wasn't Gemma.

"I'll be on my way, then," the detective said, and the customers started cheering and applauding. Alice bowed as if accepting their applause. "Thank you all," she said to them. "Just remember, it's good luck to be in Destiny—and it's certainly never dull."

———

She was right. It was never dull around Destiny. At least it hadn't been since I'd arrived here.

Even with this discussion over, things didn't appear to be calming down in this store. Not completely.

I still held Pluckie, and now I hugged her even closer. What was her opinion of these odd humans and their insinuations and accusations?

She might not understand what we'd said, but I was certain she could read the moods around her. As if to prove she recognized my angst, she nuzzled me and licked my cheek.

I watched Alice Numa for now. I'd figured after her statement that the detective would depart immediately, but she didn't. Instead, she took Gemma aside for a few minutes to talk to her alone in the small office at the back of the shop. Meanwhile, business at the store started picking up again.

The people who'd been eavesdropping all seemed eager to buy books—and to discuss with the only visible salesperson at that moment, Stuart, whether the kind of confrontation that had just occurred was a harbinger of bad luck for those who'd participated. And what about those who'd observed?

Some of the visitors hadn't heard about the public affairs director's murder, so it was a topic of discussion too.

"I have nothing to say about that," Stuart told them. "The woman wearing a suit?" He nodded toward the closed office door. "She's a detective working on the case."

He obviously had no problem dumping on Alice, or at least putting her on the spot—and using her to get himself off it. I didn't disagree. Dealing with the murder was her job, after all.

I wondered what Gemma and Alice were talking about just then. I doubted it was good for Gemma.

Frank had pulled away from the rest of us, the book still in his arms, and stood in a corner leafing through it again. Why was he still here? Did he hope to point more fingers at Gemma as a suspect before he left? If so, was it still out of spite—or self-protection?

Soon, the office door opened and Gemma came out first. Her pretty face was scrunched into what looked like suppressed anger.

Frank wasn't the only one I suspected of pointing fingers.

When Alice Numa followed Gemma out, some customers rushed over to the detective. They started bombarding her with questions about the murder and how superstitions might be related to it. And what they should buy here or elsewhere to make sure they had good luck.

Scowling toward me, as if I'd loosed the horde on her, she responded as she headed toward the door. "Sorry, I can't answer any of that. It's an ongoing investigation."

Into good luck superstitions? Well, I wasn't going to interfere. Although I did manage to point to Pluckie, still in my arms, while talking to a couple of customers near me. "One thing you can be sure of is that black dogs are lucky. And if you're going to a business meeting, running into a black and white dog will ensure your success."

Which only seemed to poke the curiosity of the patrons here. That was a good thing, since I invited them to learn more at the pet boutique next door. If they bought stuff while they were there, all the better.

I hated to disappear while there were so many questions being asked of Gemma and Stuart and while Gemma had so clearly been disturbed, but I had to get back to my store.

Well … actually, the truth was that I really wanted to get out of there. My pet boutique just gave me the perfect excuse. I didn't get away quite as quickly as Alice, but I did soon thereafter.

I'd talk to Gemma later, when things had simmered down. Or at least I hoped they would.

Things at the Lucky Dog weren't nearly as exciting—thank heavens. Or fingers crossed, as the case might be. Jeri had taken off to work at her family store, but Martha remained downstairs helping Millie. Though the place was busy, it wasn't nearly as jammed with people as the Broken Mirror.

After hooking Pluckie to her usual location, I bent and hugged her again. She was one soothing pup.

"What's wrong, Rory?" Martha asked after sidling over. She leveled her hazel eyes on me, their edges crinkled in concern. Otherwise, she was looking good, especially considering she was a senior with health issues. But the worst of her non-health problems had ended when she'd been cleared of Tarzal's murder, so I wasn't surprised that her skinny shoulders were level beneath her shocking pink Lucky Dog Boutique T-shirt or that she was standing without any apparent effort.

"Things don't seem to be improving for Gemma," was all I said. That was enough. Having gone through being the prime suspect in a murder, my boss and good friend here clearly understood.

"We'll talk later," she said with a decisive nod that shifted the folds of skin beneath her chin, then went back to her customers.

That made two conversations for me to anticipate, including one with Gemma.

Three, if I counted Justin, which I did, since my phone rang a few minutes later and, when I checked it, it was him.

"Hi," I said somewhat coolly as I walked behind a tall set of shelves to hear him better. He'd promised to send help when I saw Frank enter the bookstore next door. But the help he had sent turned out to be as disruptive as the man himself.

"Hi, Rory. I got an update about what happened from Detective Numa. There's more to it than she told you, or that I can tell you too. But I'm sure you have concerns and I'd like to let you know what I can."

"Has Gemma been cleared?" I asked.

"It's not as simple as that," he replied.

"Sure it is. I'm busy for the rest of today and this evening, but I'd like to talk to you soon." Both assertions were partly false, but after the adrenaline rush I'd experienced at the Broken Mirror that had been punched up and not alleviated by the detective who reported to him, I needed a break from Justin and his reassurances without complete explanation.

"Okay," he said, his tone subdued as if he heard my thoughts. "Tomorrow."

"Sure," I said. I could always come up with a good excuse then if I wasn't ready yet.

As I pressed the button to hang up, I was surprised a bit by the extent of regret that passed through me.

I was still weighing a relationship with Justin, after all. And at this moment, the idea seemed much too heavy.

TWENTY-THREE

I DID TURN PART of what I'd told Justin into truth a little later when I saw Gemma approach the front of the Lucky Dog.

"I'll be right back," I told Millie, who was waiting on two men with three Lab mixes. I hurried out the door.

"Hi, Rory." Gemma still appeared downcast but not as upset as when I'd seen her last in the Broken Mirror. "Got a minute?"

"I've got a bunch of minutes for you," I said. "Where do you want to talk?"

"Do you have time for coffee?"

That was more than the few minutes I'd assumed this conversation would be. Even so, I'd make the time for my friend. I'd started pondering that afternoon about whether part of my concern about her was that she had come here, to Destiny, for me. She had arrived a day early for reasons of her own, but she would not have come to this town at all if I hadn't been here.

"Let's go to Beware-of-Bubbles," I replied. I went back inside briefly and let Martha and Millie know where I was heading and that I'd return soon. They promised to watch Pluckie.

On our short walk nearly next door, my conversation with Gemma remained light about the abundance of people around. We also noted the unusual lack of lucky pennies. And again, not even any buttons. "Are there any pet-related things you can seed the sidewalks with that will bring people good luck?" she asked.

"Maybe buttons with dog faces on them," I said. "But I wouldn't want to make it anything too expensive, like hematite amulets, even small ones."

"If I think of anything I'll let you know," she said. "Same goes for books, especially on those about superstitions. Some kind of printed flyers for both of us to leave around, maybe?"

"As long as the town leaders don't think we're just littering," I replied.

We both grew silent, partly because we'd just reached the coffee shop. But the mention of town leaders unsurprisingly brought Lou Landorf to my mind. I suspected neither of us wanted to think about him at the moment.

Even so, in a few more minutes we would be talking about him and his murder, or whatever Detective Numa had said to Gemma.

We found a table for two in an inside corner. The coffee shop wasn't overly crowded just now, which was a good thing. Plus, I didn't have to stay outside since I'd left Pluckie at the store. I'd no doubt she'd be well taken care of by Millie and Martha, and her being there gave me a good reason not to stay here too long.

We took turns going to the counter to order our drinks, mine a mocha and Gemma's a latte. When we were together again at the table I leaned toward her. "Don't keep me in suspense. What did Detective Numa say to you in the office?"

She closed her cinnamon-colored eyes briefly. When she opened them again, they were moist. "No suspense there. She said what we've known all along. She believes I'm good for the murder. To the detective, Frank sounds genuinely afraid of me. Isn't that the funniest thing you've ever heard?" But she wasn't laughing and the dampness in her eyes turned into a couple of tears that tracked down her smooth, pale face.

"No," I said. "Not funny at all. But you know what is a good thing?"

"What?" She looked at me hopefully, as if I was about to impart an important statement that would be a reprieve from any bad act she might actually have committed, even murder.

In a way, I was.

"Last time, when I was trying to help clear Martha of being accused as a murderer, I felt like I was doing it pretty much on my own, just little Rory Chasen against the big machine of the Destiny Police Force."

"Big machine?" Was that a glimmer of a smile I saw on her face. Good. I was achieving something I'd tried for, at least.

"Well, little machine around here. But they have the additional backup force of superstitions."

"So what's better this time than last?" Gemma asked, sipping her coffee but keeping her gaze on me.

"Martha couldn't really do much to assist me in helping her. But you're not like her. For one thing, you're not ill. Plus, you know superstitions and you look at them from a different perspective from people around here." Holding my foam cup, I leaned toward her and raised it so we touched them as if they were wine glasses and we were at the Clinking Glass Saloon.

"Yes, but—" she began.

"Don't you see?" I interrupted. "You know you're innocent. I know you're innocent. Working together, we'll figure out who's guilty and make sure the cops get the proof they need."

Was I laying it on too thick? Allowing her to get too hopeful? I wasn't a cop. I didn't really know what I was doing.

And by making a statement like that, was I jinxing the whole possibility?

Just in case, I surreptitiously knocked on the wooden table top from underneath. Then, recalling that knocking on wood hadn't saved Lou Landorf from his awful fate, I also crossed my fingers.

As a final stab at bringing good luck to myself and to Gemma, I pretended to have an itch on my neck caused by my straight blond hair tickling it as I moved.

I used that as an excuse to touch my lucky hematite dog-face amulet.

When I looked up, I saw that a few more tables were occupied since when we got here a short while ago, and that Edie and Brandon Brownling had just come through the coffee shop door.

"Drat!" exclaimed Gemma in a soft voice at the same time. "They won't be happy to see me here in the middle of a work day."

"You are working here. We've gotten together because you have some questions about retail management, and I'm advising you."

Gemma managed a smile. "Sounds reasonable. But considering what we really were talking about—"

"Your luck is going to be just fine," I promised her. "Wait and see."

One piece of luck was that they didn't appear to scan the table area to see if they recognized anyone. Instead, they maneuvered around several and took seats at the far side of the room from us. Maybe there was nothing at all for Gemma to worry about.

But I wouldn't count on it.

"Quick," I told her. "In case we need to play the superstition card, remind me of a few concerning coffee." I knew some were bad luck, of course. Why else name this place the Beware-of-Bubbles Coffee Shop?

"Here are the ones I recall," Gemma said. She began to relate a bunch, most of which I'd heard. "If the bubbles move toward you, you'll get rich. If they move away from you, you'll have hard times. Big bubbles mean disappointing news—or a friend will arrive soon. And…" She paused. "Oh, yeah. If you see bubbles in your coffee, drink it fast because if you finish it before they disappear, you'll get some money soon. There are also superstitions relating to the prediction of the weather based on bubbles in coffee and others about spilling coffee."

"Good enough," I said. Or so I hoped. Edie's gaze had started wandering and soon settled on us. I didn't even attempt to pretend I didn't see her. I smiled and nodded, then turned back to Gemma. "So here's what I think we need to do next regarding—"

I didn't get to finish. The Brownlings, foam coffee cups in their hands, stood over us.

"What are you doing here, Gemma?" Brandon Brownling's scowl pleated his forehead and the corners of his pale brown eyes. "Would you rather we hire someone else to manage the store?" The senior's tone was hoarse as he raised his voice to be heard over the moderately noisy crowd here. As before when I'd seen them, he wore a button shirt, black plaid this time, over his baggy slacks.

"Who is running it now?" demanded Edie. She was in a casual outfit, too, but her blouse was tucked into her slender jeans. Her hair, a more vibrant silver than her husband's, looked mussed a bit, as if they'd been running around in a breeze outside—or something had upset her and she'd run her hand through it. Since the weather was fairly mild I suspected the latter and wondered why.

"Stuart Chanick is still around," I reminded them. I proceeded to give them my planned explanation of how I'd invited Gemma to join me away from the store while I provided her with some additional insight into managing a retail establishment.

Edie placed her free hand on her hip. "I hope, Rory, that you aren't attempting to give Gemma ridiculous orders about how to run our shop, the way that toad Lou Landorf did."

Toad? Although I had nothing against toads, that was an odd and nasty way to refer to someone recently deceased, a murder victim.

Or were her words a murder confession by Edie Brownling? I doubted it. But they did make me consider her, and maybe her husband, too, as more likely candidates. They hadn't liked Lou and his orders. They were protective of the bookstore in which they now had an interest.

Was that a sufficient motive to murder Lou? I wouldn't think so, but that didn't mean they didn't think so.

Just in case, I found myself scanning the parts of Edie's arms that I could see below her sleeves. No warts. I didn't see any on Brandon, either.

If they'd had physical contact with Lou and believed him to be a toad, maybe they'd develop some miserable skin condition, since a superstition suggested that touching a toad caused warts.

I nearly laughed aloud.

Brandon pushed closer to the table as a middle-aged couple moved around him. "What are you laughing about?" he growled.

I didn't answer but gently took his hand and maneuvered it so I could look inside his foam cup. His coffee drink was pale brown, signifying cream and possible other flavorings.

And, yes, it contained bubbles.

"Hmm," I said, watching the liquid.

"What are you doing?" Edie demanded.

"Reading the omens in Brandon's cup," I said, forcing Gemma's earlier comments into my mind. "I'd suggest that you drink your coffee really fast. Those bubbles seem to be moving away from you, and that could signify bad news—although it'll be just fine if you're expecting a friend, since that can also mean a fast arrival. In any case, if you drink up before the bubbles disappear altogether, some money will be coming your way. But I do wonder if it's going to rain. Bubbles in coffee can predict that, you know." I'd taken liberty with some of the superstitions Gemma had mentioned, but they wouldn't know it.

"Is everybody in this town so weird?" Edie grumbled, shaking her head. She touched her husband's hand and drew it away so I couldn't see inside the coffee cup any longer.

"Of course," Gemma said. "This is Destiny. What did your son tell you about this place?" I noticed her cringe a little, as if she feared a discussion that would rehash all that had happened before and bring bad luck spewing over all of us.

But Edie's irritable gaze grew sad. "He loved it here," she said. "Weirdness and all."

None of us spoke for a long minute. Then Gemma said, "I think Rory answered my questions for now. I'll go back to the shop now."

"Fine." Brandon gave a brusque nod. "Good thing for you we're not paying you hourly or we'd dock your wages for this flagrant breach of your obligations."

"I'd say it was a flagrant breach of something else if you happened to have killed a toad," I muttered under my breath.

"What did you say?" Edie spat.

I finally stood and looked straight at her, smiling sweetly. "I'll walk back to the Broken Mirror with Gemma," I said. "I'd like to look up superstitions about toads."

With that, Gemma and I both picked up our cups from the table, got our purses, and strode out, neither of us looking back toward the nasty store owners.

"You'd think they'd be more mellow after losing a son," I said.

"It's probably their way of dealing with their pain," Gemma responded.

"Maybe," I acknowledged. "Although I can't help but wonder if they're paying it forward."

"What?" She stopped beside me on the crowded Destiny Avenue sidewalk.

"Killing someone else to try to get over their own loss," I said, for now they had risen a bit in my estimation as possible murder suspects. Was it silly, considering how ridiculous their reference to Lou and his death had been?

Probably. But especially after this latest conversation with Gemma, I really wanted to expand my suspect list to ensure the killer was found—fast.

———

We'd only gone half a block when I saw Justin making his way through the slower tourist crowd toward us. I stopped quickly, nearly stumbling.

"Did you see a penny?" Gemma asked. She must have noticed my attention was straight ahead and not on the ground and looked that way too. "Oh." Her tone was suddenly stricken, and I moved my attention to her.

"It'll be fine," I said firmly. No matter what Detective Numa might have said, I wouldn't allow Justin to arrest Gemma or do anything else to ruin the good mood I'd helped her to build.

Or so I hoped. I crossed my fingers, realizing the wry smile on my face had everything to do with considering myself as potentially gullible as everyone else.

Was it totally coincidence that he was here? Judging by the expression of apparent relief on his face the answer was no. But I suspected he also hadn't tracked me down, or Gemma, to offer the apologies of the Destiny Police Force for what had gone on in the Broken Mirror Bookstore an hour or so ago.

I'd called him because of fear of what havoc Frank Shoreston might level on the place, and its occupants.

He'd promised to send help, but the detective he sent hadn't had to stop chaos. She did, however, need to act reasonable and encourage Frank to do so too.

She instead had leveled accusations and possibly even threats. Yes, they hadn't been overt and immediate. But she'd made it clear that the DPD maintained its sights on Gemma as its primary suspect in the Lou Landorf murder, when, of all the people who'd happened to be in the store at the time, there'd been several others with a lot more likelihood of guilt.

"There you are, Rory," Justin said when he reached us. "And Gemma. I had to track you down by asking at both stores where you were." His voice was raised since the crowd around us was shouting and diving toward the sidewalk. They had just spotted an empty tour van in the street and the driver—not Arlen Jallopia—was tossing buttons out the window. Carolyn's doing, I felt sure. It was good for her business and lucky for the tourists. Or so they would believe.

"Why were you looking?" I demanded coolly. "I assume you're not about to arrest either of us, since Detective Numa didn't do it despite her insinuations that something like that is inevitable."

The concern and warmth in Justin's gaze transformed into something chillier, too. I felt sad for an instant that I'd provoked the change. But I remained irritated about how Gemma had been treated before. And Justin had been the one to send Alice Numa to the bookstore rather than coming himself.

That wasn't fair. I knew it. He was the Chief of Police and couldn't necessarily afford the time to appear at disturbances that were most likely minor.

"I did speak with Detective Numa about her visit to the bookstore to ensure that Mr. Shoreston did nothing to harm anyone. She told me that he instead seemed in fear of being harmed himself."

"Then why show up there all the time?" That was Gemma, and her tone reflected her exasperation. When Justin looked at her, she lifted her hands as if to deflect what he was going to say. "I know, I know. He says he wants to learn all about superstitions from the books we sell so he can be sure the guilty party—me—neither gets him arrested nor murders him." My friend Gemma had always held herself up in a confident and pretty manner back in L.A., but she seemed, here in Destiny, to sag often, as if accepting the inevitable upcoming blows.

"That's what Alice told me," Justin said. "Were you two on your way back to your stores? Let me walk with you, okay?"

Sure it was okay. The Lucky Dog Boutique was less than a block away, and the Broken Mirror Bookstore was on its other side. When Gemma looked at me for confirmation, I nodded.

"Let's go," I said.

Justin planted himself between us, his pace slow but determined. He was definitely a good-looking man, even when I was peeved with him.

"Gemma," he said, "since you're friends, I'm sure Rory filled you in on how frustrating it is to be involved in a murder investigation and not believe the person most implicated is likely to be the killer." He looked at Gemma, not at me.

"Yes, and I get that. I know how hard she worked to clear Martha. But when I came to visit her, I never, ever imagined I'd be in Martha's shoes."

"I know you're also aware that we can't discuss that investigation and the results in any detail," Justin continued. "But there were a couple of things that came out of it that I want you both to remember."

Now, as we made our way forward in the midst of the crowd going the same direction as we were, Justin did look at me. I saw the message in his gaze, which didn't exactly make me feel all cheerful and relieved.

"You want me to stay out of it," I all but snapped at him. "For my own safety, as well as the good of the DPD. But I'm sure you're aware of why I won't. And can't. Not when all fingers in your department seem to be pointing the wrong way, toward my friend who's clearly innocent."

"Not so clearly," Justin said softly. "Although I hope what you're saying is true." He lifted his right hand and I saw him cross his fingers—which in itself said a lot since he was as much of a superstition agnostic as I.

I fought it but couldn't help smiling. "I know it is," I said softly, possibly too softly for him to hear among the crowd.

We had reached the outside of the Lucky Dog but I gestured with my head. "I want to see Gemma back to her place, make sure everything there is okay." Like, that Frank wasn't there. If he was, he'd better be in his corner reading, and Stuart had better be around too.

"Okay. I'll go with you." Justin's look didn't invite me to protest, nor did I want to. He continued to walk with us.

All seemed fine in the Broken Mirror. Stuart was there talking to several guys who looked like scholars or librarians. He had a copy of *The Destiny of Superstitions* in his arms and was talking about how it was organized.

I figured he'd sell a bunch. Especially with Gemma's help.

I took her off to the side before I left. "Keep in touch," I said. "I think things have simmered down for the rest of today, but you never know."

"No," she said, shaking her head sadly, "you don't."

I walked out the shop door with Justin behind me. As he'd said, he accompanied me to the Lucky Dog next door. On the way, I'd come up with a bunch of excuses why I couldn't have dinner with him that night—I'd promised Martha I'd bring something in for her. I had some important bookkeeping to do.

I didn't want to say the truth—that things involving the murder investigation were tightening inside my mind. I didn't blame Justin, at least not exactly. But I needed some space to reflect on it all. And to figure out the best approach I could take to help find the killer … and protect Gemma.

I was therefore surprised at how much it hurt when Justin spoke first and said, "I'd love to invite you to join me for dinner tonight, Rory, but I can't. Too much going on in the investigation and otherwise with the department. But we'll talk tomorrow, okay?"

"Sure," I said, trying to sound all perky.

But inside I wondered what superstition there was that was causing us to become opponents instead of allies in this especially difficult situation.

TWENTY-FOUR

WE DID TALK THE next day, but that was all. One phone call late in the afternoon, from Justin to me. He was checking in, probably because he said he would. Nothing new to report—or, if there was anything new, he wouldn't admit it to me, let alone tell me what it was.

I was in the Lucky Dog when he called, as I was most of that day. I stood behind the glass case containing amulets and charms in supposedly lucky shapes, straightening out the shelves. At the moment there was a slight lull in which we had no customers in the shop, which was unusual, and each time it happened the emptiness was brief.

It was a good time for him to call. An omen of some kind? Neither he nor I believed in such things.

"Sorry I haven't more to tell you," he said as our short conversation wound down. "I expect I'll see you tomorrow, though, at Lou Landorf's memorial."

I had heard, of course, about the memorial to be held for Public Affairs Director Lou, but because this was Destiny the ideas for when, where, and how were all interwoven with which superstitions would bode best for all those choices.

Since he'd been a believer—even if knocking on wood had turned out not to work for him—the idea was to do something different, but in keeping with this town's foundation.

From what I'd eventually gleaned, the decision was to celebrate his life in the place he'd died—the park on Fate Street. Carolyn Innes confirmed it when she stopped in at the Lucky Dog a short while after Justin's call. She had her two long-haired dachshunds Helga and Liebling with her. Both immediately scrambled over to exchange sniffs with Pluckie, who appeared delighted to see them.

Today Carolyn was wearing jeans and one of her black T-shirts on which a black cat was depicted as outlined in gold, decorated with button eyes. Her non-button, real blue eyes looked as inquisitive and amused as usual.

"I thought I'd come in and see you first, Rory," she said as she reached me at the cash register counter, "but I'm going to visit Gemma too. Have you been told about Lou's memorial?"

"Only that it's likely to occur this weekend. But specifics? No."

"I figured," she said. "I've been talking up how Gemma and you are now members of our community and some locals seem quite happy to accept that, but not everyone. Especially since you seem to have an affinity of some kind to the killings that have occurred. People consider that to be bad luck, so even with your success here at the shop and your great talks on animal superstitions there are still some reservations about how to act around you. Not from everyone, of course, but a few of our citizens." She leaned closer and whispered, "I shouldn't mention it, and don't let it go any farther, but that includes our cat lady." She backed away and continued, "Same goes for Gemma, too, considering the shop she's managing, and the fact that she's a murder suspect."

I'd been opening my mouth to protest from the moment Carolyn started to talk, but she didn't let me butt in. And now I especially, despite her warning, wanted to ask about the mysterious cat lady I'd heard rumors about before—but apparently everyone considered it bad luck to talk about her. This was the most anyone had said to me about her, and Carolyn seemed unwilling to say more.

Instead, she kept speaking. "Now you're going to tell me how wrong everyone is, aren't you? You can be sure I'm not among those who're less than pleased to see you still here. I'm delighted that you're now a Destiny resident. And I don't blame you at all for being so involved in the only two murders this town has seen in ... well, forever. No matter what some of them say, you're not a bad luck omen."

The expression on her face appeared sincere—all except for the smile on her lips.

I couldn't help it. I giggled a little at the absurdity of what she said. And the fact that some of it was all too true.

"Don't tell your skeptical buddies that I still don't much believe in luck being governed by superstitions," I said. "I'm willing to change my mind, of course, if I see irrefutable proof. So why don't you let them all know that I'd love for them to tell me what to do to bring good luck to myself and everyone here, including Gemma. And you. And them." I paused. "And if their suggestion is to knock on wood, maybe we should remind them of poor Lou Landorf."

"Speaking of whom, here's the deal. His memorial will be held at 1:00 p.m. tomorrow in the park where his body was found."

I nodded. "I'll be there."

"And here's the Destiny part of it. We're all to bring a flower to place on the site where he died. Every one of us is also to get up and recite a superstition dealing with death. No one will be wished bad luck if the idea they bring is spoken first by someone else, but the Vardoxes are going to record it all and put it up on their website, as well as listing all the spoken superstitions in the next edition of the *Destiny Star*. Can we count on you to be there?"

"Of course," I said. I'd have to go talk to Gemma, too. Between us, we should be able to come up with the perfect superstitions to proclaim in memory of Lou.

In gratitude to Carolyn, and because I love dogs, I gave Helga and Liebling some special dog treats. Pluckie, too, since I couldn't leave her out. I also gave a couple of balls decorated with black cat profiles to Carolyn's dogs. Pluckie had her own. In fact, she was spoiled by the number of toys she had. But how surprising was that, with her human mom running a pet store? I paid for them but still couldn't resist.

And then I managed to work it in. "Carolyn, you and some other folks around town have mentioned a cat lady, but no one will say more. Please tell me who she is, and what does she have to do with cats?"

Carolyn's eyes widened, and she drew closer to me. "It's supposed to be bad luck to talk about her. But because it's you—and you know I don't necessarily buy into superstitions—well, I'll risk a little. All you need to know is that she keeps track of our black cats, and only she knows how many there are. She makes sure they're fed and have someplace to stay at night if they're not otherwise owned by Destiny residents."

"Then the one I saw a while ago up on the mountain, when Pluckie was in danger, is okay?" That had been a scary experience all around, and I'd been so worried about my dog that I hadn't tried to make sure the cat got down safely too—although I felt concern about it afterwards.

"Yes. She doesn't tell us stuff like that, but word gets out if a cat is hurt or disappears."

"Good," I said, forbearing from shaking my head. Apparently cat superstitions had a champion here, and so did the feral black cat—or cats. But I still didn't know much more than I had before.

Surely the pet boutique manager could be let in on that secret someday, right?

Carolyn and her gang soon left. A short while afterward, I got a text from Gemma. She, too, was attending the memorial. Would I go with her?

I texted her back: Yes.

———

The next day, Sunday, Gemma and I both elected to close our stores for a while, not surprising considering that our helpers also wanted to be at Lou's memorial.

Would tourists feel upset that Destiny's citizens weren't around to sell them stuff or take them on tours or whatever? Maybe, but the word was put out there that it would be bad luck for anyone who'd known Lou, even a little, not to come to his ceremony. Even tourists, as long as they knew what Destiny was all about, would understand that no one, in town or otherwise, dared to risk it.

Although dogs were usually welcome at the park, I chose not to bring Pluckie because of the large number of people likely to be present. I left her leashed to her usual counter at the shop and made sure she had plenty of water and toys of her own within reach.

Once I'd spoken with Carolyn yesterday, I'd also gone upstairs to Martha's apartment to tell her what was going on. Unsurprisingly, she already knew. Despite the suspicions leveled on her previously when Tarzal was murdered she was a true member of the community, and now that she had been exonerated she was treated accordingly. She told me quite a few people had called to tell her and even ask if she needed help to get there. I promised her she wouldn't. Either I'd bring her, or Millie would. And, as previously promised, we talked a bit more about my concerns for Gemma.

Now, she was downstairs and I helped her get settled into her wheelchair near the Lucky Dog's door. I then went to the few customers who happened to be around and explained the situation. One couple hurriedly purchased the toys they'd been examining. A group of visiting college kids was nice—or superstitious—enough to express sympathy and promise to return later.

Millie, who was joining us, pushed Martha outside, and I locked the door behind us. Jeri had told me she would also be there, but she was attending with her family.

While Millie continued to handle Martha's chair, I hurried next door to get Gemma. The bookstore was empty of customers. Presumably she had also shooed away any who had been there. Stuart was with her, though, and said he was joining us. She, too, locked the door as they left.

Unsurprisingly, the sidewalk on Destiny Boulevard for the short distance we had to traverse it was busy, since both locals and tourists were there. When we turned onto Fate Street there were still a lot of pedestrians and I didn't recognize all of them. Presumably the tourists here were heading for the park too. To mourn? Maybe, but I suspected they mostly wanted to see and hear the aspects of superstition that would go on at Lou's memorial.

As we'd heard, a couple of people who worked at the Bouquet of Roses flower shop stood at the corner of Destiny and Fate selling individual roses. Nearly everyone stopped to buy one for a dollar each—possibly a bargain, but I figured the Bouquet owners and staff would have been informed that to gouge more for this would bring them bad luck. Maybe that would even have been true, if those of us needing to bring a flower leveled a curse on them had they made it difficult to secure one.

Martha, now holding two pink roses for Millie and her, sat patiently in her chair while our assistant paid for them. Gemma, Stuart, and I had already bought our own.

"Do you have a superstition about death picked out to recite?" Martha looked from Gemma to me.

"We talked about several possibilities," I assured her. "How about you?"

"Oh, you know me. I've got a bunch. And you, Stuart?"

"Since I edited *The Destiny of Superstitions*, I've got several in mind too," he assured her.

We were soon on our way again—or as much on our way as we could get in this crowd.

The park was as busy, when we arrived, as I'd anticipated. Of everyone there other than the cops, I probably had the best knowledge of where Lou had been found, but I didn't have to mention it or point out the area. The crowd already formed a semicircle around it, standing on the grass beneath the sparse trees facing the ficus bushes, surrounding Mayor Bevin Dermot. The density even obscured the picnic tables at the park's edges.

Speaking of cops, they were everywhere at the fringes of the crowd. I saw Officer Sweelen and her cohorts in uniform, including Officer Bledsoe, whom I'd met before, spread out as if told to form a fence around the area. The detectives were there, too, although not as precisely spaced at the perimeter. I recognized Alice Numa and Richard Choye, and figured that the other two people standing there facing the assembly and wearing suits and scrutinizing frowns were probably detectives as well.

Justin was also present. In his typical blue shirt and black trousers, he stood off to the side of where the mayor paced at the front of the throng holding a microphone in his hand and checking his watch often. Justin didn't seem to pay a lot of attention to the mayor, though. Instead, he watched the assembly intensely, as if he expected someone there to step forward with a weapon—maybe even a stake carved into the shape of a curved fist, like the one that had been used to stab Lou.

As if he sensed me watching him, he turned to where I stood near the crowd I'd come with, off to the left of the multitude and toward its back. Our eyes met as if we'd planned it. Maybe, in some manner, we had.

This was a solemn occasion, but I found my lips curving in a small, discreet smile. Which was ridiculous, considering the tone of our most recent conversations.

At the sound of Bevin clearing his throat into the microphone, I looked away, somewhat relieved by the distraction.

"Ladies and gentlemen," the mayor screamed. No, he had simply turned up the volume in the public address system too high. He fiddled with it. "Sorry," he continued. "Ladies and gentlemen, welcome to Destiny's remembrance of one of our most outstanding citizens, Public Affairs Director Lou Landorf." He paused, then cleared his throat. It sounded moister this time, and I wondered if the mayor was tearing up as he talked about his deceased subordinate.

He said he hoped everyone was aware of how superstitious Lou had been, and consequently how well he had fit into the Destiny culture. "I hope you all have come with a superstition or two about death and dying that you can recite as we say our farewells to this extraordinary man."

He looked off to his right side. That was when I noticed that both Celia and Derek Vardox were there, each with a camera aimed at the mayor. I'd heard that they would record sound as well as pictures and had no doubt that some of what went on here today would soon be up on the *Destiny Star* website—and in articles printed in the paper.

Also among the crowd I saw Jeri there with her family. They must also have closed Heads-Up Penny Gifts. Other store owners I knew were also there. And Serina, my hostess from the Rainbow B&B, stood off to one side talking to a number of people I recognized to be guests at the inn.

Frank Shoreston was present, too, standing among a bunch of people I assumed were tourists. Not to mention the owners of the Broken Mirror Bookstore, the Brownlings and Nancy Tarzal.

Arlen Jallopia, Martha's nephew, joined us and stood behind his aunt. So did my pal Carolyn Innes, and she acknowledged having closed her button shop for the occasion.

"Now, as many of you know," Bevin continued, "I often sent Lou away from Destiny on a very special mission. Of the visitors who are here, how many of you met Director Lou Landorf in your home-towns or elsewhere, or saw him in theaters or being interviewed on local TV stations about our wonderful venue of superstitions?"

Quite a few people in the large audience raised their hands, roses held in some of them. Lou had clearly been successful at his assignment.

"That doesn't surprise me. And how many of you were actually given orders by our Lou to show up here?"

Nearly everyone kept their hands raised.

Bevin's laugh was almost a tearful choke. "That was Lou for you. He was okay about following orders some of the time, but he much preferred giving them, then making sure whoever received them fol-lowed through—even those he was supposed to report to, like me."

Was that a complaint against the dead man? Maybe. I'd certainly heard of Lou's telling Bevin what to do, as well as other people. The mayor obviously liked to be in charge. Could that have been a mo-tive for murder?

Was Mayor Bevin the guilty party?

Like everyone else who'd known Lou Landorf, he'd been under my consideration, and he would remain there.

I shot a quick glance toward Justin. Damned if he wasn't also looking at me.

He must have been on the same wavelength as I was, thinking the mayor was a viable suspect.

Or maybe he just knew me well enough by now to realize that I'd glom onto the possibility as I attempted to clear my good friend.

"But we all loved Lou," Mayor Bevin was saying, "notwithstanding our sometimes clashing with him. Right now, I'm looking forward to the time that our Destiny Police Department finally determines who harmed our dear public affairs director and achieves justice."

234

When he paused, someone started to applaud, and it grew. Now when I again looked at Justin, his expression was grave, and he nodded as if in full agreement. Which probably was the case.

But he could also be considering what the mayor had said as a criticism of his department—and him.

"And now," Bevin said, "let's pay our dear Lou, who knocked on wood about nearly everything, the honor of remembering him as one of Destiny's greatest advocates of superstitions. First, please pass the flowers you brought forward. Did you know that flowers have a lot of superstitions associated with them, both good and bad?" He didn't wait for any response but said, "The red, violet, yellow, and orange ones that our flower shop in town sold to you should be just fine, though. Red ones in particular symbolize life blood."

I hadn't known that. On the other hand, I'd figured the people at the Bouquet of Roses flower shop would have been aware of omens related to flowers they sold and would have acted accordingly.

Bevin had some of his aides collect the flowers and lay them on the ground where Lou had lain. "Now," he continued, "I'd like you each to line up and speak into this microphone as you relate a superstition relating to death."

I wasn't really sure this was a good idea—although it couldn't harm Lou Landorf, since he was already dead. And the one superstition he had believed in, or at least acted on all the time, hadn't saved his life.

Even so, since this was Destiny, I wasn't surprised about the number of people who participated.

The superstitions and omens mentioned ranged from how pointing at people can supposedly kill them, to how it is theoretically a good idea to provide illumination to people who have died, including on the anniversary of their death to show them the way home.

One person mentioned how covering your mouth while you yawn is an excellent idea since it prevents your spirit from slipping out and keeps the devil from entering.

There were superstitions I was aware of regarding how ominous it supposedly was to have birds fly into your home—and of course recalled the one that Lou had seen inside before his death. And opening an umbrella while inside a house can lead to a death.

To my surprise—or maybe not, since she was becoming the town's expert on superstitions, or at least superstition books—Gemma made her way through the crowd to recite a superstition.

Bad idea, probably, since she remained a suspect. But maybe by putting herself out there, in everyone's view here at the memorial, it would show that she had no fear of being arrested. That she didn't do anything to harm Lou.

Today she had dressed in a charcoal blouse and black skirt, appropriate attire for mourning at a ceremony like this one. "I've heard," she said after taking the microphone from Bevin and looking into Celia Vardox's camera, "that we may be expecting rain later this week. We can keep our fingers crossed that it happens, since one superstition I'm aware of is that it's supposed to be lucky for a dead person's soul if it rains during his funeral. This is Lou's public memorial, but I understand he'll have a private interment later this week, and that's more like a funeral." She turned to look at the spot where Lou's body had been found. "All my best wishes for you and your soul, Director Lou." Her voice cracked as she finished. I supposed people could think she was acting, but I knew better.

When I glanced at Justin, he appeared somber but his gaze was far from accusatory. Good.

I wondered if Gemma's participation would force Stuart to go in front of the crowd, but despite the editor of the premier book on superstitions being present, he stayed near where I remained with Martha and Millie.

I chose not to speak, but had I gone up to the microphone, the omen I'd mention was that a howling dog portended death. I'd heard dogs howling on multiple occasions since arriving in Destiny, and several times people actually had died. Did I believe in this one?

I'd be foolish not to.

More superstitions. Were all the people here remembering each of them? I wasn't. There were so many I started tuning them out.

But of course the topics of death and dying were optimum ones for coming up with superstitions—since people tried to control things around them by engaging in superstitious actions.

There's no controlling death and dying, though. Unless one happens to be a murderer.

Was Lou's murderer here? Whether or not he or she had been present the other day in the Broken Mirror Bookshop, when we'd discussed that possibility, I'd little doubt that the person was at this memorial.

Sure, it could have been a tourist Lou had lured to town by tales of the amazing nature of Destiny but who'd had an unlucky time. That tourist could still be here, trying to find a way to stay away from the cops' attention.

More likely, in my estimation, was that the killer actually knew Lou better than that.

Yet as time had continued since his death, I hadn't yet zeroed in on who it was. Suspects, yes. Evidence or even feeling convinced, not.

As fewer people headed toward Mayor Bevin and his microphone, I looked around. No expressions on anyone's faces said *It was me!*

But when I again looked at Justin, I read both amusement and frustration, as if he knew, once more, what I was up to.

Soon, the ascension to the microphone ended. The memorial was drawing to an end.

And as the mayor thanked everyone for coming and wished us all good luck, I found myself again preventing a smile as Justin maneuvered his way through the crowd in this direction.

TWENTY-FIVE

BUT IT WASN'T ME who Justin greeted first. "Hi, Martha," he said, bending to kiss her wizened cheek. "Are you okay?"

Grinning up at him with her off-white teeth showing, she assured him she was. "Millie's taking me back to the shop right now, and I'd really appreciate it if you'd accompany Rory there in a few minutes."

She shot a sharp gaze first at him, then at me, as if communicating to both of us that we should stay together and talk.

Sweet lady, and I knew she sensed the attraction between us. But this wasn't the time.

Justin apparently wasn't going to argue with her. "Sure," he said. "I've got a couple of people I need to touch base with here before I go, but I'd be happy to walk to the store with you, Rory."

"That's okay," I said. "I'll head there with Gemma and Stuart." They stood nearby, and I glanced at them. Not that I really needed company, but I didn't mind being with friends. "No need for you to go out of your way, Justin."

"Oh, but we're about to dash off right away. With all these people talking superstitions, some will probably want to buy books." The gleam in Gemma's eyes told me that she also was attempting to leave me with Justin, like it or not.

But he was the man who might wind up having her arrested. Why would she wish him on me?

Unless she was more convinced than I was that I could protect her…

I doubted it. But if there was any possibility, I had to grab at it. And that meant hanging out for a while with Justin. Any attraction between us had been put on indefinite hiatus anyway.

"Okay," I said, looking at him almost defiantly. "I've got some things to talk to you about. So, yes, let's walk back that way together."

That meant I watched as the others I'd been with headed as quickly as they could down Fate Street, considering the crowd around them. I then observed Justin hold a brief meeting with those who reported to him who'd been at the memorial. At least it was fairly quick.

He joined me again near one of the picnic tables where I'd sat down to wait. "You ready?" he asked.

He looked somewhat harried, so I said, "Sure, but you really don't have to—"

"Your store's on my way back to the department anyway." Cutting me off that way didn't bode well for a pleasant and friendly conversation. Maybe for the sake of our non-relationship I should insist on going alone.

But before I could say anything else, Mayor Bevin joined us.

Despite his usual leprechaun outfit, consisting of a green suit jacket over darker pants, he looked anything but like the cute, friendly, lucky creatures that leprechauns were supposed to be. Definitely not like the one depicted on the pin on his lapel.

"Justin? Glad I caught up with you. I was afraid you'd get away before we had a chance to talk."

I glanced toward Justin's face. He didn't look excited about talking with the mayor, but the politician was his boss of sorts.

"I—" I began.

"We'll only be a minute, Rory." Justin obviously didn't want me to go running off without him. But did he want me to hear their conversation?

Apparently neither man minded. The mayor sat down beside me on a bench, looked up at Justin, and said, "This was a difficult day for all of us, Justin. Especially because I wasn't able to tell all those in mourning that, despite the terrible tragedy of Lou's death, we had learned who had killed him and justice would be immediately served."

"I understand, sir." Still standing, Justin shifted uncomfortably, resembling a child whose teacher scolded him for bad behavior in class. "I can assure you that the investigation has taken priority at the Destiny Police Department. We will have an answer soon, I promise you."

"Not good enough. We need it right away." Bevin stood, shaking his head forcefully enough that both his silvery hair and beard rippled. "Now," he emphasized loudly. "And we need some success on that other investigation, about what happened to that tourist who apparently fell off a mountainside. Is your department near closing that one?"

I hadn't heard of any final determination there, either. I recalled how upset Lou had seemed about that situation, too, before he'd been killed.

It was definitely a problem for Destiny and its potential for attracting visitors. And it was also definitely a problem for Justin. Couldn't they just officially conclude it had been an accident? From all that had been made public, it didn't look like a murder.

Lou's death, though . . .

The mayor brought his short, plump body closer to Justin, facing him. "You know I went out on a limb a couple of years ago when I hired you, but I found myself listening to Lou and his insistence on getting his own way. I liked you, too, of course, but he pushed me to choose you from out of town rather than promoting anyone here. Bad enough that you don't have anything definitive about that tourist's death, but it would be really ironic if you don't solve Lou's murder fast and well." Bevin's full lips pursed. "I'd found a way both he and I liked that kept him from being around giving me orders. He enjoyed traveling and being Destiny's tourist emissary. He should just have stayed away. He might still be alive."

I'd seen moisture in the mayor's eyes before, and now it returned. Maybe he hadn't liked following his subordinate Lou Landorf's orders, but it appeared he would miss them, and Lou, from now on.

"We'll talk again about this soon, Justin. Real soon." The mayor rose and strode off.

"Now are you ready to go?" Justin's tone and expression as he addressed me were both unreadable, but I knew he couldn't be feeling great.

"Yes," I said. "I think it would be a good thing for both of us to get out of here."

The crowd had thinned so we had no problem negotiating the Fate Street sidewalk south toward Destiny Boulevard. Neither one of us spoke at first. But the silence grew uncomfortable. I was dying to know what Justin was thinking.

Bad choice of words, though. I wasn't dying, but Lou remained on my mind.

"Are you going to miss Lou as a friend?" I finally ventured.

Justin glanced down at me, then again stared straight ahead. "Not really. I certainly knew he'd been involved in the decision to hire me. Since I moved here we got along fine—mostly, at least, until this tourist death fiasco. But I'd owe him, and the town, closure in his murder even if that hadn't been true."

I didn't disagree. But I was definitely concerned that, since Gemma had gotten the DPD's greatest attention in the matter, she would become even more of a target now.

"Look," I said. "I know I'm not a cop or anything official. But I know Gemma's not guilty of anything other than coming to town to help me and staying to help those bookstore owners. I'll do anything to help prove that."

"Including finding the murderer yourself?" Irony dripped from Justin's tone, but when I looked up at him this time his handsome face looked more amused than stoic or angry.

"Done it before," I said with a smile. And then I grew more serious. "I'd be glad to act just as your sounding board if you want to bounce ideas off me. Do you have any real evidence against anyone?" Not Gemma, of course.

"No," he shot back. Then more gently, "It hasn't been long since Lou was found, and I've got a number of people in the department still researching the kind of lawn decoration that was used as the murder weapon. Several stores in town sell them."

"The Heads-Up Penny?" I'd seen some there at the gift shop owned by Jeri's family. "Where else?"

The Bouquet of Roses flower shop and the Knock-On-Wood Furniture shop, he told me. Neither was surprising.

"And before you ask," he said, "my guys have checked who the fist-shaped knock-on-wood stakes were sold to recently. Most were tourists, and those who were locals still had the ones they bought, mostly stuck into the ground to decorate their lawns at home. We don't know yet where the murder weapon came from or who might have bought it."

"What about the store owners themselves?" I cringed to think that Jeri's family might be involved, but it was a possibility.

"We're still looking into that, too, but none seem likely."

Justin was at least talking to me now, out of frustration or friendship or hope—or concern for his job. But the fact he'd told me very little before didn't mean that he had withheld anything helpful.

At this point, it sounded as if his department based their suspicions more on who'd said what to whom and when, rather than having anything concrete to base an arrest on.

Which was good for Gemma … maybe. But I couldn't count on it.

Justin gave me a goodbye kiss when we reached the Lucky Dog. "Thanks for letting me vent a bit, Rory," he said. "And though I can't really take you up on it, I appreciate your offer to help."

I forbore from snorting in frustration at him. Instead, I smiled. "At least I feel somewhat more confident that Gemma's not about to be arrested for something she didn't do," I said.

"I made no promises," he responded, and then he left.

I checked that all was well at the pet boutique before jumping in to wait on a couple of customers. A short time later, making sure that Millie and Martha were okay with being in charge again, I took Pluckie out, then visited Gemma at the Broken Mirror to tell her about my walk.

"So you did get from Justin that he's not about to arrest me?" She sounded relieved.

"As I said, he made no promises. But he also didn't point to anything that made it sound as if they had a bunch of evidence against you."

"That part's good, at least." She pivoted away from me. It was getting late, and at the moment there weren't any customers in her shop. She had already told me that Stuart had gone off with the Brownlings and Nancy Tarzal to talk about strategies in marketing *The Destiny of Superstitions* in places beyond Destiny, so we were alone in the Broken Mirror. "You want to try something superstitious, Rory?" When she turned back to me, the smile on her face looked too mischievous for words.

"I don't know—"

"Come on. It'll be fun. Although ..."

"Although?"

"Unless you're willing to stretch a bit in what you believe, nothing'll come of it."

I might not admit it to her, but she had me intrigued. "I'll try," I said. "Now, tell me what this is about."

She motioned for me to follow her while she wended her way around some of the tall bookshelves in the store.

We wound up standing in front of one of the mirrors hung on the wall near the back, one with painted zigzags representing a break in the mirror's surface.

A mirror hanging here had actually been broken a while back, but that was one of those things we weren't really supposed to think about, let alone talk about.

I looked into the mirror and saw myself, with the backs of the tall shelving units behind me.

"Okay," I said. "What now?"

"Now, I'm going to get you an apple, then leave you alone here."

I knew suddenly where this was heading. I'd read parts of *The Destiny of Superstitions* too. "And you believe I'll then see the reflection of my true love over my shoulder? Gemma, my true love is dead, so even if I see him—"

"What if it's Justin, Rory? I've seen the way you two look and act around each other. You're fighting it, and maybe he is, too, but I really think the two of you have something."

"What if I don't see him or I see someone else? Or what if the mirror breaks?"

"Not going to happen."

But I felt relieved when I heard some noise and turned to see a bunch of giggling college-age girls enter the bookstore. "None of it's going to happen today, Gemma, but thanks. I guess. And as far as in the future, I'll only do it if you do it too. Maybe no one will appear to me, but Stuart will appear to you." But not Frank Shorester, I hoped.

"Spoilsport," Gemma grumbled, but she was smiling. "Okay. We'll both do it one of these days. Maybe that's the kind of superstition destined to come true."

TWENTY-SIX

I DIDN'T SEE JUSTIN in any mirrors for the rest of that Sunday. Not that I expected to.

Gemma and I had dinner together that evening, though. Pluckie was with us, so we grabbed sandwiches and drinks from Wishbones-to-Go, then ate in the B&B's otherwise empty dining room. Just us, which turned out to be a good thing. I wasn't sure where our hostess Serina was, but I was glad she wasn't there to eavesdrop.

At first we discussed Lou's memorial and how touching it had been—and compared notes on whom we'd seen there and how they had acted.

Neither of us could say that anyone's reactions or lack thereof showed with certainty who the killer was. We both had suspicions, though. We also both agreed that the murderer had most likely attended. The DPD had taken that position, too, so we weren't alone.

Then our discussion turned to the future. Not who would see what man in the mirror when we looked for the right reflection, but what would happen if we both decided to remain in Destiny to see how our own destinies progressed.

That meant not staying forever in this B&B—and that was why I was glad Serina wasn't listening. I told Gemma what little I knew about local residential communities, such as where Justin lived, and the few apartment complexes I knew of.

She ended that conversation with a deep sigh. "As much as I'd like to make plans, it's too soon for me to think about such things. I want to be sure first that I'll be staying in Destiny to run the store."

"Is there any question that the owners want you to?" I felt somewhat blindsided. I thought that was a given.

"No," she responded. "But if I'm arrested for murder—"

"You won't be," I vowed.

I only hoped that was a promise I could keep.

I thought about Gemma a lot while walking Pluckie for the last time that evening, then going upstairs to bed.

Seeing one's true love in a mirror? Hah!

But I did check over my shoulder after washing my face for the last time and looking into the mirror over the sink in my bathroom. I could see into part of the bedroom.

No Warren. No Justin.

When I looked far enough into the reflection, I did notice Pluckie lying on an area rug near the far wall. I smiled at my sleeping lucky dog in the mirror, then turned to join her to give her a good night hug.

I didn't dream of either Justin or Warren that night. A good thing. Justin had once told me that dreams were harbingers, and I didn't need to guess the meaning of any such thing right now.

———

Monday was usually a busy time at the Lucky Dog Boutique despite the fact the weekend had ended. The next day was no exception. Good thing Pluckie and I had joined Gemma for breakfast at the B&B and walked to the stores early, since I wasn't sure if I'd have an opportunity to stop in at the bookstore and say hi, although I hoped to.

Martha stayed upstairs most of that day, but Jeri came in early. I didn't ask, or even hint, about the possibility members of her family had taken one of the decorative superstition stakes they sold at their gift store and used it on Lou. Why would they?

I wasn't about to inquire about possible motives, either. At least not without having even an off-beat reason to suspect her family, which I didn't.

Except for their access to those stakes.

Pluckie was busy that day, too, since a lot of our customers brought their canines in. It was my lucky black and white pup's responsibility to greet them and make them feel at home with nose and butt sniffs. Or so I told any customers who remarked on how friendly Pluckie seemed.

Things at the Broken Mirror must have been a bit less frenetic that day since Gemma called and offered to bring lunch in to me and whoever was working at my store. I accepted. But it turned out she was busy, too, and couldn't stay to eat with us. She had left Stuart in charge.

"Is he staying here much longer?" I asked Gemma as I reached into the paper bag she'd brought and pulled out an egg salad sandwich for me and a ham-and-cheese for Jeri that she had picked up at the 7-Eleven. We stood by the door since she'd made it clear she had to leave immediately.

She shook her head, and her pretty features sagged sadly for a moment. "He tells me he'll need to head back to his New York offices within the next week, and he's not sure if and when he'll be able to return."

I thought he had an interest in buying the bookstore, but maybe not. Or maybe he'd tried and hadn't been able to reach any agreement with the owners. "I know he's been helpful to you," I said, knowing she was itching to leave the Lucky Dog but wanting to keep talking for now. "But will you miss him in other ways too?"

She nodded. "Yes, I think so. But if you're asking whether I anticipated seeing him reflected in the mirror, the answer's no." She stuck out her tongue, grinned, and left.

If Stuart was leaving soon, that meant I—and oh, yes, the DPD—would need to determine quickly if he was a viable suspect in Lou's murder. The only motive I could attribute to him was that he, too, was interested in Gemma. But if knocking off prospective romantic rivals was his game, why was Frank Shorester still alive?

Same went for considering Frank a suspect. On the other hand, as to both of them, maybe not enough time had passed for them to feel comfortable offing another opponent...?

I supposed Stuart could have shared one of the motives that was attached to Gemma: anger that a government employee had dared to give orders as to how to run the bookstore. Even if Stuart had expressed some interest in buying the store before, and even if he hadn't liked Lou's edicts, it would be much easier to negotiate, or just walk away, than to murder him. And those orders certainly hadn't motivated Gemma to kill.

Nevertheless, I was pondering this as I watched Gemma hurry through the nearest bunch of tourists to return to her shop.

I found myself pondering it again several hours later while taking Pluckie out for a walk to clear my own head, too, after the constant throng at the pet boutique that day. Jeri was leaving soon, but Martha had come downstairs and Millie had called and promised to spend an hour or two there before we closed.

That allowed me time to breathe a bit. But as I inhaled deeply when Pluckie and I came from the side of our shop onto the sidewalk, I saw Frank entering the bookstore. Again.

I recalled the last time I'd seen him go in there and how concerned I'd been. This time, I didn't anticipate anything in particular to go wrong. I hoped.

Was he still researching superstitions on how to stay safe from a murderous former girlfriend like he'd claimed before—even as he put himself in that former girlfriend's presence in this store?

Or maybe he was seeking superstitions on love to toss at Gemma and try to win her back. Or to get retribution against her and the remaining guy she still had some interest in if he couldn't get her back—like proving, perhaps, that Stuart, and not he, was murderous.

Something else, such as trying harder to find, or manufacture, proof that Gemma was guilty?

Pluckie and I returned to the pet shop. There were enough people at the Broken Mirror that I doubted Frank would try anything nasty today any more than he had on other visits.

But about ten minutes later my phone rang. "Rory?" Gemma said. "Could you come over here?"

———

I didn't know her reason for inviting me. I simply told my assistants I'd be back soon and headed over there, sans Pluckie.

When I arrived, Detective Choye was there too. Dressed in a short-sleeved white shirt and black slacks, he stood near the corner where Frank was now seated, and the two of them were engaged in an intense discussion.

"What's going on?" I asked Gemma, who met me at the door. The bookstore had several sets of customers in it but they didn't seem to be looking for help—not now, at least. Stuart was talking to a couple of senior men, though, at the far side from where the other discussion was taking place.

"I hope you don't mind. I just need a little emotional support right now." She glanced toward where Frank and Choye were talking, then shook her head. "Let's pretend that I asked you for some help with a question I had about managing this place." She waved me toward the small office in the far corner and I followed.

"What's up?" I asked once she'd shut the door behind us.

"That's just it. I don't know. But every time I approach them they shut up or start talking about how wonderful *The Destiny of Superstitions* is. Maybe I'm just paranoid, but I have a feeling they're both talking each other into certainty that I'm the one who killed Lou. Or maybe the detective is pushing Frank to tell him specifics about why he's so peeved with me, and trying to figure out what evidence he can collect about it."

"Just because you're paranoid—" I began.

"—It doesn't mean someone isn't out to get me," she finished. "Yes, yes. I'm a librarian. I know the ending to that quotation, more or less. I'm hoping the world isn't out to get me." She sighed. "But I'm pretty sure those guys are."

"Let me see if I can find out," I said.

"How?"

"I'll wing it," I told her. We left the office, which turned out to be a good thing since Frank was chatting with Stuart, but the detective was leaving. I sized up the possibilities quickly, then gave a low wave to Gemma that only she'd be able to see and followed Choye out the door.

He was already in front of the Lucky Dog when I caught up with him, apparently on his way back to the police station. The sidewalk crowd wasn't too heavy so moving forward wasn't difficult. Nor were those around us speaking loudly, although they did seem to be dodging cracks in the sidewalk.

"Hi," I said. "Can I talk to you?"

"Sure, you can talk. That doesn't mean I'll listen. Or answer." He looked down at me briefly with a half smile, as if he'd cracked a joke. He didn't slow his pace, though.

Good thing I enjoyed walking; I had no trouble keeping up with him.

"Can you tell me why you were just at the bookstore?"

"Sure. I'm keeping a close watch on your buddy Gemma. We're still collecting evidence before we arrest her."

Shocked, I nearly stopped walking. Choye slowed for a second, too, and began to laugh. "Had you there, didn't I? That's true, by the way, but I was actually there because that guy Frank called and said Ms. Grayfield had been threatening him again as he sat there deciding whether to buy a book."

"Doesn't that sound rather familiar?" I asked. "Frank's been saying nasty things about Gemma since they both got to town and he learned she isn't continuing their romantic relationship. We talked about that before." We were walking again. I couldn't help glancing at some of the people going in our direction and against our flow, not as many tourists as there were sometimes but quite a few dogs were on leashes beside them. Fortunately, a lot of them appeared headed the opposite direction from us, in the direction of my pet boutique.

"Yes, we did." He paused, then continued. "I know you speak a lot with Chief Halbertson. I do too. He must like you."

"We're friendly enough," I responded, rolling my eyes. "But—"

"Just so you know—and I shouldn't be mentioning it—there's talk going around at the department that he shouldn't be so friendly, especially not to you. That's going to get him in big trouble if he doesn't let us zero in on the primary suspect in the Landorf murder and arrest her, just because he's giving her the benefit of the doubt because of you."

How odd that this man, this detective, was talking to me about such things. And if they were true, it was terrible, for both Justin and Gemma.

"Look," I said. "Gemma didn't do anything, and that's undoubtedly the reason your boss hasn't authorized her arrest."

"There are those who think otherwise," he said, "both in and out of our department. They believe that our chief sometimes makes decisions for reasons other than reality."

We stopped because a crowd filled the sidewalk at the Break-a-Leg Theater, standing in a ticket line. I didn't know what was playing. I didn't care.

"Like you?" I asked.

"I've said enough," Choye said in a low voice, bending to talk right into my ear. "And if you ever mention it I'll deny it and say you're making it up to protect your friend. Thing is, I actually like our chief. I'm hoping you'll pass enough of this along to get him to do the right thing."

And arrest Gemma? I'd have to think about the wisdom of saying anything to Justin. But if what Choye said was true, I didn't want

Justin to be doing anything to help me, or my dear friend, that would ultimately wind up harming him.

Feeling a little desperate, I asked, "Who is making those claims?" Or was just Choye doing it, trying to use me to get Justin to authorize Gemma's arrest? Was he attempting to protect another suspect? If so, who? And why?

If it wasn't him pushing for an arrest, then who? Detective Alice Numa? She was the only other one I'd much interaction with, but there could be others with the same opinions Choye had expressed.

Still, Alice undoubtedly had an interest in getting this case resolved quickly, especially since I'd heard Lou blame her for not finding answers to the other puzzle still rocking the DPD.

But would she be willing to do anything to get a result here— even have someone innocent arrested just to get a supposed suspect in custody?

Why wouldn't she run this by Justin? He'd been blamed at the same time by Lou for not concluding the investigation into that tourist's death more quickly. Maybe she had and he had refused to listen, not because of any feelings he might have for me but because he in fact had doubts of Gemma's guilt.

Did I dare talk to him about any of this? I didn't really care if I got the two detectives in hot water, but could my doing so harm Justin—and Gemma?

"Go back to your store," Choye said as a slight opening appeared in the crowd and he started to move forward. "I've said all I'm going to."

TWENTY-SEVEN

I FORCED MYSELF TO concentrate on business after returning to the Lucky Dog. That was never hard to do since I loved my work, dealing with people interested in our products and even learning all about the superstition angles and pretending I knew them.

I'd been here long enough that I really did know quite a few, especially relating to our merchandise.

Plus, I had the help of Millie and Pluckie late that afternoon. I exchanged banter with both of them as well as with our customers, talking up superstitions and dog toys and paraphernalia.

Pluckie didn't talk back, but she did seem to have fun modeling collars and leashes, and showing how the toys should be played with. We sold a bunch of things that afternoon, which made me happy.

Even so, in the back of my mind—and maybe too much in the front of it—I kept returning to my conversation with Detective Choye.

I hadn't known him before, when suspicion was leveled on Martha after Tarzal's murder. He apparently hadn't been assigned to interrogate either Martha or me. She and I had both talked mostly to Detective Alice Numa. And to Justin, who'd acted professional but had done what he could to protect Martha, who was almost like his mother.

Alice hadn't been protective of Martha then. She certainly wasn't protective of Gemma now. Just the opposite. Was she one of those claiming that Justin was acting improperly by not taking Gemma into custody? If so, what evidence did she think would justify an arrest?

Then there was Choye himself. I now thought Gemma and I had been somewhat wrong about his conversations with Frank. They might not have been discussing why all fingers pointed toward Gemma, even if that was Frank's vengeful goal.

Instead, Choye had acted as if he was pushing to find real answers in a way that benefited Justin so his boss wouldn't be harmed by failure, never mind Lou's prior accusations against the police department and Mayor Bevin's current ones.

Failure that might be caused, or exacerbated, by what the detective saw as the police chief's possible interest in me.

Or was that just the way Choye wanted things to look?

Interest or not, I genuinely wanted to help Justin succeed and find the real killer, who wasn't Gemma. Consequently, Choye and I had something in common—if I understood his motives correctly—even if he didn't think so.

But Justin wanted me to stay out of the whole thing and not get involved.

Did he know about the possible controversy within his department? He definitely knew Mayor Bevin's opinion of him.

All right. I needed to talk to him now, preferably in person. But not anyplace we'd be seen by residents of Destiny. That, definitely, would be bad luck.

So how? And where?

I was getting hungry. The shop's closing hour approached, and dinnertime would arrive soon. But even if Justin was available, I couldn't meet him anywhere in Destiny, not even his home. He had neighbors, and citizens of Destiny watched out for each other—in good ways and bad.

We weren't far from Ojai, and both Justin and I had cars. It would be more efficient if we rode together, should we decide on dinner in another town. But efficiency and saving gasoline weren't the point.

We had dined together once at an intimate cafe called Randie's along the highway from Destiny but on the far side of Ojai. Its food was okay but not gourmet, and its prices were on the high side, which meant its clientele wasn't huge—which for now was a good thing. The likelihood of us being recognized was a lot less there than around here.

I went into my store's backroom to call Justin, since I didn't even want my staff to hear. I reached him right away.

"Rory? I was going to call you. There are some things I want to talk to you about. Are you free for dinner?"

"Sure," I said in a pleased tone, as if the idea was new to me. Even so, I told him where I wanted to meet—and that I really hoped for privacy. I didn't explain why. I probably didn't have to.

He agreed that Killer and he would meet Pluckie and me there in an hour.

———

Since we'd eaten there before, we knew the dogs were welcome. We sat on the dimly lighted back patio with hardly any other diners around. The inside rooms had a reasonable crowd, but not here. Which was good.

Justin had offered to drive us all, but I'd declined without saying why. We ordered our drinks—merlot for me, amber beer for him, and water for the dogs. I studied the menu without meeting his gaze.

"Know what you want?" he asked in a minute. I nodded. A small Caesar salad looked good to me. I didn't have a big appetite after all. It had been smashed down by what was in my mind.

We soon ordered our meals. Justin was going with a veal dish, which also sounded good. I figured I'd get a taste, which would be enough.

A taste. As if we really were in a relationship and shared meals.

I wondered if any superstitions applied to sharing food. I'd heard it was supposedly good luck to have seven people at a table, but if there were thirteen at least one would suffer bad luck. Tasting each other's food, even splitting a meal? I hadn't a clue.

When our server, a college-age guy in a brown knit shirt and matching slacks, left to place our orders, Justin looked across the table toward me, leaning on his arms. The top buttons of his blue shirt were undone and his sleeves were rolled up. A hint of beard darkened his cheeks and a hint of irritation darkened his blue eyes. In all, he didn't look happy, almost as if he knew why I'd wanted to get together—to ask questions and possibly scold him.

But I also wanted to warn him.

"So," he began. "What's up?" Why hadn't he started with what he wanted to talk to me about?

Or maybe they were the same thing and he knew it.

I prepared a smart retort, then let my shoulders slump. "Concern," I replied in a low, gloomy voice. "And not just about Gemma."

"About what, then? Or who?" His tone suggested he didn't really want to know. That irritated me.

"You," I snapped. "If you're not doing your job right because you're trying to look good to me, you'd better stop. Although—"

"Although what?"

"Although you'd still better not arrest Gemma."

I wasn't surprised to hear a short bark of laughter.

"Were you talking to Choye?" he asked.

"Well … yes, but—"

"He's a nice guy. Dedicated to the department and to making it run smoothly. Even dedicated to me. But that sometimes leads him to off-beat conclusions, and not only about cases but about what's going on around us too."

"He sounds like he may be your champion," I shot back, wanting to see Justin's reaction.

"Yes, in a way. I know he's trying to protect me. Or at least that's what he thinks he's doing."

Maybe, but I didn't mention my doubts.

Our server brought dinner rolls over. They looked delicious, but the delay frustrated me.

Justin handed the basket to me first, and I took one of the small and crusty breads. After pulling off a couple of pieces I'd give to Pluckie later—and possibly Killer, too—I put a touch of margarine on what was left and watched Justin do the same.

"The thing is," I began, after taking and chewing a bite, "I want you to realize that Gemma's innocent, and to avoid arresting her because of that, not because … because … you believe I—"

"Choye's assuming I'm trying to impress you by leaving your friend alone, even though she's guilty," Justin asserted.

"That's what I gathered. And he says he's not the only one who thinks that. Others in your department are getting unhappy with you, he says. We already know the mayor is frustrated that there hasn't been an arrest yet." I was saying too much, but I was concerned for him.

"Did Choye tell you who else in the department is unhappy?"

"No, but if I had to guess, one would be Detective Numa." I reminded him of the talk the detective had with my friend, and what Gemma had subsequently told me. "I assume she hasn't changed her belief that Gemma did it."

"Not that I'm aware of."

The rest of our meals were served then. I felt almost as if I'd related everything I needed to say. Except...

"You're really not doing anything to jeopardize yourself or your career because of me, are you?" I blurted the question almost without thinking.

"Not at all."

"Then do you have any evidence against anyone, let alone Gemma? Do you know who killed Lou?"

Justin had carved a small piece of veal scaloppini off and reached to put it onto my plate. His movement stirred Killer, who all but put his nose on the table.

Justin, like me, had saved some roll for the dogs. He gave each of them a piece.

The delay was understandable but frustrating. I wanted to hear his answer.

When it came, I didn't like it. "No," he said. "Like I've been telling the mayor and everyone else, we have suspicions but no answers yet."

———

The meal was tasty, the company excellent. The conversation? Enjoyable on some level, since it was with Justin. But after our initial salvo we just skirted over anything conceivably important relating to the murder. Maybe he couldn't say more. I understood that.

I also didn't like it.

I really wanted to know, to understand, what the atmosphere was like for him at his department. Was he ultimately going to feel he had to give in to pressure and arrest someone just for the sake of having a person in custody?

And would he have to make it Gemma so it wouldn't look like he was so smitten with me that he'd protect someone guilty to impress me?

But discussing his job further was apparently off limits for the rest of that night. And whatever attraction there was between us seemed to be lurking where I barely sensed it.

As a result, I talked to Pluckie and Killer a lot, too, mostly about food and another dog who came out on the patio.

It dawned on me finally that Justin hadn't started talking to me about whatever it was he'd indicated earlier that he wanted to discuss. I asked him.

"We did mention it before, kind of." He had finished his entree and was eating another roll, watching it rather than me.

"What was it?" I asked, looking directly at him. Darn, I liked the guy. But I didn't like how this evening was turning out. We seemed both to be working hard at friendliness rather than it being a natural reaction between us.

He did look toward me now. And smiled. "I figured it would be fruitless for me to tell you again to butt out."

I laughed. "That's true. My response? I'll butt out if and when I'm sure Gemma's safe. And when you're safe, too—or at least your job is. If that means I have to skirt around you and find the killer myself—"

"Just be damned careful," he interrupted. "Part of my job is protecting the public, and I'll do that even for a member of the public who's purposely endangering herself for a mission she shouldn't have anything to do with."

———

That pretty much ended our dinner. He allowed me to pay my share, which I figured was as much to make it look to me like this wasn't a date as to ensure that if someone happened to recognize him they, too, would consider this to be just a meeting between friends. Fortunately I saw no one I recognized so I didn't believe that would be an issue anyway.

We walked Pluckie and Killer together outside the restaurant, then Justin accompanied us to my car, which was in the same lot as his.

Would he kiss me good night, or were we estranged enough that he wouldn't even give me a peck of friendship?

"Just be careful, Rory," he said. "Don't do anything foolish. And keep in close touch with me, especially if you decide to put yourself in danger."

"But I—"

He did shut up my response with a kiss, warm but not aflame with romantic interest, which made me feel sad. I nevertheless unlocked my car door and opened it.

Pluckie jumped in, with Killer watching.

Just for fun, I pivoted, planted a much hotter kiss on Justin's lips—holding him close so he couldn't flee it—and then turned again to slide into the driver's seat.

"I don't suppose I could tell you the same thing," I said, "but if you put yourself in danger, please be careful."

TWENTY-EIGHT

WITH PLUCKIE SNORING SOFTLY on the floor beside me, I lay in bed that night thinking. That turned out not to be a good idea. Or maybe it was a great idea.

I kept rehashing not only my dinner with Justin, but also all that had been going on recently, who'd been saying what about Lou Landorf's murder, who all the suspects were, or at least those I knew about, and what evidence there was to point fingers at anyone... like the stake that had been used to kill him.

To my surprise—or maybe not—those thoughts started coming back to a central theme.

No, a central person.

I knew I was reaching for a conclusion far from Gemma, but was I going too far? Was I making things up in my mind?

Not entirely. But the motive made sense—if one could consider anger a motive.

People had killed for less than that. And Mayor Bevin Dermot had been angry with Public Affairs Director Lou Landorf recently.

He'd been angry with him before too. Or maybe it had just been irritation then. Had it built up over the years?

Or was I just stretching the possibilities?

After all, this wasn't the first time I'd considered the mayor a potential murder suspect, or even a suspect in this case.

Detective Choye had mentioned that people both in and out of the department were talking about Justin, suggesting that he not act so friendly toward me. Did that include the mayor?

For now, I needed more information, possibly on the somewhat historical stuff.

Could I learn, without asking too many questions, more about what I suspected?

I wasn't sure, but there was a source I could try.

Thinking about that finally let me get some sleep.

———

I stayed quiet about my thoughts the next morning when I met Gemma and Stuart downstairs at the busy breakfast room of the B&B. After a delightful day-awakening meal thanks to our hostess Serina, Pluckie and I did our usual thing these days of walking with Gemma and Stuart to our shops.

Inside, my nerves were grinding, ready to go. But I needed to do a little preparation first anyway.

Fortunately, as usual, too, I arrived at the Lucky Dog around nine o'clock and we didn't open till ten. On most days, I spent that time reorganizing shelves, checking and ordering inventory, and looking into the online records I kept of our sales.

Today, I got online first thing. I visited the *Destiny Star* website. I knew the Vardoxes updated it often but hadn't paid a lot of attention to whether they maintained archives on it.

Fortunately, they did. Unfortunately, those archives only covered the past few months. I needed to search longer ago than that.

I did some other checking online but found nothing particularly helpful. Older newspaper articles might be useful, though, so I decided to go to the *Star*'s offices later and see if they had any on their computers or microfiche, or whatever, that they'd make available to me.

Meanwhile, I'd continue to fret and stew and wonder if I was simply going nuts out of worry for my friend. Or friends.

Or if my mind actually had glommed onto a real solution.

———

That day turned out to be a difficult one for breaking away from the store.

First, Jeri called and said her mother had a stomach virus. As a result, Jeri wasn't going to be able to come in to the Lucky Dog to help out. She'd never been anything but clear that her family's store, Heads-Up Penny Gifts, came first, so I couldn't argue or even cajole her.

"I hope your mom feels better fast," I said, meaning it not only because it was polite to say so.

Martha wasn't coming downstairs to help out, either. She didn't feel ill, just tired, and with all the health issues she'd had not long ago I was the one to insist that she take a break.

Millie, fortunately, was there. But this Tuesday, when she arrived mid-morning, she came up to me at the cash register when we had a lull in customers. She appeared a bit uneasy, like a youngster who'd broken something and was scared to admit it.

"Everything okay?" I asked, when what I wanted to say was that I was leaving her in charge for a while.

She looked down toward the floor, where Pluckie sat. Her youthful skin turned pink as she blushed. "I wanted to ask, Rory … I mean, I kind of have a lunch date. I hope that's okay. I won't be longer than an hour, I promise."

What could I say to that? She was a wonderful shop assistant and was completely reliable most of the time. Plus, she helped out with Martha and was generally ready at an hour's notice if I needed her to come in on days off to help with a big crowd.

One longer lunchtime than usual?

"That sounds great, Millie. Of course you can take the time off. I'll be eager to hear how your date goes, and even more so who it's with."

Her flush grew even redder. "Maybe, if it goes okay."

I considered calling Martha's nephew Arlen to ask his schedule that day. If he had no tours pending, maybe he could run the shop. I'd already confirmed that his skills were adequate to do so, even though Martha had made it clear she wanted me in charge and not him. But when I called Destiny's Luckiest Tours and asked for him, the owner, Evonne Albing, let me know that Arlen was completely booked till evening.

I was beginning to think I was fated not to go to the *Star*'s office that day. Was I cursed somehow? Or was it instead good luck not to be able to get away and do the research I craved?

Had I been in Destiny too long already? A normal person wouldn't assume that every possible good or bad thing in her life was caused by some form of luck.

Still, the more time that passed when I couldn't do the research I wanted, the more obsessed with it I became.

Besides, maybe I was obsessing over nothing. Just reaching, as I had done before. The sources of information I wanted might not even exist any longer. When the next lull in customers occurred, even though Millie had left for her lunch date—or maybe because she'd left, since she wouldn't overhear what I did—I called Celia Vardox to find out.

"Oh, sure, Rory," the newspaper co-owner told me as I watched out the front window and spoke into my phone. "We figure it takes too much memory and all to keep versions of our paper on the website for very long. But we do maintain copies, both physical and on the computer. Fortunately, the room where we keep them wasn't affected by the fire." She paused. "Plus, you'd have to check, but I think the Destiny Library keeps copies on microfiche."

The library. Of course. If I'd asked Gemma for her opinion of what to do, that would have been her first suggestion.

When Celia told me that Derek and she would close their office around seven that night, which was also when I closed the Lucky Dog, I knew what I'd do. It might even be better for keeping my search secret to go to the library. Assuming it stayed open longer.

It did, although not much longer. The library website indicated it closed at eight on Tuesday nights. That should be long enough for me to get started, although I'd need to leave Pluckie at the Lucky Dog.

Millie returned after lunch with apparent stars in her eyes. Stars she could wish upon? I didn't know, but she wasn't ready to talk about her date. We were so busy that I didn't feel comfortable leaving her there alone to watch the shop. I sold several lucky amulets that afternoon, along with the usual and fun superstition dog and cat toys in a greater quantity than usual. Lots of pet food and doggy accessories too.

Martha did come downstairs for a short while, although she noted that my orders to her to rest were good ones. With my help, she headed back up the stairs a short while later—not tripping, fortunately, even if tripping on the way upstairs heralded an impending wedding in the family. I wasn't aware of any romantic interest Arlen had anyway, and he was Martha's closest family. And though I now was sort of a member of the family, that certainly wouldn't have suggested a future wedding on my part. No guys in my life that might fit that superstition anyway, with Warren gone and Justin and I not getting along especially well now.

And with what I was about to look into . . . well, if I was right about the mayor, his boss, Justin would probably not want anything personal between us. That gave me a pang of sorrow—but it didn't change anything.

Before I closed the Lucky Dog for the evening, I walked Pluckie briefly, then gave her some of our lucky dog food kibble, laced with canned food, too, the remainder of which I put into the refrigerator in our storeroom. "You be a good watchdog and take care of this place for me, Pluckie," I said, smiling as I watched her scarf down her meal. I left her loose in the shop after carefully checking to make sure all doors and windows were locked.

I hurried down Destiny Avenue toward the Civic Center. At this hour, I actually could hurry since the crowd was a bit sparser than during the day.

I reached the delightful antique library building within five minutes and went inside. I immediately went to the help desk and asked the librarian there, who appeared to be nearly as old as the facility, where I could find copies of the *Destiny Star* from a couple of years back.

Amazingly, they had them not only on microfiche but also scanned into their computer system. The Vardoxes might have made them available, or this senior facility had even more modern ideas than I'd have given them credit for.

The librarian, whose name was Maude, showed me where to sit and how to get into the records.

They were easy to use. I'd already determined that the *Destiny Star*, although it called itself a local weekly newspaper, didn't contain much news in the general objective journalistic sense. It promoted Destiny and its superstitions and its citizens.

I wasn't surprised, therefore, when several articles from a couple of years ago described the loss of Destiny's prior police chief, who'd been hired away by Sacramento.

More coverage was given, then, to the search for a replacement, including within the then-members of the Destiny Police Department. That included Detective Richard Choye and Detective Alice Numa.

Both were interviewed in the paper. Both had been professional in what they'd said and how they'd reacted to the opening.

Both had expressed an interest in getting the job—most especially Alice.

More articles had been written about Mayor Bevin Dermot and his staff, including Director Lou Landorf, and what they looked for in a replacement. Apparently Bevin had been all set to hire one of the town's own.

Lou, not so much.

I knew now how much Lou pressed and gave orders and insisted on getting his own way. That was probably one of the contributing factors to his death.

The mayor's dislike of his attitude then, even though he'd buckled under it, could have stayed with him all this time, exacerbated recently by Lou's pushiness on his return to town and irritation that his work to attract tourists was being jeopardized by a recent tourist death. He'd pushed everyone with any potential of resolving it. Including the mayor?

I continued reading about all that had gone on back then, when Justin had gotten his job, thanks to Lou, but he was not necessarily the mayor's first choice.

Interestingly, the Vardoxes had also gone into who else, who local, had wanted to be promoted into that position.

Someone else had been angry then.

Someone else had been angry now.

I'd wondered whether the mayor could have remained angry and resentful that long. He'd found a way to deal with Lou, though— getting him out of town often.

What if others who hadn't been in charge hadn't gotten over it? One other.

The other who had been publicly chastised by Lou Landorf before his death.

Could Detective Alice Numa have harbored a deep resentment against Lou that long?

Had she harbored a greater one against Justin that she could be using now to make him look bad ... and potentially lose his job for not having someone she considered a genuine suspect arrested?

Surely she hadn't been Lou's murderer, though. Not for something so long ago. Or was she?

I had a feeling now that she was at least somehow involved.

Or was I just reaching for someone, anyone, to point at to throw suspicion off Gemma?

I at least needed to look into this new angle, and hope I found answers, one way or the other.

TWENTY-NINE

I COULDN'T EXACTLY ASK Justin what his relationship with Alice was, although I'd seen them together enough to have the impression it was professional and mostly cordial.

I realized I probably was just grasping at proverbial straws, trying to find something to point fingers away from Gemma.

And the mayor? Was I giving up on him simply because it would be terribly difficult to point fingers at him?

I didn't think so. Pointing at a cop wouldn't be much easier.

I needed some proof.

I left the library soon afterward. I decided that obtaining printouts or even just mailing links of the helpful articles to myself might cause questions about why I'd looked them up, so I decided not to, at least for now.

But what should I do next?

I pondered that on my way back to the Lucky Dog to get Pluckie. The sidewalks were nearly empty now, although I saw fairly large crowds in the Shamrock Steakhouse and the Black Cat Inn's restaurant across the street, and a lesser one as I passed the Apple-A-Day Café. The Beware-of-Bubbles Coffee Shop was closed at this hour.

The answer, of course, was obvious, but I fought it internally. That was partially because I knew I should heed Justin's warnings about staying safe.

But logically? The only way I could get the information I sought was to talk to Alice Numa.

Then I figured out how.

———

Was I being foolish? Sure. But it was about time that we got some answers around here.

I still wasn't actually certain how Alice was involved, if at all, but I had my suspicions and hoped to learn the truth tonight.

And hopefully stay alive doing it.

"We'll be fine, Pluckie," I told my little dog as I stood behind the counter at the Lucky Dog. And crossed my fingers, just in case that kind of thing worked.

Pluckie was loose, and she came over and stood on her hind legs, her front paws on my thighs as if she wanted to comfort me.

I appreciated it, and her. And hoped I wasn't lying.

I looked out the front window and saw that the usual Destiny old-fashioned streetlights were on, the sidewalks were nearly empty, and there were no cars cruising Destiny Boulevard that I saw. Then my eyes opened wide.

Barely visible in the dim light, a black cat walked along the sidewalk, crossing right in front of the store.

Maybe this wasn't such a good idea. I turned away, ready to call Alice and tell her we'd talk some other time. But that was when a knock sounded on the glass, startling me—and it shouldn't have.

She was here. I didn't believe in ill omens anyway.

I drew in my breath, then gathered all the strength I needed to greet the detective. With Pluckie right beside me, I walked forward and opened the front door.

I glanced out again. I didn't see the cat any longer. I knew that Gemma and Stuart had headed back to the B&B without me. I'd told Gemma hours ago that I was going to the library at closing time and she shouldn't wait.

I hadn't checked, but Martha was probably upstairs asleep, or at least in bed watching TV. Although she helped often during the day at the store and also attended some Destiny events as long as someone was helping her, she never came downstairs at night.

Pluckie and I were virtually alone here with Alice.

And the black cat outside.

"Hello, Ms. Chasen," the detective said, striding in. It may have been off-hours for her, but she wore her typical pantsuit, in charcoal this evening. Also typically, she wore a scowl. "So what do you want to talk about tonight?"

I smiled grimly. "I'm sure you can guess." I thought about how, more than a week ago now, a door to the shop had opened unexpectedly, which Justin had said could be a harbinger of an unwelcome guest. Well, I'd invited Alice, yet I couldn't say she was exactly welcome.

"Your buddy Gemma and how she murdered Lou Landorf?" Her return grin looked much too amused.

Holding back the negative retort that sprang to my lips, I said, "How about if we sit down?"

She agreed, and I led her through the shop and its rows and shelves of pet superstition paraphernalia, through the mesh drapery decorated with decorative dog bone shapes, and into the back storeroom. There, I waved her toward one of the chairs at the card table in the center.

She complied without saying a word. She merely stared at me as I joined her. Our hips met as I moved too closely around her to get to the other side of the table. "Sorry," I said.

Pluckie sat at my feet, and I bent to pet her while assuring myself I could handle this.

"Would you like a bottle of water?" I asked Alice next, delaying the inevitable.

"No thanks. And I can't stay all night."

I didn't want her to. And in fact, there was good reason to get this party started. I needed to get it over with.

"Okay," I finally said, my voice low and my eyes on hers, then down again toward Pluckie, who looked at me uncertainly and wagged her tail. "Here's what's been on my mind, and I wasn't sure who to talk to about it." I paused, then said, "You might know that I've become friends with Chief Halbertson."

"Just friends?" Alice's tone was scornful.

"Pretty much. I won't go into detail, but although I sometimes feel attracted to him I won't let it go any further."

"Because of the guy whose death got you to come here?"

She knew about Warren walking under a ladder. Thanks to circumstances a while back, everyone who lived here probably did.

"That's right." It wasn't entirely true, but I wasn't about to admit that. "Anyway, you probably also know I've been trying to figure out what really happened to Lou Landorf."

"Right. Sticking your nose in where it doesn't belong. Again." She shifted back in her chair and started to look bored.

I figured I'd better kick it up a notch. I needed her full attention for what I was going to say.

"Some people might think that, but what I'm trying to do is protect my friend Gemma. I know she didn't kill Lou."

"Right. You know that." She shook her head disdainfully.

"Yes, I do. Especially now … because my snooping has given me suspicions of something else. Someone else."

"Let me guess. Frank Shoreston. He's on everyone's list." She again leaned toward me. "But I've talked to him probably more than anyone else after the director's murder. Yes, he's got a lot of resentment toward your friend Gemma and maybe thinks he can exact some revenge by keeping her in our radar. But what he's said makes a lot of sense."

"Maybe. I assume it's because Gemma and Lou were arguing about how to run the Broken Mirror Bookstore. That argument would also work to indict Stuart Chanick or the owners, Nancy Tarzal or the Brownlings. Or all of them together. Or even Mayor Bevin since Lou and he argued a lot. But that's not what I'm talking about."

"Then what, Ms. Chasen, are you talking about?"

I bit my lower lip. "Not what, actually. Who."

"Then—"

"Police Chief Halbertson," I cut in.

That stopped her. Her deep brown eyes opened wide. "What, exactly, are you suggesting?" she demanded.

I hesitated. "I'm not completely sure. I guess … well, you know Justin better than I. Could he have been … upset when Lou started pushing harder to get answers about how that poor tourist died here a few weeks ago?"

"Lou wasn't only taking that out on Justin," Alice reminded me. That was true. I'd heard him berate her too.

"I know. But, well, once again you know more than I do. I can tell you what I heard, though. A couple of years ago, Lou supposedly pushed Mayor Bevin to bring in someone from out of town to become police chief, stuck his neck out a bit when he insisted that Justin be hired. Employing someone who didn't absolutely believe in superstitions for an important job like that might have been bad luck for Destiny, but Lou ignored those warnings. Maybe he came to regret it and was angry and accusatory and all that."

Alice looked a lot more interested now. "Then you think Justin's a good candidate for having murdered Lou Landorf?"

Murdered was a strong word, but it fit—although Justin didn't. Not in my genuine estimation, at least.

I knew that at least a few people had considered him a potential suspect in Tarzal's murder, but that had made even less sense than this situation.

I crossed my fingers under the card table, not only for luck but because I was lying. I hoped.

"Yes. I've been thinking about it a lot and believe Justin's a good candidate for having been the killer."

Alice made a noise deep in her throat. "Interesting possibility."

"I'm sure you've considered it," I said, although I doubted it. Unless she had been thinking about a way to frame Justin for it if anyone suggested her as a likely suspect.

"Perhaps," she acknowledged.

"If so, maybe he's been giving hints or pointing you and Detective Choye toward Gemma, maybe even planting ideas or evidence to frame her."

She didn't say anything but appeared to be considering my idea.

"The thing is," I continued. "Well, like I said, you know Justin a lot better than I do. And for a lot longer. You met him before, when he came to town for the job, maybe even earlier, when he interviewed. What did you think of him then?"

"Honestly? I thought there were others who were more qualified."

Like you, I thought. "Did you tell Mayor Bevin or P. A. Director Lou that?"

"Oh, yeah." No hesitation there.

I hesitated now, since I was considering getting into an area that could turn into a dangerous quagmire if I weren't cautious. "I gather they didn't believe you, or at least didn't agree. Which is a shame. I had the impression, from the time he returned to town from his mission to attract tourists, that Lou and you were … good friends." I was making some assumptions here and expected her to deny it. But I did recall some glances she'd leveled on the public affairs director.

She looked at me, and I shook a little inside, unsure what would happen next. "You could say that," she finally responded, no inflection in her voice at all.

"So … well, how angry were you when he started berating not only Justin but you, too, for not finalizing the investigation into that tourist's death, blaming you for it?"

Okay. I'd done it. Said what was really on my mind, not just tiptoeing around the possibility of Justin being a viable suspect but making my real suspicions more apparent. Would she realize it right away? Or would she just consider it part of the conversation?

She was too smart for that. Her dark eyes flashed, and she stood immediately behind the table. The abrupt movement caused Pluckie to bark. I noticed again Alice's substantial build. At least I didn't believe she had a gun hidden beneath her suit jacket, unless it was well hidden. That was the reason I'd "accidentally" gotten too close to her before and bumped hips, but hadn't felt anything. She wasn't wearing her utility belt.

"Are you accusing me now, Ms. Chasen? Is that your plan—to point fingers at anyone and everyone to try to get eyes off your buddy Gemma?"

"Not just anyone," I responded softly, touching Pluckie to comfort her—and to try to keep her near me and as safe as possible. "Only you."

I froze, watching her reaction. She didn't laugh. She didn't yell. She just looked at me.

"Who have you told about your ridiculous suspicions?" she demanded.

Only one person, actually, and I wondered if Justin, who'd acted as my hero before, might be on his way here to ensure that I got out of this situation all right.

Because, as soon as Alice had arrived, I'd prepared for my conversation with her by pushing the button on the phone in my pocket to call him and let him listen in.

What I'd have liked at that moment would be to hear him come through the door at the front of the store, which I hadn't locked behind Alice. Better yet, right here, from the alley and through the door into the storeroom where I sat.

I heard neither.

Had I assumed too much? Had my phone even worked?

Maybe it didn't matter. Alice might be mad at me, but she hadn't admitted anything.

She did take a step toward me, though, and I recalled her pending question. "I haven't told anyone," I lied, again hiding my crossed fingers. Although, unfortunately, I might not be lying. I couldn't confirm whether Justin had heard anything.

"That's good." Alice's hard tone matched the livid expression on her face. "You know, I'd considered carrying a weapon here tonight, even though I'm officially off-duty. Too bad I didn't. On the other hand, I suspect I'm a bit better than you at hand-to-hand combat. And if I start fearing for my life because you come at me with a box cutter or something else—I'm sure I'll find something with a sharp point in this room that I can use once you're unconscious—then I can 'defend' myself."

Pluckie was barking again now, obviously sensing the tension in the room. I couldn't bend to quiet her and certainly couldn't pick her up.

"Don't you know it's bad luck to find a knife?" I asked, hating how my voice squeaked. "I read that in *The Destiny of Superstitions*."

"Oh, I won't just find it. I'll consider it a gift from you."

"I think that's bad luck, too," I said. *Justin, where are you?* But of course I couldn't count on him.

Yes, I'd been foolish, but not entirely so. It just so happened that I did have a weapon of sorts.

The phone I hoped was blurting all to Justin was in one of my jeans pockets. A strong mesh leash I'd wound into a tight coil—one that had decorative representations of horseshoes stamped onto it—was in my other pocket. I reached in and grasped it.

That was when Alice launched herself toward me, hands outstretched as if she was about to grab me.

"No!" I screamed, as Pluckie barked and tried to bite her. She reached out and knocked my dog to the floor. Pluckie yelped.

Furious, I took the leash and tried to wrap it around Alice's throat, but she not only stopped me, she yanked the leash away.

"This'll do fine." She laughed as she started to wind it around my throat instead, even as I kicked at her and tried to stick my thumbs in her eyes.

But she was right. She had training. I didn't.

Justin was right too. I'd put myself into danger, thinking I could protect myself—and I was apparently wrong.

"No!" I tried to shout, but gagged.

"No!" shouted another female voice, startling me. It apparently startled Alice too. The leash didn't tighten further. We both turned, and I saw Martha, in pink pajamas, rush in from the door to the stairway to her apartment. She held an umbrella in her hand—one decorated with smiling doggy faces and with a very pointed end—and she aimed it toward Alice's middle as she continued to run.

"No, you old bitch!" Alice shouted, stretching to grab the umbrella before it could reach her. She wrested it from Martha's hands, and my dear old friend gasped as she was pushed to the floor.

Alice now held the umbrella. She pulled it up and started to slice it downward to stab Martha.

I rushed at her. So did Pluckie. And in the ensuing tangle, the umbrella, still in Alice's hand, opened.

An umbrella inside a building. Open. A bad omen for the one who'd done it. I felt a tiny bit better as my shoulder slung against Alice's left breast, knocking her sideways, away from Martha.

"Bad luck to you, bitch!" I yelled at her, even as she regained some balance and tried to launch herself at me this time.

"Freeze, Numa!" came another shout. This time male. This time recognizable as belonging to the chief of police.

Justin was here. He'd burst in the back door to this storeroom, as I'd hoped. Holding his service weapon up to his face to ensure perfect aim, he pointed it toward the detective who was his subordinate … as well as his number-one murder suspect and more.

THIRTY

"Of course I was listening to you," Justin said a while later.

Detective Choye and some uniformed officers had been right behind him when he'd stormed into the back of the Lucky Dog. They'd quickly arrested Alice and taken her away.

I wasn't thinking of her as Detective Numa now. But the likelihood that her days on the DPD had ended was the least of her problems.

"Me too," said Martha. We had all gone upstairs to her apartment once the excitement in the shop had ended. It was getting late, and Justin and I had wanted to make sure she was okay.

Not only was she okay, but she invited us for tea—herbal, she promised, so it wouldn't keep us awake when we finally went to bed.

Pluckie now lay at my feet beside the plush sofa where I'd settled myself by habit, facing the matching antique-looking chairs where Martha and Justin now sat. Martha looked right at home here with the teacup and saucer on her pink pajama-clad lap. Surprisingly, the atmosphere suited muscular, masculine Justin as well.

The edges of Martha's hazel eyes drooped a bit with fatigue, but otherwise she looked hyped and happy. As well she should. She'd saved me—and wound up utilizing a superstition to boot! Once word could get out about this night, Destiny residents would be jazzed.

"So you came downstairs because you heard voices?" Justin addressed his pseudo mom. "I've warned you before to be careful and not just—"

"I'm okay," she cut in. "Rory's okay. And I didn't see you there to save her, not when she needed you."

Those were kind of my thoughts too.

"If I could have gotten there any faster, I'd have helped her," he said. "Although not as colorfully as you, and not as appropriately for Destiny."

"Then don't scold me. I'm good luck." Martha grinned.

I grinned too. But when her grin turned into a yawn I said, "I want to hear all about what other lucky superstitions are on your mind, Martha, but not tonight. I have a feeling that when our adrenaline starts winding down, we'll all be exhausted. Although Justin may still have some work to do, right?"

"Right," he said.

A few minutes later he accompanied Pluckie and me back downstairs after making sure Martha locked her apartment door behind us. No, he assured me, he didn't think Alice had any accomplices, but Martha's well-being and safety were a priority of his.

I knew that. His cajoling was a major reason I'd stayed here in Destiny to help Martha with the Lucky Dog.

The store was still full of his guys now investigating what had turned into a crime scene. I let Justin lead Pluckie and me around the minor chaos till we got outside.

There, near the front of the Lucky Dog Boutique, was the black cat I'd seen before. Or at least I assumed it was the same one. It was standing still now, looking around at the small crowd of tourists and a few townsfolk staring and pointing toward the store.

"I knew something was going to happen tonight," I told Justin. "I saw that kitty outside before Alice arrived."

"Did he cross your path?" Justin's tone sounded amused.

"Not really."

"Then—"

Before I could finish, a figure came around the side of the store, a person who appeared dressed entirely in black. I assumed it was a woman, because she seemed short and ... well, I just did.

Whoever it was, she scooped up the cat, then turned to look in my direction. I couldn't really make out any facial features, but I did see her nod in her hoodie, then she and the cat disappeared around the corner.

"Is that the woman I heard about?" I asked, turning to look at Justin. "The one who supposedly keeps track of Destiny's black cats and sometimes takes care of the feral ones?"

"I assume so," he said.

"Who is she?"

"All I know so far is rumors—and that she calls herself, unsurprisingly, Catrice."

"I never saw her before, or at least I don't think so," I said, then couldn't help asking, "Is she real? Are the cats?"

"Add that to your lists of unknowns about Destiny and superstitions," he replied with a wry smile. "And don't forget that it's supposed to be bad luck to talk about her."

I wasn't surprised when Justin insisted on driving Pluckie and me to the B&B. He'd driven here because it was a lot faster than walking, he said.

Our conversation in the car was cool, relaxed, and completely off the subject that was on our mind. I was glad but suspicious. He surely wasn't going to let me get off that easy, was he?

He waited outside our lodgings while Pluckie took care of her last business for the night, then he walked us to the door and waited till I used my key to open it.

"Rory?" he said, looking down at me as I turned to say good night.

"Yes?" I checked the expression in his eyes to determine if this was it, and he was about to chew me out. I'd disobeyed him, after all. I'd put myself into danger, somewhat intentionally.

"We'll talk," he said. Then he bent toward me and his mouth got busy on something a lot more fun than talking, and so did mine.

"Good night, Justin," I breathed a long minute later, then hurried inside and shut the door.

———

The next morning, Destiny was on fire—figuratively, fortunately, and not literally. I didn't need to look up superstitions relating to blazes.

Instead, rumors flew. Residents did all they could to encourage good luck superstitions to come true for everyone there, including tourists.

That was what Serina told me at the B&B as soon as Pluckie and I came downstairs for our short morning walk. Destiny was in turmoil.

"It'll be okay," Serina assured me. Then she scrutinized me with an intense gaze. "You know something, don't you?"

"Who, me?" I asked innocently. But I figured the truth would come out if it hadn't already—unless, of course, talking about this situation was labeled bad luck.

As I walked Pluckie down Fate Street in the direction of the park, I saw a lot more tourists than usual at this hour heading that way too.

My phone chimed to let me know I'd received a text message. I pulled it from my pocket.

From City Hall? It said, "Town meeting at Break-a-Leg tonight at 7:30." Oh.

All store owners and managers had to register with Destiny's administration, so I wasn't surprised they had my phone number. I felt sure that, whatever would be said this evening, the spin Destiny intended to give on what had happened last night and otherwise would be provided.

Far be it from me to do anything but follow the rules, because doing so would provide good luck, or so I figured we'd be told.

Unless, of course, the approved story was full of lies that would hurt Gemma or me. Or Justin, of course. If so, I'd defy rumors and tell the truth.

By the time Pluckie and I returned, Gemma and Stuart were downstairs in the breakfast room. My friend nearly elbowed her way through the crowd of guests to get to me. "Is what I've heard true?" she demanded, looking at me with wide, hopeful eyes. Today, she wore a black T-shirt with the outline of an open book that said "Read More" over a black skirt, and she looked pretty, as usual.

Now I felt certain she'd never have to wear prison garb, so I smiled. "Depends on what you heard."

She leaned closer. "There's been an arrest in Lou's murder, right?"

"Could be."

"And you had something to do with it, you louse. Why didn't you let me help you?"

"Because," I replied, gazing wryly into her face. I'd no intention of saying any more than that. I didn't need to explain to her or anyone else what I'd done or why I'd done it, not even Justin. Well, maybe Justin...

Unsurprisingly, I did see Justin a little later that day, after the four of us—Gemma, Stuart, Pluckie, and I—conducted our usual walk to the shops. The only thing surprising about it was the timing, since an exhausted-looking police chief appeared in the shop the moment it opened at ten.

"Can I have a few minutes, Rory?" he asked.

I glanced toward Jeri and Millie. Only Jeri had been scheduled to come in but both arrived early, asking for information. The only dirt I passed their way was that they should come to the town meeting later.

"Sure," I told Justin. Rather than going into the backroom where eavesdropping was likely, we went out the rear door into the empty alley. I brought Pluckie, who immediately began to sniff the air, then the ground.

"I just wanted to give you an update," Justin said. "Here's what we're gathering so far, although Alice has lawyered up and hasn't confirmed or denied much."

But the word "much" was the key. She had talked a while before deciding to shut up.

I recalled one day in the Broken Mirror Bookstore when Alice had agreed with the speculation that Lou's killer was there. Now I knew how true that was.

The story now believed correct by the DPD was that Alice had resented Justin from the first, since she had wanted to be promoted to police chief. She had even been secretly dating Lou Landorf back then to butter him up and get him to support the idea of promoting her.

She'd been resentful when he hadn't, but he'd told her he was waiting for a much better position for her. And lately, the idea was being bounced around to start the new, official security team within the department that Lou had mentioned, one that would deal directly with tourists and their issues. Lou had suggested it, in fact, and Alice was being considered to head it. She liked the idea, since to visitors to Destiny she would become the go-to cop, the person they'd all love and revere because she would help straighten out their problems.

"The death of the tourist threw a monkey wrench into that idea," Justin said, shaking his head. "Alice might actually have been good at that position. But Lou was furious about the death of the tourist up on a popular mountain lookout and the bad publicity it gave Destiny—especially since his current assignment was to attract lots of tourists to town. Lou lashed out, like he always did. He blamed me for not finding the reason right away. He blamed the whole department. And that included Alice. He made it clear he wouldn't recommend her for that exciting new position thanks to her failure."

"But it wasn't her fault," I said. "Was it?"

"No, but Lou was never the most understanding person, especially when riled. Alice and he had still been dating secretly when he was in town, meeting infrequently late at night mostly outside Destiny, but when they were short on time they met in the park. They apparently had quite a torrid affair going that had started a couple of years ago, but they'd been surprisingly discreet, considering who Lou was. No one knew about it, although that's still under investigation. It ended, though, when the tourist died and Lou got angry. To make matters even worse in Alice's estimation, he started flirting with newcomer Gemma. His murder? It was premeditated by Alice."

Alice hadn't admitted this part, he said, but apparently she had seen the kind of stake used to kill Lou in Heads-Up Penny Gifts and had intended to buy one for Lou as a peace offering. It was his kind of thing, after all, with the carved fist on the top representing knocking on wood. But anger caused her to steal one instead so nobody would know she had it. Then she'd convinced Lou to meet her one more time in the park—and used it on him.

"She was apparently hopeful that Pluckie would be the one to find him, since she knew you sometimes went to the park on your morning walks," Justin said.

"Lucky us," I replied.

"Alice is one of those Destiny residents who tries to pretend she doesn't fully embrace superstitions, but now she's sure bad luck is raining down on her—not because she's a murderer, but because she accidentally opened that umbrella indoors when trying to protect herself by hurting you. Oh, and she also saw that black cat cross in front of the Lucky Dog when she was on her way inside to get you. She'd considered entering another way but knew that would be bad luck too."

There was a superstition about needing to enter and leave through the same door to prevent bad luck, although why she couldn't have sneaked in and out the alley door I didn't know. Maybe because sneaking would look bad for a cop supposedly trying to investigate a crime, if anyone saw her.

And that cat. Was it wholly coincidence it had happened to be there that night, or was the cat, and perhaps the cat lady, somehow psychic? I wondered if I could find out. Without talking about her.

"Alice also considered you bad luck, by the way. You came to town at a time she was trying to find a subtle way to curse me. Instead, you helped me solve the first murder in years here. You apparently brought me good luck." He smiled at me.

I smiled back.

"Okay, then," he continued. "In case you were wondering, I was listening to your conversation with her the whole time over the phone. I wanted to be there and shove you out of the way and shake you. But ... well, I was also upset."

"Because I was the one to figure out it was Alice?"

"Some of that, yeah. But mostly because you'd put yourself in danger."

We shared a brief, though hot, kiss.

"I've got to run, Rory," he said sadly as he broke it off. "See you at the town meeting tonight?"

"Absolutely."

———

I talked to Gemma later that morning at the Broken Mirror, whispering what had happened and swearing her to secrecy.

"Thank you, thank you, Rory," she exclaimed, hugging me beside the cash register as Stuart waited on a group of customers.

Then Gemma let her own bomb drop. "You know, Rory, I've been aware since I arrived here about all the controversy relating to that tourist's death. I wondered if it could be superstition related—what around here isn't?—and did some research." She quietly told me what she'd found and her suspicions about it.

"Weird!" I exclaimed. "And surely someone in this superstitious town considered it. But I'll let Justin know."

———

Mayor Bevin Dermot occupied the entire stage at the Break-a-Leg Theater that night. He held a microphone and paced and wished everyone good luck over and over even as he informed us all about his version—which was to become the town's official version—of what happened.

His audience was huge, at least for Destiny. The theater seats were all occupied, and people stood in the center aisles and along the wall.

The Vardoxes stood just below the stage, filming him and typing notes on their tablets for whatever article they intended to put into the *Destiny Star* and on their website.

I sat along an aisle near the front, with Gemma and Stuart and Carolyn. Most other Destiny residents I looked for were there, too, as well as Nancy Tarzal and the Brownlings. Martha was there in her wheelchair, helped along by assistants Millie and Jeri.

"Now," Mayor Bevin said, "it's bad luck as well as bad form to talk about former detective Alice Numa being arrested for the murder of our dear Public Affairs Director Lou. It's an ongoing investigation and I don't want myself or any of you to mess up evidence or the prosecution or anything, so we can't talk about the situation any more than we could the last one, since it'd be bad luck. We all do need to cooperate with the police, though, and answer their questions honestly and all that. In case you're wondering, she claims her bad luck was caused by accidentally opening an umbrella inside, and having her path crossed by a black cat." He paused. "She is a Destiny resident, no matter what."

It was, unsurprisingly, public now that Alice had been arrested. No one was even trying to keep that quiet. But where and how she had gotten caught, and how her supposed bad luck had affected it, weren't directly part of the mayor's discussion.

The why and how she'd allegedly killed Lou wouldn't be discussed here either, I figured.

I saw Justin standing at stage right, nodding. With him were Choye and some of the uniformed cops I recognized.

"In any event, I want to thank our police chief Justin Halbertson for his efforts in the investigation and for coming to a reasonably quick solution, assuming it's correct, of course, and that a trial proves it."

He glanced toward Justin, who just nodded. Not exactly the most rousing approval of him or his team's work, but it was okay.

I was also glad that no one else seemed to have picked up on my involvement. If the mayor knew, he was apparently keeping it to himself.

Maybe he considered it bad luck to talk about it.

"I've got my fingers crossed," the mayor continued, raising his right hand to show that was true, "that all goes well and that the resolution is quick. Will you all join me?" He gestured with his hand, and pretty much everyone in the audience did the same thing.

When that was finished, the mayor still had things to say. "Now, you all may know that some of what happened could have been precipitated by that terrible event, the death of Sherman Ambridge, one of our treasured tourists, a few weeks ago. Sherman was a super-stitious man and a frequent visitor. He had brought some business associates and they were apparently also enjoying our ambiance, maybe even considering opening a retail store here. But they all went up one of our mountains on a hike and Sherman supposedly disap-peared. His body was found the next day. As a result, an investigation was conducted to determine if it was an accident or a homicide—and it took our investigators a while to make a determination. And in fact, they just resolved it today."

He paused, possibly for effect, and leveled a glare at Justin, who looked straight back at the mayor, clearly not apologizing.

"Because Destiny's reputation was at stake, particularly our good luck, Lou was especially upset, and his anger toward our police de-partment was obvious. I can't say whether that was a factor in what happened to Lou." He didn't have to. Anyone who knew any of the circumstances was aware the answer was in the affirmative, although indirectly. "In any event, the investigation has been closed. Sher-man's business associates claimed he had wandered off and they couldn't find him. It was getting dark and they called 911 and got off the mountain. Did someone push Sherman? There is no evidence, verbal or physical, that that was the case. However ... "

His pause was dramatic and lengthy. The audience was his. Ev-eryone watched and waited, some with mouths open as if to encour-age him.

"His comrades there finally admitted that Sherman had had aspi-rations of exploring the local mountains near Destiny. Therefore, he'd done some research into superstitions relating to mountaineering."

"Mountaineering?" someone in the audience exclaimed. "Oh, my lord! Was he attacked by an eagle?"

Yes, Destiny folks—including the police—knew superstitions. Apparently the local medical examiner had been told to factor this into the tourist's autopsy and it had been dropped as a possibility since there was no evidence the man had been attacked.

But this was the superstition Gemma had come up with, and when I'd suggested to Justin that he ask the victim's friends if they'd any knowledge of it—and whether their dead friend had known it too—he had pushed them to talk.

Sure, they had discussed superstitions before and any potential relationship to the guy's death, but with Justin's unrelenting persuasion the truth had finally come out.

"Not exactly, but an eagle was definitely the reason he died. He saw one at the lookout and tried to capture it, but he missed it, and that's when he fell. His friends had been too upset and embarrassed to admit it before now—especially since they were afraid tree-huggers, or at least animal-huggers, would say it was an appropriate outcome. Sherman had wanted to kill the eagle and extract its tongue so he could stick it into his collar for good luck while mountaineering."

A lot of upset groans and calls resounded through the audience, including Gemma's and mine.

"No one would have wished death on him for that," Bevin finally continued, "but—"

"Except the eagle," someone shouted. Laughter resulted, and then Bevin called for a moment of silence out of respect for the dead tourist, whether or not he'd earned any respect.

Bevin finished soon after that.

I had left Pluckie at the Lucky Dog and went to get her. Then I joined a large group of people at the Clinking Glass Saloon, including

Justin, whose reputation as chief of police was now polished again, and no longer tarnished.

———

It was early Friday evening, the day after Mayor Bevin's presentation at the theater.

Because of all the goings-on, I had deferred my next "Black Dogs and Black Cats" talk till next week.

Word must have somehow gotten out about my involvement in solving Lou's murder, or Alice's capture at the Lucky Dog Boutique, or whatever. My store had been exceptionally busy all day.

Fortunately, my assistants both were there, as was Martha. They were discreet enough not to say anything about what they knew had transpired here a couple of evenings ago for fear of bringing bad luck on themselves—in the form of the wrath of Destiny's mayor and police, if nothing else.

That didn't keep them from zipping their lips in an obvious way when asked whether our store had been connected with the arrest, suggesting it was true even if they wouldn't discuss it. Smart ladies.

Now our store was closed and Pluckie and I were at the Broken Mirror Bookstore. Gemma had asked me to come over. She had something she wanted to discuss with me.

Good stuff, like where could we move to together in Destiny?

Or bad stuff, like she'd had enough and was returning to the L.A.-area library where she worked?

I didn't know, but I hoped it was the former. In fact, I found my-self crossing my fingers on the way to the shop.

I looked for black cats, and even the black cat lady, but saw neither.

The Broken Mirror was still open, although I didn't see any customers. Not even Frank was there—not a surprise, since he had stopped us outside the theater last night and said goodbye to Gemma, maybe forever. He'd had enough here in Destiny. He was going home.

To my surprise, Gemma had had tears in her eyes as she hugged him and wished him well.

Stuart was there, though, talking to the Brownlings. I had heard he had decided at last to make an offer to buy the store before his required trip back to his employer. Was it happening now?

Gemma, seeing me, motioned for me to follow her to the back of her store.

There, she said, "It's finally time. Enough has happened here in Destiny. We need an inkling of our own fates too."

"You mean seeing if there are any reflections of our true loves in the mirror?" I asked in a scoffing tone. Not going to happen.

Or I didn't want it to … did I?

"Exactly." She reached toward the back of a nearby shelf and extracted an apple wrapped in a paper towel. "Eat," she said. "And then look."

I didn't have a good excuse not to now, except for common sense. But what the heck? I took the apple from her, ate a few bites, then turned to stare toward the back wall and into the mirror with the stylized decorative painted-on cracks.

And gasped.

Justin's image was behind me.

I turned quickly and nearly sighed in relief. He wasn't an illusion. He was there, in his blue police chief shirt and dark pants and with a big, handsome smile on his face.

"Hi, ladies," he said. "I didn't mean to startle you, Rory, but Martha said you'd headed over here. I wanted to invite you to dinner. Both of you, if you'd like to come, too, Gemma."

"Thanks," she said. "I have plans." But the huge, complacent grin on her face suggested that her plans had been met. I'd seen Justin in the mirror.

Maybe she and Martha had plotted this appearance, but did it matter?

"Well … sure," I said. I figured we'd talk about what came next in the Alice Numa investigation and eventual prosecution.

Instead, Justin surprised me. Turned out he invited Pluckie and me to his home for dinner that night. Not for take-out, either. He was a reasonably good cook, at least on his patio grill, and we had homemade hamburgers and onion rings, along with a delicious Mediterranean-style salad.

Pluckie and Killer got tastes of the well-cooked meat, and I helped Justin clean up afterward.

No need to go into details, but I soon found myself in Justin's arms … and staying the night.

Maybe that mirror superstition was real—or it had made me vulnerable to one night of pleasure, at least.

Justin took us back home very early the next morning after more kissing and … more. He promised to call later.

By the way, I did ask Gemma that day if she'd seen anyone in the mirror after I left, and if so, was it Stuart or Frank?

Yes, she said to the first question. And neither, to the second. It was someone she hadn't recognized, who hadn't been there when she'd turned around.

But she was delighted to be staying in Destiny to learn who it was. She still wasn't sure whether Stuart's offer to buy the store had been accepted, though.

This time, for a change, I didn't dispute whether superstitions could come true.

© Christine Rose Elle

ABOUT THE AUTHOR

Linda O. Johnston (Los Angeles, CA) has published forty romance and mystery novels, including the Pet Rescue Mystery series and the Kendra Ballantyne, Pet-Sitter Mystery series for Berkley Prime Crime, and the Superstition Mysteries and the Barkery & Biscuits Mysteries for Midnight Ink.